COSPLAY CUPID

A GEEKY, SECOND-CHANCE ROMANCE

COLORADO GEEK SERIES

ALICIA WILDER

Rocket Books

1

———

She always saved the wig for last.

It was the moment she became the character. From super-powered spies to plant-wrapped villains, over-powered witches to goth detectives. And today, a classic, returning to her very first cosplay choice, in all its red, blue and gold glory—the superhero princess herself, 2017 version.

Melanie had perfected the costume since then: Invested in real boots and a much better wig, one with more shades than black. She wasn't really tall enough to be Diana, but the heels helped and of course her thighs seemed much longer in the high-cut bottoms.

She darkened her eyebrows and painted on bronzer to keep her pale white skin from appearing too witchy next to the dark hair. Tucking the last strands of her own mousy, brown hair up under the netted wig cap she was wearing beneath the wig, she examined herself in the mirror.

She looked good. Hell, yeah, she looked great.

The costume's attitude settled over Melanie as she adjusted the "W" on her gold headband. No longer the shy accountant people knew Monday to Friday, she raised her chin and stood with her pelvis forward. She was a feminist icon. She was a goddess. She was sexually desired and culturally revered.

But even a superhero had to share the bathroom sometimes. As she stomped into the bedroom like she was taking over the house, she almost bumped into Chris.

Wearing his own usual uniform of loose pants and a t-shirt, pale from lack of sunlight, and with greasy hair standing on end all over his head, he glanced past her to the bathroom. "How am I supposed to shower in there?"

Melanie aimed her chin back over one bare shoulder. Her robe was on the floor, costume bag on the toilet seat, makeup all over the sink. The bathroom was a mess.

Her boyfriend was hunched like he was too tired to stand upright, even though he was tall enough to affect their choice of apartment. As usual, his eyes were anywhere but on her costume. She was like a child caught playing dress up. His brown eyes seemed to pass right through her. *No.* Melanie held on to that vision in the mirror and the reason why she cosplayed in the first place: It brought out her flawless goddess within.

In her boots, she was almost as tall as Chris, who always looked like he just came in from playing baseball. She squared her hips and put her hands on her hips. Power pose.

"I'll get it," she said and pivoted back into their small bathroom. She swept everything into her polka dotted costume bag and dumped it onto the floor outside the bathroom door since there was no storage space in the room. She gave the sink a quick wipe with toilet paper and declared it good enough for Chris.

"Are you sure you can't come?" she asked, because she always did. He was more into video games and board games than comics, but all kind of nerds were welcome at cons.

"I'm sure. Gotta work. But you have fun." He waved and shut the bathroom door without glancing back at her. No kiss goodbye.

When they first got together, he always came to cons with her. Now, as she headed toward the front door to meet her Uber, bracing to bear the raised eyebrows of her driver as they caught sight of her costume, she'd never been more alone.

The glow of Chris's computer lit up the living room. His earphones sat on the coffee table, waiting for him. Oblivious to the smell of the garbage coming from the kitchen, he'd sit there for hours, doing whatever he considered "work" that day, and then she'd end up taking out the garbage when she got home that evening.

She should grab it on her way out, but she didn't want anything to get on her costume. She paused. He probably wouldn't leave for hours and by the time she came home that evening, tired, the whole apartment would stink like the alley behind their apartment building.

Fiiiiine. Better to do the chore now.

Melanie crossed the strap of her themed tote bag over her chest. She gathered up the trash bag in a hurry and held it well away from her as she managed the lock on the door with her hands full and her bag sliding off her bare shoulder. She rage-dropped her keys once.

A partnership should mean having a little daily help for tasks like this, shouldn't it? Honestly, considering she did all the chores anyway, she might as well live alone.

She marched down the stairs outside their apartment building, straining her back with the way she was holding the trash bag away from her costume. The early-May Denver air was a little chilly for someone as barely dressed as her, and she shivered a little as the breeze hit her bare shoulders. But she was too dedicated to the costume presentation to let a coat ruin her outfit.

She was almost to the dumpster when the strap of her tote bag dropped off her shoulder, sliding down her arm. She automatically tried to catch it, a mistake because when she swung the garbage bag toward her, the sharp edge of the gold eagle emblem on her chest sliced the plastic bag open and wet coffee grounds spilled down her cleavage.

Melanie froze, unable to accept what had just happened, the garbage bag clutched to her chest. A fly buzzed nearby. The smell of trash in the alley almost made her gag. Something wet trickled down her arm. *Oh no, no, no.* Melanie dropped the bag, and an empty Chinese food carton and a banana peel squelched onto the asphalt at her feet. She jumped away to save her boots, cursing, but quietly, so no one would glance out their window and see the hot mess from apartment four.

She slowly looked down at herself, praying it wasn't as bad as it felt. There was a brown stain on the cloth part of her bodice. *Shit.*

Her phone buzzed in her tote bag and she heard a car drive off from around the front of the apartment building. She knew without checking that it was her driver abandoning her as a no-show fare. As if she didn't have enough going wrong without her Uber rating taking a hit.

Standing amid the mess, she took a deep breath of trash air. Her trash boyfriend upstairs was supposed to take out the garbage every Thursday night before the dumpster was emptied and could *never* seem to remember until it started to rot, forcing Melanie to do it rather than sit in the kitchen drinking her leisurely Saturday morning coffee as the smell crept through their apartment like an unpleasant third roommate.

And now instead of only ruining her morning coffee, Chris was ruining her outfit and threatening her superheroic aura. Sure, he'd apologize over forgetting the trash yet again—with that "sorry, mom" expression, as if they were a sitcom couple and she was the boring housewife.

But she's not *boring.* She's in public wearing a flashy, pantless costume. Did Chris even appreciate her playful daring? *Clearly not.* Even though he used to encourage this side of Melanie.

What would Diana do? She knew the answer. Melanie might not be the confrontational type, but the superhero she was wearing had no fear.

Leaving the trash where it was, she stomped back up the steps, enjoying the thunking sound her boots made with every step. Her heart was beating wildly. She glanced down at her chest to check that nothing was popping free. Melanie didn't really have the boobs for a heaving bosom, but the brown coffee grind smudge she could see on her tight bodice kept her anger fresh.

Chris lifted half of his headset off one ear when she came in. She slammed the door against the wall in the hallway, but he barely glanced up.

"Back so soon?" Chris asked.

Hair damp from one of his two-minute showers, he was already lounging on the couch with his computer in his lap, gaming or coding—half the time she couldn't tell the difference between his work and play. It used to be a joke but became an impediment to conversation.

Don't hesitate, Melanie.

"Our lease is up in November," she said, like someone—some character inside of her—was speaking from far away. "After that, we might need to rethink our living situation."

The words came out because she'd been thinking about this. Last year, when they re-signed with their landlord, they'd briefly talked about finding somewhere else this year. Somewhere a little bigger, perhaps in the suburbs. "Maybe something with a yard for a dog," Chris had said, and they'd both known they were talking about the next big relationship step. That felt like so long ago now.

The sentence hung out there after it passed Melanie's lips, and she couldn't take it back. For a second, thinking about last year and that conversation that was almost from another life, she wanted to; she wanted to take her costume and makeup off and be quiet, not speak up, not confront this problem that had been hanging over them for months. Be the Melanie that was content with what, while it might not be the perfect relationship, was a reliable one. She could let this go—her costume would recover, she could still make it to the convention on time—tell Chris she was just blowing off steam and nothing had to change.

But then a cool breeze drifted in from outside and ran over her mostly-naked skin. The heeled boots lifted her posture and lengthened her back. The pressure lifted from her chest and she knew, even if she was inspired by her character, she was doing the right thing *for her*.

"What's that supposed to mean?" Chris glanced at her, then back at his screen. He kept clicking, clicking. Must be playing a game. A game that was apparently more important than their entire relationship dangling by a shredding thread.

Melanie gritted her teeth and breathed through her nose and out her mouth. *I am Diana.*

She was doing this wrong—she wasn't being clear, she didn't have a plan—but it was so hard to get the words out in the first place that she forced herself to keep going, to ride the wave of anger at him for not paying attention when she was finally able to speak up. "I'm so excited to go to this convention and talk to people who actually look at me," she snapped.

He glanced at her again, clearly still distracted by his screen. "What does that have to do with anything?"

She grabbed for the whip at her waist to give her nervous hand something to do. She'd like to use it on him. If only it was the real thing. If only she could get some *truth* out of her boyfriend.

"Just what I said," she said slowly. "It's refreshing to get some attention and talk to people who care about the same things I do."

Chris sighed, clicked one more time and lifted the headset off, putting it down on the coffee table. He got up on his knees to see her over the top of the couch, but leaned to one side, then the other, stretching. He had no right to be tired, considering he had barely moved three steps this morning. "What, like superheroes and comic books? I guess I just don't have a lot to say about that stuff. You don't care about my games and I don't hold it against you."

"And maybe that's a problem." Melanie wasn't sure that was the *real* problem, but she hadn't quite figured out what was, so this seemed like a good place to start.

"Maybe you're making it a problem." His voice came out slow, like it was an effort to even respond, and it seemed accusatory to Melanie, as if she was the one making him tired.

Her hand clenched around the gold-painted leather in her hands as she attempted to hold on to her anger and her stupid voice wavered in the face of his doubt. "If it's a problem for me, that means it's a problem."

"Fine," he said, dropping the word on a deep exhale. "But it never *used* to be a problem."

So unfair. "Well we used to talk and we used to share activities."

Chris scrubbed both hands through his hair, making it stand up. He got this slightly-glazed, rumple-headed appearance after spending time on the computer. It had been adorable once, back when it was an hour or two of concentration at a time, before he started working from home and gaming every night "to unwind" and was never not on there.

"OK," he said with a second deep sigh. *Like* I'm *the unreasonable one?* "So you want me to go to the convention with you? Is that what you're trying to say?"

Their conversation was going in circles. Her next move was to shout, "I want you to *want* to go to the convention with me," and then he'd say she couldn't force him to feel a certain way or something else that was accurate but didn't even come close to addressing the yawning gap between them.

Melanie turned around and stomped to the kitchen, leaving the front door open behind her. She wiped at her chest with a wet paper towel. It created a wet stain but at least the brown smudge and coffee grounds seemed to wipe away. Chris hadn't even noticed the mess.

When she opened the cupboard beneath the sink to throw the paper towel away, there was a dirty paper towel in the trash can, without a liner in it. Chris apparently didn't notice she hadn't put a new bag in when she took the old one out.

Melanie closed her eyes and put her hand on the coil of her whip. As cheesy as it was, having the prop there seemed to get her closer to her own truth. Accessing that had been so difficult lately and instead she'd been skating along, afraid of what might change if she didn't keep the peace. Afraid of losing their relationship and afraid to start over. *Just plain afraid.*

She didn't know what she wanted, exactly. But she knew what she didn't want: The life she'd been living. Pretending Chris wasn't driving her crazy. Doing activities alone that they used to share.

Her skin prickled when she heard Chris follow her into the kitchen. He stood there, waiting for her to turn around. Did he expect her to back down, change her mind? *No.* She was going to draw a line. She tossed the paper towel in the trash can with the other one and closed her eyes to concentrate on her inner voice.

"What I'm saying is," she began, struggling to speak her thoughts. "That with our lease expiring in November, I need some space. I need to figure out what I like again. Without you. Because you...you take up a lot of *room.*"

She turned to Chris. Long and lanky, he filled up the kitchen doorway, and she flashed back to the first time, early on in their relationship, when he came to her apartment to provide "IT support." She'd been overwhelmed by how cute he was, how easily he'd fixed her computer and then turned the contents of her fridge into dinner for two. Now, he was leaning on the doorframe like he couldn't stand upright without the support. *Times have changed.*

Thinking about her computer made her realize one thing she knew she wanted. It was like it'd been written on the backs of her eyelids and now that she'd stopped and asked herself the question, she could finally see it there.

"I want to spend the next few months going to conventions and dressing up and spending my time with people I enjoy being around," she told him. "Which does not include you right now."

Chris stared at her, unblinking. He leaned forward for a moment, his forearms flexing, and then drew back. For a moment, she wasn't sure he was going to respond. "And what am I supposed to do?" he finally asked.

She raised her chin. "Whatever you want, Chris. Keep doing

exactly what you're doing if you want," she continued, gesturing to include his sloppy clothes and poor posture. "But at the end of the convention season, if something hasn't changed, we need to go our separate ways because something about this—us—isn't working."

His eyes skipped away from hers to the floor. "How are we supposed to fix it if you're off traveling all summer?" he asked, but it seemed like a rhetorical question. Then he raised his eyes and aimed a laser glare at her, like he was trying to make it her problem.

Melanie imagined his frustration bouncing off her wrist bands like bullets. They hadn't been partners for a long time, she realized. This was no longer a *them* problem, one they were confronting together.

"That seems like a *you* problem," she said. It was not that she didn't care. But this was how she was going to manage her problem with them and he could manage *his* problem however wanted.

She turned to leave, shoving past him, because she was running late and her phone kept buzzing in her hand, filling up with messages from people she *wanted* to talk to.

"Melanie..." he called after her. "You can't be serious."

She turned back to him and struck the power pose again, for courage. "You cannot be serious that you didn't think we had problems."

He stood there in the hall looking confused, like an overgrown child. "Are we breaking up?" he said, like the question just dawned on him.

Melanie swallowed, because she *didn't* want to break up with him. She was pressing her hands so hard into her sides, the metal edge of her bodice dug into her fingers. Chris had been at the heart of her life for so many years now that her knee-jerk response to his question was *NO*. She didn't want to lose him.

"I don't want to break up with you."

She saw the expression on his face, like the words she'd said made him think he could wipe away everything else she'd managed to express. The truth was, she didn't want to lose him, but he had already been gone a long time.

She added: "But I don't see any other solution and I'm tired of working so hard to make us work. So...November."

Their eyes met in silence. And Melanie wondered, again, if she'd been too harsh. Maybe she should have slept on it. Maybe she'd regret this tonight, when she came home tired, or in the morning, when they could be having coffee and eggs together in the kitchen.

"You could have just *talked* to me," he said.

And she heard a snap inside her head, switching her from empathy to defensiveness. How dare he put this all on her. She swallowed back her anger, shook her head and backed away. "I'm tired of trying to talk to you, too."

She shouted over her shoulder as she walked out. "And clean up the mess by the dumpster!"

2

Five Years Ago

Melanie wore superhero in disguise: the vintage t-shirt, bomber jacket and baseball cap. She'd been so excited about the movie—one of the first big first female-led superhero films—that she'd bought the outfit pre-made and worn it every Saturday for a month after the movie came out, even while out running errands or with friends.

That Saturday, she went into a grocery store to grab sushi to eat at home in front of the TV and a tall, lanky man surprised her when he walked past her in prepared foods by the deli and gave her a two-fingered salute.

"Evening, Captain," he said. He was tall and his long-legged walk almost had him past her before she could respond.

Melanie flushed so hotly that the faux leather jacket felt like a plastic straitjacket. She wore the costume out specifically because it was subtle. "You know me?"

She raised her eyes to his and started to sweat at the back of her neck when his attractiveness level registered. Nervousness made her wanted to look away, wipe any expression off her face and walk the other direction. Normal Melanie would have. But she wasn't just Melanie that day. She was wearing combat boots in a grocery store. So Melanie put her hands on her hips and raised her chin.

"'Grunge is a good look for you,'" he replied, straight-faced.

She laughed and scanned him up and down. He was wearing joggers and a battered hair band t-shirt. "I guess you're not wearing that ironically," she said, nodding at his shirt.

He grinned back. "You mean your Nine Inch Nails shirt doesn't express your soul?"

If she'd met him on a dating app, she would have swiped left. Too attractive, not nerdy enough. On an app, he probably was one of those guys whose profile was just photos, no words. Or said something taciturn like "6'6 if you're into that."

But she stood and talked to him for a few minutes in the grocery store, and he asked questions about her outfit like it was normal to be wearing a costume in a grocery store. Then he listened as Melanie burst into an excited tangent about her love of the movie. They exchanged numbers. Melanie had never done that before with a random stranger she met in public.

After he'd recognized she was in costume—and didn't mock her for it—it didn't matter that he might be a little bit of a bro. Both Melanie and her character liked him.

A month later, Chris asked her why she'd never gone to a con before. "Too many people," she'd said. "I'm not that kind of geeky."

It was her people, he insisted. She could wear her costume and everyone would know who she was, not only him. He kept bringing it up. A true superhero would wear her disguise with pride, he told her.

He bought them tickets, and Melanie was too frugal to refuse, so she let him drag her to her first comic convention, the local one in Denver. It was amazing. People there wore costumes that ranged from photocopies to creative interpretations. No matter how realistic your outfit, fellow fans still got excited when they recognized you.

They went every year, together, for the next three, and Melanie thought of Denver convention week as their informal anniversary.

DENVER - now

Breakfast was coffee and yogurt. It was Melanie's yogurt, but they were out of cereal and it was easier than fixing eggs. No dude should be caught eating yogurt, but he could get away with it because he was in his own home and he didn't buy it himself.

Often, when he got so caught up in his work that he forgot to eat, he ended up so exhausted at the end of the day he lost track of things, like Melanie getting home from work and any plans they might have had. Chris was trying to do better.

He should go to the store, considering they were out of everything. He suspected Melanie expected him to go while she was gone this weekend, but she hadn't said anything. About that. She'd said a lot of other things before she left this morning that Chris was very carefully not thinking about.

When she came out of the bathroom in her costume, he would have promised her five trips to the grocery store if she'd spontaneously used that whip on him—and *that* was a kink he didn't know he had. And then she bent from the waist to gather up her clothes and make-up in the bathroom and he thought he might spontaneously combust.

Keep your eyes on her face, he'd reminded himself repeatedly. He'd heard Melanie's rant about costumes not being fetish-wear and "cosplay is not consent" a million times. It was never directed at him, but it was delivered very passionately before and after and sometimes during pretty much every convention.

Also, right after they'd moved in together, he overheard her telling her sister that she would never date a man who treated his girlfriend as sexual property just because they lived together, and that "Chris would never act like that." He tried to live up to all compliments given behind his back, as a general policy. They seemed so much more meaningful than ones delivered to his face.

He'd woken early that morning, jostled by Melanie when she

hopped out of bed to get ready for the convention center. Chris had rolled over and dozed off again because it was the first chance he'd had to sleep in after a month under deadline on the work project his team had finally turned in last night.

He'd gotten up before she left to say goodbye and then ended up wishing he'd stayed in bed. He'd thought he could finally relax a little and then another problem was dumped in his lap.

Once Melanie left, taking her cloud of irritation with her, Chris decided it was a day to re-play an old favorite. He just couldn't with something new today, so he pulled out the original *Bioshock*. There was comfort in going through the familiar levels, and the only choice he had to make was whether to save or harvest the Little Sisters. He harvested them all because he wasn't in a saving mood.

He was on call, so he had to put the game on hold a few times to respond to idiots breaking something, though never anything that difficult to fix. No actual coding emergencies; the IT equivalent of the common cold.

How pissed was Melanie this morning, really? It was hard to tell, since she never told him when she was upset with him until she boiled over and snapped, saying things she usually took back later.

But it seemed like she didn't buy his excuse about having to work when he'd told her he couldn't go with her to the comic convention. Fair, since it was an excuse. He really didn't *want* to go.

The idea of getting up early on the rare day he could sleep in just for all that fuss—the dressing up, the standing around all day in those flickering fluorescent lights, making small talk with people whose catalog knowledge of the *Doctor Who* timeline could put literally anyone to sleep—pushed him to run in the other direction. Not that he runs, anymore, not for months. He can't ever find the time or energy.

Anyway, Melanie didn't really need him to enjoy those conventions; she took such joy from them on her own.

He ordered a pizza for lunch, or brunch, or once he started to get hungry around 10:30 and told himself to be proactive. He left it on the coffee table the rest of the day so it was easy to access whenever he got hungry, and didn't notice it was afternoon until his supervisor Jenny sent him a Slack message.

Jenny on Slack:

(1:22 p.m.) dude, take a break already

Chris on Slack:

(1:22 p.m.) I haven't moved from my couch all day, I'm fine

So he couldn't walk more than a few feet away from his computer while he was on call. He was fine. Who needed fresh air, anyway?

For the first time that day, he picked up his personal phone and swiped down for notifications. No messages, not even from Melanie checking in. He used to get those.

She probably wouldn't be home for dinner. She'd go out with her "fandom friends." She'd be so caught up in one of her fandom conversations, talking with her hands, her face lighting up with her passion for the subject, her breasts heaving in that costume, that she'd lose track of time. So he ate another slice of pizza, not worried about waiting to eat with her.

He got up to use the toilet and glanced around the living room, which looked a bit like a freshman dorm room. Like before you learn independent living and basic hygiene are not mutually exclusive. There was an empty soda liter bottle, and crumpled napkins under the coffee table, the pizza box on top, plus his sweaty ass-dent in the couch. At least he'd showered this morning.

In their small apartment, the mess looked big. He and Melanie were constantly on top of each other, which was fine before he'd started working from home, but now made him feel like he couldn't finish a thought. Chris did not compact into small spaces very well; he was tall and therefore all of his things, like his shoes and pants, were huge as a result. His stuff was usually scattered all over the apartment after a day of not paying attention to where he tossed it. To solve the problem, he mostly never put shoes or real pants on anymore.

He sat down, which was his biggest mistake, because then he didn't want to get back up to clean. This happened a lot. Working from home meant he had no excuse to put cleaning on his "to do later" list and sometimes that was a heavy responsibility. Especially when he wanted to focus on getting his work done, and then to relax when he was finally done.

If he lived alone, he wouldn't have to worry about straightening up. Was that why Melanie had brought up November? Chris's frustration about things like having to clean up to Melanie's standards never lasted long. After all, if he lived alone, who would have picked out this hella comfortable couch? What human being would he have a conversation with that wasn't through the computer? Whose yogurt would he eat when he was too lazy to go to the grocery store? He once had a roommate who bought nothing but brown sugar pop-tarts and noticed if one went missing. But Melanie said nothing and bought extra yogurt cups every week.

He didn't deserve her.

Chris leaned his head on the back of the couch and listened to the game's soundtrack. He'd been on the save screen for a while, trying to decide whether he was at a good pause point in the game. Did he want to continue or default back to the last level? It was like a metaphor for his life. Inertia kept him glued to the couch, exhausted at the idea of racing around working on a to-do list. He could hear the dripping kitchen faucet that their landlord still hadn't fixed in the kitchen.

His personal phone buzzed. He sat up and grabbed it, thinking it was Melanie. He groaned when he saw a text from MOM on the screen.

Mom: Are you getting enough iron? I just read that exhaustion can be a symptom of anemia

Mom: Are your hands cold?

Chris: I'm just normal tired mom. I've been working a lot.

Mom: You were too tired to go out with your girlfriend? That's not normal tired!! (zzz's emoji)

Mom: You need to make sure you're dedicating quality time there

Chris: It's fine, she knows I'm working.

Mom: Are you eating and drinking water?

Chris: Yes!

Mom: Does she check on you? I'm not sure this is normal. It could be more serious than anemia.

Chris: Don't worry so much. I'm busy, gotta go.

Mom: Check in when she gets home so I know you're safe!

Chris tossed the phone aside. Moms. His mother seemed to think Melanie was his babysitter.

He glanced idly around the messy living room. She might have a point.

But it wasn't like he was incapable of cleaning up after himself. He sat forward and picked up his controller. Melanie had her thing; she couldn't judge him for his.

He'd get to everything else later.

~

From @miz_anna_doll:
Denver, Colorado
(picture of a little girl dressed as a My Little Pony)

Cutest site I've seen today! Come out to booth 217 to get your book signed! #DenverComicCon

From @melly_89:
Denver, Colorado
(picture of Melanie in costume)
"It's not about deserve, it's about what you believe." #DenverComicCon
Liked by @miz_anna_doll and 10 others
@miz_anna_doll: Amazzzzing!!!

From @deadpool.superfan99:
Denver, Colorado
(picture of a woman wearing a skin-tight costume)
Good on the inside/Bad on the outside or vice versa? #DenverComicCon
Liked by @crimefightingshswizzler and 49 others
@miz_anna_doll: Good! Definitely!
@hannabanana_79: Good! Omg!
@giovanna.marchant: @Here's hoping you're at least a little bad. Drinks tonight at 9?

From @geeks-who-speed-date:
Denver, Colorado
(cartoon picture of a costumed embrace)
Come on out at 1 p.m. for speed dating at #DenverComicCon! You could meet your partner, sidekick or archnemesis (if you're into that kind of thing - we don't judge)

Liked by @miz_anna_doll and 209 others

MELANIE WALKED into the con doubting her choices. It was much cooler inside the convention center and she wished she had a little more material on, the sweat from standing in line outside evaporating rapidly. Chris had barely *looked* at her outfit and maybe he wouldn't be the only one who ignored her. Maybe she couldn't really pull off this look—she wasn't the right height and her boobs were smaller than they should be—and maybe she looked silly trying.

But almost immediately, a little girl who looked about nine pointed at her and started screaming out her character name.

The little girl's parents approached, cell phones out. "Do you mind if we get a picture?"

Melanie smiled and put her hands on her hips, adopting the power pose.

So it started.

She had already appeared in five strangers' photos by the time she made it to the main convention hall, a massive space that currently looked like a birthday party held in a Costco.

The merchandise floor was in the basement of the convention center, basically a huge concrete warehouse broken up by colorful banners and bunting organized through the alphabet on overhead signs every few aisles. There were tall fabric-lined booths stacked with hats or corsets for sale and booths stacked high with books; experiential booths you could walk into after standing in line and get an immersive experience with the latest TV show or movie; booths over in Artist Alley where artists sat waiting to take a commission or talk about their work. It was a visual mess and very overwhelming.

But it was the best part of the convention—better than the panels or celebrity guests—because here Melanie got to stop and chat with friends who followed the convention circuit with their booths and purchase their books and drawings. She always supported her friends with her purchases, but everything else she usually spent two or three cons eyeing before buying. It seemed as though Chris now silently judged everything she brought home in her superhero tote bags.

Best of all, the reason she really loved the convention floor, was that every few steps, she was stopped by someone shouting her name—well, her character's—and asking for a picture. Like she was a celebrity. Like she was admired and beautiful. Like she had a team of people helping her look perfect when she went out.

Not like real life at all.

Real life was sending emails to get approval from three people at work and then "circling back" to remind the people who didn't respond and re-approving changes from the same endless cycle. It was spreadsheets with shortcuts that she was constantly forgetting. It was the plant on her desk that couldn't decide if it wanted to live or die.

Real life was how, last night, the big gesture Chris made was offering to move his show to the computer so she could watch her own on the TV. He looked like a cute, messy-haired, Golden Retriever while he did it, eager to get her approval before he went back to his own thing.

Real life was spin classes where she wore her sweaty hair down so she could secretly listen to her own music instead of the instructor's cultish exhortations of "you can do this" and "your thighs are music to my ears!"

It was worth it to have those thighs in this costume, though.

Of course, the tall high-heeled boots are her little secret for *lifting* (the butt) and *separating* (the thighs). Even superheroes needed a little help.

"Hey princess! Is that you, Melanie Greene?"

Melanie turned and saw one of her favorite artists waving at her from behind the large corner booth, which was piled high with colorful graphic novels. Anna did art for a children's franchise, so her booth was always packed with the younger convention-goers, and she often dyed her hair pink or purple or both and put it up in pigtails. She looked, in other words, like she could be one of the ponies in her art. But in a cute way. She was so outgoing that, upon first meeting last year, she forced Melanie to be her friend and didn't take her shyness for a "no," and then introduced her to a ton of other "convention regulars."

They hugged across the booth table.

"Damn," said a male voice behind Melanie when she was standing on tiptoes with her rear end out to lean over the table. He wasn't so bold as to touch her, so she didn't deign to give him a look. Hazards of cosplay.

"You've got a featured table!" Melanie commented when she let go. The corner tables at the convention were more expensive than the ones lined up down the aisles.

Anna brushed off the vinyl tablecloth with a flourish. "Ta da! I've finally made it. Well, more the ponies than me. But..." She gestured at a smaller stack of books, her side project with a small press.

"How's sales?" Melanie asked.

"We're going to break even on copies," Anna said, touching her fingers to the top copy of her retelling of a Greek myth using squirrels. The cover showed a squirrel standing on two back feet, holding a sword.

"Awesome!" Melanie matched Anna's grin.

"Oh. My. God. Do you follow the convention on IG?" Anna started bouncing up and down a little. Anna, who was petite and peppy, had similar energy to both her young audience and the animals she wrote about. "Mel, they have cosplay speed dating later, do you want to go with me?"

Melanie imagined a room full of hot men in costume, presumably with geeky hobbies like her own, and was tempted for a hot second. She could find someone different. Someone who adored her costume.

"Well," she said. "I would but I don't think my boyfriend would appreciate it."

Anna slapped herself on the forehead. "I am *such* an idiot, of course not, I'm so sorry."

"You're not an idiot." Melanie didn't blame Anna for forgetting about Chris; she'd never met him. He stopped going to cons with Melanie before she met Anna. She decided it was not the right time to explain the complicated status—maybe off? Maybe not?—of their relationship.

"You have to tell me all about it," she told Anna.

Anna laughed and put both hands on her bright red cheeks. "I probably won't go. I'll chicken out at the last minute if I have to go alone."

"You could meet a Brony!"

Anna grinned. "Oh, I've met plenty of Bronies. They are…interesting." Very long pause, because Anna struggled to say anything derogatory about anyone, even men who loved childrens' books about ponies. She rushed to add, "I mean, there could be a hot one! Somewhere."

Melanie laughed. "Well, don't settle, Anna. You deserve the best."

Anna leaned over and hugged Mel again, but quickly, as a crowd of both little girls and adult men were approaching the table.

"OK, I'll circle back later," Melanie said and waved before she turned to move on.

"Can we get a picture?" Two of the adult men holding Anna's pony books stopped her. Despite Anna's dismissive talk, one of them was actually pretty cute in a beefy, buzzcut way.

"Of course," Mel smiled and posed with them. They were both very polite and kept their hands to themselves. Maybe this was the type of man who would show up at the convention's speed dating later.

As she held her big, showy smile for the shot, a tiny thought wormed past the glow of attention: Had she settled?

When she and Chris first started dating, she didn't think she had. He had a career and interests outside of beer and football. He spoke honestly about his past relationships. He read books, once in a while.

He'd even been to therapy before. And he always had *ideas*. Spontaneous trips to water parks on week days; learning to roll sushi for dinner; using felt instead of plastic for her costume boot wraps. They were opposites in some ways—Chris, messy and spontaneous; Melanie, a list-maker and planner—but they met in the middle. He added a lot to Melanie's life, drawing her out of her apartment and out of her own head.

But lately...

Lately was OK sometimes; sometimes they flowed in the natural patterns of a relationship they'd developed a long time ago. There were days they connected through sheer product of their overlapping routines. But many days, their relationship seemed increasingly like a chore on their to-do list: She could put a lot of time and attention into it, but why, when he wasn't? At the end of the day it was just another box to check off.

And they both spent so much time in their apartment now that the walls were starting to close in.

One of the Bronies, the cute one, pulled Melanie back to the convention, the crowded aisle and echoing room. He extended his hand to her, tucking his cell phone away with the other. "Thanks so much. You look amazing."

She took his hand automatically, smiling while turning away. It was only after letting go and taking several steps away that she realized he'd slipped her a business card.

This had never happened to her before. She had been touched inappropriately and gotten plenty of long looks down her cleavage, but no one at a con had actually been bold enough to give her his number. And on a business card, with his full name and work address!

She tucked it down her bodice with no intention of using it. At least she knew her costume was working on *someone*.

In aisle K-M, serendipity hit because she ran into a comic book dynamic duo at the same time. They laughed and paused to admire each other's costumes. Then a nearby comics fan wearing a t-shirt featuring all three of them asked for a picture of them together, prompting everyone in the aisle to stop and pull out their cell phones. It created a roadblock that lasted for at least 10 minutes before everyone got their shots. The flurry of iPhone cameras with their shutter sounds turned on was like paparazzi, except more friendly.

She never talked to her two fellow cosplayed colleagues, but they came to mind the rest of the day and she hoped that under their masks, they were hot. It made the fantasy a little sweeter.

Before Chris, Melanie used to worry about her costumed fantasies. Even with Chris, every once in awhile she would think about someone she met at a con wearing a mask or spandex leggings to give her that little psychological push she needed to fall over the edge of a climax. Sometimes wearing a costume of her own while they had sex got her there.

He never wore a costume, to a con or not. He always had ideas for costumes—usually something complicated or weird, like something mechanized or a *Borderlands* character—and every con they would make plans to put one together for the next one. He'd been working on the Hulkbuster idea for a few years. But he never followed through and she didn't even know where those robot parts were now.

But he seemed to like *her* costumes very much. They turned him on as much as they did her. And that made it OK that Melanie liked to pretend to be another person, in public and sometimes in bed. It made it OK that sometimes her characters seemed more real than she was, that she hid her hobbies from everyone who knew her.

And then, suddenly, it wasn't his thing anymore and now Melanie had to re-find her love of cosplay because her dirty little secret was that she wasn't a true fan of any one fandom. Melanie dressed up because she liked to dress up. She liked to disappear into another character.

Cosplay was her fandom. Fandom was her cosplay.

~

Anna: (1:44 p.m.) You should bring your boy on Sunday! Is he free? I want to meet him

Melanie: (1:44 p.m.) He can't, but hopefully someday!

Anna: (1:44 p.m.) Nooooo

Anna: (1:46 p.m.) Are you wearing a different costume tomorrow?

Melanie: (1:46 p.m.) No, I'm sticking with this one. I worked so hard on it. Idk I am still a little in love with it

Anna: (1:47 p.m.) You are STUNNING in it. I stan

Anna: (1:87 p.m.) I'm moderating a panel at 5 if you want to come, it's in room 213. Otherwise I'll be in the booth, text me!

Anna: (1:48 p.m.) If I get a free minute you have to help me stalk Tom Welling

Melanie: (1:48 p.m.) lol ok

CHRIS HAD RUN out of excuses. Jenny told him to stop working—"it's a Saturday, everyone else is phoning it in, dude"—and he spent another hour playing *Bioshock* and eating cold pizza.

But he hadn't heard from Melanie and it was possible she might still be angry. He knew from experience that she could hold a grudge all day if he didn't intervene to apologize or buy her something that made her smile.

He typed out a message to her a few times:

Hey, can we talk? *Ugh, the worst.*

Are you OK? *Too vague.*

Are we OK? *Too needy.*

Eventually, he gave up and just played video games. He was so familiar with *Bioshock* he thought he might beat it again in a day if he kept at it.

But a few hours later, he was staring down the list Melanie'd written and put on the table that led into the kitchen from the front hall.

Bean sprouts, she'd written. He didn't even know what those were.

Plain 2% Kefir. What the hell? He didn't even know how to say that to ask someone in the store where to find it.

95% ground beef. He didn't know what that meant. What was the other 5 percent?

The last time he got groceries, he forgot the list and tried to work off his memory and messed everything up. He didn't realize what a big deal it was to Melanie that her broccoli be fresh, not frozen, and her kombucha be no-sugar-added. Melanie gave him that pursed lips and sigh that expressed disappointment in a way that reminded him unpleasantly of his mother. And he resented her for it.

He'd rather order groceries to be delivered, but Melanie said the order was usually wrong and they didn't pick the right ripeness of fruit or something. That kind of thing really bothered Melanie; Chris considered it a minor tax for the convenience.

OK. Do this and then don't move from the couch the rest of the day. Not a great incentive. He'd rather skip the groceries and go straight for the couch instead, maybe to sneak in an afternoon nap after only getting six hours the night before. But he thought of Melanie. He didn't want Melanie to get stressed out on Monday when she had to go to work and there was nothing to eat in the house.

Plus, she might be less angry with him if he checked something off her to-do list.

OK, *their* to-do list. Chris pinched the tight muscles around his neck and tried to remember when he stopped thinking of household chores as part of his job, too.

Probably when he ended up the lead on projects he wasn't supposed to be leading and had to start leaving his Slack notifications on 24 hours a day.

Leaving the apartment, he realized that he hadn't been outside in a couple days. The weather was perfect—blue sky, dry heat. He thought about adding a fun errand onto his list, trying to trick himself into having an outing instead of an errand, but stopping for coffee or ice cream was the kind of thing he would do with Melanie and it didn't seem the same by himself. He didn't want to enjoy the day; he wanted to get it over with.

He knew the list was not going well when he started with the "avocados - 2 ripe, 2 green" and they all looked green to him.

Chris gave sidelong looks at the other people bustling around the crowded store who seemed to be moving with purpose, picking their fruits and vegetables without hesitation. What was wrong with him that he could write a hundred lines of clean code in a morning but this seemed so hard?

He ended up grabbing four random avocados and hoping it turned out OK. It probably wouldn't, but he was going to go crazy sweating over every item on the list.

He moved quickly through the store after that, trying not to think too hard about any of the items. He stumbled across the Kefir by accident when he was getting yogurt, and that almost made up for wandering repeatedly up and down the "ethnic foods" aisle trying to figure out if coconut milk was Indian or Mexican, and whether shopping in that aisle made him complicit in racism.

He drove home, ready to do nothing the rest of the day. He carried all the bags in one finger-achingly heavy load up the apartment building stairs and left everything that didn't need to be cold in a heap on the counter.

Bioshock time.

As the game was loading, Chris checked his phones. Personal phone: Nothing. Work phone: DMs from Jenny and his other coworker Tim, each complaining about the other. He responded "sorry, dude, that's insane" to both of them.

Jenny responded immediately, asking if he had time to fix a problem Tim created.

Chris on Slack:

(3:15 p.m.) I thought I wasn't supposed to work so hard.

Jenny on Slack:

(3:16 p.m.) Never listen to my advice.

It was supposed to be a joke, but Chris didn't feel like laughing.

Lately, the more he worked, the less he got done and the less he cared about it. But he didn't want to leave Jenny in a lurch and it probably wouldn't take long, so he signed on and found the open bracket that broke the code within minutes. It only took him 20 minutes to fix it, but that left him thinking about work and the new project he had to start Monday even though the old project was going to require more revision.

With his head back on the couch, the controller in his hand, and the game's music playing, he fell asleep for about half an hour. He could tell his mouth was open the whole time because it was dry when he woke up. Very attractive. Good thing he was home alone.

Checking his phone again, there were no notifications. He stalked Melanie's Instagram. She looked like she was having fun at the con. She'd posted pictures of herself with other people in costume and her Story was full of stuff she spotted and thought was cool. Her voice when she narrated some of the clips was high-pitched and hyped up over everything. These things gave her so much energy. He both liked it and was intimidated by it at the same time, because Chris hadn't been able to match that level of energy in...he didn't know how long. When he'd gone to cons with Melanie in the past, he vaguely remembered enjoying it. And not needing a nap after. (His mother kept telling him he must be Vitamin B deficient but Chris thought he had a surplus of Vitamin Work.)

When she came home, her bag would be full of new t-shirts and toys and her eyes would be full of stories and he'd have missed something important to her, and that seemed bad. But Chris didn't have a lot of energy to stress over worrying he was a bad boyfriend. Add it to the pile of things stressing him out.

He ate another slice of meat lovers' pizza and opened a new liter of Dr. Pepper so he could focus on his game.

Denver Comic Con Schedule
Saturday Events:
1pm - Cosplay speed dating! Come find your player 2! (hetero/cisgender)
2pm - Cosplay speed dating round 2! (LGBTQ+)

MELANIE'S BOOTS had a mind of their own and they were walking her right where they wanted to go.

The sign on the door read: Cosplay Speed Dating!

There was a line of men in costumes—lots of clowns and video game characters, plus an eye-catching superhero who must have been burning up inside his full-body leather—in the hallway outside. A man in a brown coat and tight pants was holding a clipboard at the door. "You want to join us?" he asked her hopefully.

Melanie shifted from foot to foot. Apparently she did; she was here. But should she join? Well, the answer to that was obvious: No. But now she was standing here with all these men sizing her up and turning around and walking away felt hella embarrassing.

"Do I have to stand in line?" she finally asked, because that seemed like a good out. She was definitely not up for any lines at a mid-sized comic con. What was this, San Diego, aka Melanie's dream comic con? No, it was not. She got ready to huff and march away.

"Nope, women go right in." He swung open the door behind him and waved her in like a VIP at an exclusive speakeasy. The room beyond looked mysterious and full of potential alternate lives.

She couldn't say no. But after she crossed the threshold into the large meeting room, Melanie went hot all over, like she'd crossed an invisible line. This was messed up, what she was doing. There was no justification. She still had a boyfriend. Didn't she? Yet she couldn't help wondering what life would be like with someone new. She wanted to know what else was out there.

She stood awkwardly, arms akimbo, right inside the door. Most of the other women in the room had adopted a similar pose: hips cocked or arms crossed, very few of them sitting. Empty chairs with blue cloth-covered seats, like the kind you found at church, were lined up against the wall around the room, with a matching empty chair sitting directly across from each of them.

The room was lit with fluorescents and was about the least sexy atmosphere she could imagine, which helped Melanie start to breathe again through her panic. This was not dating; this was a convention game.

It was fine. She would see what the options looked like without committing to anything.

And after all: If Chris cared what she did at these events, he would attend them with her.

She grimaced a little, tugging her bodice up higher on her chest. That was probably a double standard. She basically, sorta-kinda broke up with him, but it was still so new and quasi-unofficial. She could go home tonight and take it all back, she knew she could, and Chris would let her.

Her own hypocrisy was stunning. What was wrong with her?

She didn't want to have to *ask* him to want her.

Standing in this room, Melanie finally knew exactly what she wanted: She wanted to be seen. The way Chris used to see her. Sure, she wore this costume to get looked at, in a way no one looked at her at her government office or on the street in regular clothes. But she wanted to be seen by the people important to her. And her own boyfriend refused to do that for her anymore.

She looked around the room for Anna, not sure if she wanted to see her or not; but she didn't. Anna clearly knew herself better than Melanie did: She'd said she would chicken out.

"Alright, ladies, if you would all take a seat." The space captain from outside strode in with his clipboard. "This is a great crowd, thank you all for coming."

He explained the rules, which allowed the women to stay seated for the entire event. Mel sat down, shifting her whip to one side and trying to subtly unwedge her suit as she did by crossing her legs then uncrossing them. This was really a costume meant for standing up. She was showing a lot of skin. She sat up as straight as possible, tucked one foot behind the other and kept her knees locked together as they fell to one side. She was sitting exactly the way her grandma always taught her a lady does.

Being a lady was apparently incredibly uncomfortable.

But this was good. This was her punishment for being here.

Melanie looked around the room at all the other body language signals of female discomfort. And she thought, what would my character do? In the unlikely scenario that Diana was at speed dating—maybe undercover or something—she would own the room. She would sit up straight not to avoid flashing the room but to own her height. If she towered over the men who came in, so be it. If she couldn't make conversation, that was not her fault. She was desirable and needed no man.

Melanie repeated this to herself and tried to believe it applied to her.

Mal blew a whistle and the men hustled in. A kid without a costume who couldn't be more than 18 years old sat down in front of Melanie. Great.

"You look amazing," he said, eyes glued to her breasts. She

resisted the impulse to cross her arms, knowing it would push her boobs up higher.

"Thank you. Where's your costume?" she asked.

"Oh, I don't have one," he said. *Obviously.*

"Seems like a missed opportunity to me." She smiled. He was still looking at her cleavage. It was hardly massive, spill-over cleavage, but in this bodice it was definitely *there.* Ordinarily, this was when Melanie would ask another question and avoid the elephant in the room. But Melanie was not just Melanie today. She put one hand on the whip coiled at her side and snapped the fingers of her other hand at her eye line. "Up here, No-Costume Boy."

His gazed darted up and he startled, as though just realizing she had eyes. He barely blinked for the next three uncomfortable minutes.

Her next conversation was with a clown. His outfit was pretty good—even his hair was green, though it looked like it might be leaking a bit into his scalp—but the conversation was similar to the last one.

"We don't have to talk," she finally told him. "We can just sit here catching up on Instagram."

So they did.

Then the dude clad in red leather sat in front of her. He'd removed his mask and his face was pretty cute. His hair was a sweaty mess standing on end and he ran one hand through it but it stayed matted. He kept shifting in his seat, like his fake—or possibly real— leather pants were uncomfortable. He flashed his number sign at her, as directed, and Melanie jotted it down on her paper.

"Pretty hot in there, huh?" Melanie asked, gesturing at his suit.

"Pretty hot out here, too." He grinned, sitting back in his chair and raising his eyebrows suggestively—up, down—at her. But he landed on her gaze instead of lingering too long lower. She laughed, caught by surprise.

"Thank you?"

"No, thank you. You didn't fake the details."

"Oh." She touched her whip, running her fingers over the textured leather. "It's mostly just store-bought. I'm only a little crafty."

When she realized what she was doing with her hand, she clenched it. This character wouldn't get nervous over a compliment. "It's mostly attitude, anyway," she added, raising her chin.

He grinned. "I could see *that* from two seats over." He gestured at where he came from. "I couldn't wait to get over here."

"I thought your type leaned more assassin." Melanie enjoyed the ping-pong vibe of banter. It gave her a vague sense of nostalgia and helped her relax.

"Well, maybe this is the crossover no one knew was meant to be."

Melanie grinned. "I'd read that fanfiction."

He laughed. "I'm more a talker than a writer, but I'd read it too."

Their host blew his whistle and her companion groaned.

Melanie smiled. "To be continued on Livejournal, I hope."

He stood. "A man can only dream."

Flirting with another cosplay character wasn't *that* bad. After all, she didn't even know his name. He gave her the boost she needed to get through the rest of the men. And she was not tempted to flirt with anyone else. She coasted through the rest of them, mostly stereotypical geeks who genuinely had to be dragged into conversation. She made another dated reference to Livejournal—the entry point for Melanie's own love of fandom—and the next guy gave her a face that instantly aged her. Good thing she didn't say MySpace.

At the end of the event, Melanie stood up, straightened her outfit, and went to the table to find the sheet of paper marked with her number that was supposed to be filled with contact information from the men who were interested in her. If she'd written down an ID number for someone interesting who gave her his info at the end, it was a match. As she picked hers up, there were huffs of disappointment around the table at empty sheets or missing key numbers. One of the other women, un-costumed, glanced at Melanie's full paper, then at Melanie. "You would," she said, as if Melanie offended her. The woman left her half-filled form on the table.

Melanie wandered out of the room with her own paper. The host waved at her. "Thanks for coming!"

She waved back absently.

The clarity about her relationship had been coming and going all day, almost as if the strength of her costume ebbed and flowed, but the results of this event were a revelation. At home, she went unnoticed but here...men were *interested* in her. Or they were interested in Melanie in costume, anyway.

It thrilled her for reasons Melanie didn't want to examine too closely, because in general she was not a person who liked to be noticed by a lot of people. But in costume, everything was different. In costume, Melanie could admit to different needs.

Melanie looked back down at her sheet, which had numbers covering both the front and back in various different handwriting and colored ink. The only "date" on the sheet with an ID she remembered was the leather-clad cosplayer. His phone number was there, next to his identification number, in slashing, left-angled handwriting.

Flirting with him had reminded Melanie of the first years she dated Chris. In the early years, he made it so easy to tease and be teased. He was so laid back that even the times Melanie had brought up something serious, he'd made her laugh.

Relationships were more than a three-minute conversation or lust over a hot look, she reminded herself. Newness wears off.

But weren't relationships also more than sharing dish duty and occasionally turning toward another person's body in the middle of the night?

She wanted both.

~

WHEN MELANIE CAME HOME that night, she walked straight past the living room, through their bedroom to the bathroom and closed the door.

"Hi," he said as she walked past the couch, but she didn't respond.

Fair enough, Chris decided; she'd been wearing her costume and makeup all day and must have wanted to take it off.

She was in there for half an hour, silent and then, eventually, making the usual evening noises. Chris moved from the living room to the bedroom to wait her out.

Melanie had a weird privacy thing about toothbrushing. She didn't like to hear anyone else brushing their teeth or be seen brushing hers either. She'd leave the bathroom door open while she peed but not while she was cleaning her teeth. Chris used to tease her about it all the time, as they both learned each other's quirks, but it became the norm once they moved in together.

So Chris sat propped up in bed while she finished up behind the closed bathroom door and thought hard about how hot his girlfriend looked in her costume and not about how badly he wanted to close his eyes.

He used to be interested in sex; he should be interested. Maybe at least one part of his body was still interested, but it took a lot of mental effort to let it take over and that exhaustion was a struggle itself. It was like he'd tucked that other Chris into a drawer in his mind and didn't know how to pull him back out when he needed him.

And then the struggle was its own condemnation, saying something about him that wasn't manly or tough, and that made it even less likely to come naturally. It was a vicious cycle.

Melanie was yawning when she exited the bathroom in a small minty-fresh cloud. She paused and looked at him on the bed, her makeup-free face entirely blank.

Melanie had a part of herself, a passionate, playful part, that she held at arm's distance from him. She didn't used to. Chris used to be able to access that Melanie whenever he wanted to, without even trying. But he used to be able to access that part of himself, too. Now, most days, playfulness was something he locked up somewhere—not even in the same drawer as his libido, but somewhere even more remote, like his mother's attic—and he couldn't find it without climbing rickety stairs and braving cobwebs. It was too much work.

But on the weekend of a con, that part of Melanie should be closer to the surface. Chris wanted to see that Melanie, the Melanie of her social media. He wanted to bring her out to play. But even trying seemed like an insurmountable task.

"I guess you can sleep in here until we find a better solution," she finally said, and sat on the edge of the bed to lotion her feet.

Chris opened his mouth and hoped for something brilliant or else provocative to say. Nothing came out. Feeling like his skin was the barrier to being able to speak honestly, to spill his soul to the woman he loved, he scrubbed a hand over his face.

Melanie finished her task, turned the bedside light off and got under the covers, curled up on her side away from him.

He laid there, staring at the ceiling as his eyes slowly adjusted to the darkness. He didn't want to lose Melanie but coming up with ideas to woo her back made the sluggish gears in his brain grind. Could he come up with something before it was too late? And then, before he could come up with a plan, he fell asleep.

3

Five Years Ago

After the second con they went to together, Melanie was a little tipsy and a lot more outspoken than usual. The crowd of costumed people, the geeky conversations and many drink specials always surrounding the convention centers seemed to go straight to Melanie's head. Chris loved seeing her less inhibited than usual. It was like watching her lizard brain come out to play.

She went big for the occasion. She was wearing a costume that took her a century to put on and required being green all over. They walked in the front door of Chris's apartment and she turned to him and said, "You."

"Me," Chris said, agreeably. He dropped his keys on the front table and started side-shuffling toward the kitchen to get them both some water.

"Stop," she said, and Chris stopped. He raised his eyebrows at her. Melanie was not one to order people around. But then she was shoving him face-front into a wall and putting her leg between his, rubbing her groin against the back of his thigh. Chris didn't resist her hold on his arm, more than a little turned on. She was humping him and not being very gentle about it. He let her mash his face into the wall and breathed out of one side of his nose as she tried to get herself off. She smelled like hairspray and the thigh he was able to get his other hand around was slick with makeup.

"Couch?" he suggested.

She let go of him. "Go kneel in front of it," she ordered.

They didn't kiss or get naked, because her makeup would have gotten everywhere. She took off her raggedy skirt, put down a blanket and spread her legs on the couch. Then told him to lick her. And he did, taking her orders the whole time. Stay there. Harder. Lighter. Make circles with your tongue. It wasn't just hot because she was ordering him around. It was hot because he made her come harder than he ever had. She let him do that by giving him explicit directions. She made him do that by getting in touch with her green goddess side.

She'd be back to her usual buttoned-up look and spreadsheet addiction the next day, but Chris would always know her playful and carefree side. *That* Melanie was his alone.

And that was when he knew that he was in love.

Denver - Now

When Anna invited Melanie to go for a late lunch with her and a bunch of other artists after the final panel ended early on Sunday afternoon, Melanie agreed. A month ago, she'd committed herself and Chris to attending her niece's dance recital that evening, but she was putting off going home and finding out whether Chris still wanted to go with her.

Besides, Melanie was starving—eating didn't go well with her outfit and the food inside the convention hall was limited to mostly pizza and hot dogs anyway—so she'd agreed without asking Anna many questions.

They arrived *en masse* at an underground barbeque place down the street. It was poorly lit but smelled amazing—presumably, there were no vegetarians in their group. Shelled peanuts and red-checked tablecloths covered the tables. They pushed several together to make one long table for their crowd. Melanie sat down and found herself between a video game character with working lights on his suit and, improbably, the leather-clad superhero from speed dating.

She knew it was the one from speed dating, as opposed to some other red leather'd cosplayer, because he immediately took off his mask and made a "surprise!" face at her.

They exchanged hellos. Hers was a little stilted; he seemed less shocked to see her than she was to see him. He put his mask on the table between them.

"It's not awkward because you never texted, why would you think that?" he asked, breaking the silence. His joking seemed a little forced, but maybe he was nervous.

"Have you ever seen *her* text?" she asked, gesturing up and down her costume. She had his number, still folded in a tiny square, at the bottom of her tote bag. She didn't plan to use it but she liked knowing she had the option. She unfolded her napkin and took a few peanuts.

He grinned and shrugged. "Fair enough."

Melanie decided to try a little harder. It was nice to be chased, but it would be nicer to make a new friend. "Your costume is great, by the way. You wearing it all weekend?"

"Definitely. This thing cost me..." he grimaced. "Well, I won't be going on any other vacations this year, let's put it that way."

Melanie kept shelling peanuts, even though they weren't really that good. Not salty enough. "Same."

He took some peanuts of his own and asked her about upcoming movies starring female superheroes. Melanie was often asked her opinion on the movie versions of the characters she played, so she'd given it a lot of thought. She could easily rant about certain female heroes not getting their own stand-alone movies until 20 movies into the franchise for a solid half hour. Only the waiter interrupting to get their drink order made her stop.

"But they've defeminized her," Melanie concluded, when the

waiter moved on to others at the long table. "It's a stereotypical male action movie with a female star at the center."

"I never thought of it like that." He took a swig of his water but seemed thoughtful, not dismissive. "But what would a real female action movie look like?"

"I don't know…" Melanie's fervor started to fade and she was abashed by how passionate she'd become. She hated being challenged when she was speaking mostly from emotion, because she never knew how to back up a gut feeling. "I guess it would confront how sexualized her costume is head-on or address how much harder she had to work at becoming a sharp-shooter or, you know, doing a pull-up. Just sort of address the differences to being a woman."

"That's not sexist?"

It seemed like an honest question, so Melanie answered it. She turned in her seat slightly to face him. "It's not sexist to acknowledge that women are different from men, I don't think."

Their waiter brought their beers and a basket of fries and they both paused to order food.

Melanie put her napkin in her lap and tucked another one in her cleavage. It was awkward but, particularly after the trash incident, she really didn't want to get anything else on this outfit. He laughed at her a little.

"What's your real name?" she asked, trying to distract him from how ridiculous she must have looked.

"Oh I don't know, I think I might want to keep that a mystery." He grinned at her a little out of the side of his mouth as he picked up a fry.

It was a little annoying, because nobody IRL could get away with remaining nameless. Sometimes deep geeks confused real life with the fandom; maybe he was one of those. But she laughed, shrugged, and focused on her food. "OK, then, Mr. Mystery."

"Shhhh, don't give my secret identity away," he hissed before he took a bite. "I'm just messing with you," he added, speaking around his bite.

Across the table, Anna squealed as she described her new fuzzy green slippers. In the next breath, she pivoted to advise on creating an in-home podcast recording space: "I find that if you get three to four garment racks and fill them with clothes, you can create a makeshift booth around your computer desk and that way you don't have to sit in your closet while you record. I get the kind on wheels so that I can move them around more easily."

Melanie didn't know what it was about this group of strangers but being with them was like coming home. She wasn't even wearing her own clothes, wasn't doing anything that signaled her competence on any subject, but she felt accepted, as if she could jump into any conversation around the table and have something to contribute. It had been a few months—all winter—since her last convention and she'd forgotten this feeling of being seen around fellow geeks.

For example, now Anna and Robin discussed Stjepan Šejić's new hardback and Melanie shouted across the table at them, "I loved it! Definitive!"

Her mystery companion and the space robot on her other side compared the X-Box and Nintendo Switch over her head and she teased them for liking both *Halo* and *Animal Crossing*.

"Real gamers are diverse," chided the red devil next to her, teasing her.

On her other side, the man whose helmet opened at the bottom and allowed him to shovel food in, grunted. She got the feeling he was the kind of nerd who didn't know how to talk to women, especially women with cleavage. She wouldn't hold it against him. "Want another drink?" she asked, standing. His giant head clumsily nodded.

Her speed-dating partner followed her to the bar when she went to ask for another round. Between their rowdy group and the other costume-clad groups filling up the downstairs restaurant, they seemed to have overwhelmed their waitress.

There was a family of normies sitting at a table in the corner that also looked overwhelmed. Guess they didn't check the event calendar before they came downtown that weekend.

"Care for something a little more stiff than a beer?" he asked, leaning against the bar next to her.

Melanie tugged down at the hem of her battle skirt, then tugged up at the top of her bodice. "I've got a family thing later and my older sister is judgy, so probably not."

He laughed and ordered a whiskey on the rocks. "So...I've been wondering if you're ever going to use that piece of paper I wrote my number on earlier today."

"Hmmm," Melanie said, which was her way of not answering the question. The clichéd response crossed her mind: *I have a boyfriend.* It wasn't exactly true. Especially after last night, laying stiff next to someone she used to curl into (he never said anything, he never even *tried*). Still, there was an asterisk in her head and she didn't know how to escape it.

Would Diana slide out of a difficult conversation by pretending it wasn't happening?

"Who says I kept the paper?" she asked, tiptoeing the line between direct and ignorant.

"Really?" He turned to her as he leaned on the bar, one hand on his glass. It was kind of a sexy pose in the skintight outfit. "Why would you come to speed dating and not keep the numbers?"

She smiled without showing her teeth. She hoped her air was "aloof and mysterious," not "frustrated and bitter." She didn't have a good answer for him. "Exercise?"

He huffed and swirled his glass on the dark wood countertop hard enough that the ice clinked. "Fair enough. But...I think you'd be missing out."

"Oh really?"

He shrugged. "I come to a lot of these cons. We might see each other again. It'd be nice to plan ahead instead of hope for, you know...serendipity."

"Solid movie reference. Not very geeky, though." She wagged a finger teasingly at him. She was avoiding his meaning again, faking that she didn't understand, but she couldn't seem to stop herself.

He bumped her hip with his own. "I'm just saying, it's low commitment. But your call, warrior princess." He took his drink and wandered off with it.

Diana had it easy, in some ways. She was in love with Steve and she stayed in love with him forever. She never second guessed her decision not to move on.

But not every woman accepted being alone once their great love ended.

Melanie wasn't sure yet how to move on.

CHRIS MET Melanie at the door. Instead of saying "hello," her sister, Lynn, greeted her with: "You look tired."

Chris watched as Melanie swallowed something sarcastic, not wanting to deal with her sister's punishment, and nodded. "It's been a busy weekend." She and Lynn hugged.

"Your boyfriend was here on time," Lynn noted, turning to Chris. Even though she didn't like him, she'd use him to score points against Melanie. He'd put on jeans and a black t-shirt for the occasion, but Lynn still called it his "bed-to-couch" outfit when she saw it. She'd said it to his face, as if it wouldn't offend him. He hadn't reacted, because she was Melanie's sister and Chris tried to follow Melanie's strict do-not-engage policy. Lynn had given Melanie the cold shoulder for more than a week in the past over the tiniest confrontation, and Chris didn't want to give Melanie any more reasons to be mad at him.

Melanie hesitated, but hopefully not long enough for her sister to notice, and then leaned in and gave him a quick hug. They wouldn't normally kiss in front of Lynn, anyway. Things were nowhere near normal between them, but Melanie didn't seem mad that he'd shown up. She'd texted him that he didn't have to come tonight, but he knew she'd needed an ally against her sister.

Lynn was barely tolerable without someone else there to

exchange glances with over her sister's passive aggressiveness. Melanie put up with it because she wanted to keep her niece, Amelia, in her life. Even though Amelia showed no signs of loving superheroes yet, she did love to dress up to dance, so Melanie always said there was still hope of convincing her cosplay was fun.

Of course, that would require getting past the gauntlet of Lynn, who frequently told Melanie cosplay was "frivolous and immature."

As far as he knew, Melanie hadn't told her sister where she'd been all weekend. Thanks to Lynn's oversized, judgmental presence in her head, once the conventions ended, Melanie put all her costumes back in the closet and kept her hobby hidden from everyone but him.

"Amelia's already backstage," Lynn continued, leading the way down the aisle in the small auditorium to their seats. Melanie followed Lynn, and Chris followed Melanie, silently. "Her makeup took an hour. The lip stain she's required to wear got everywhere."

"I could help with her makeup, if you want," Melanie volunteered.

"It has to be done to precise standards, Melanie," her sister said, as though Melanie didn't know how to follow directions or, heck, even create new eyebrows in the middle of her forehead.

Melanie glanced over her shoulder at Chris, who made a talking head out of his hand and slapped it with his other one. Melanie nearly tripped over someone's foot in the aisle. At least he could still make her laugh.

Once they found their seats, Lynn immediately started down her list of important status updates: Work. Relationship. Home. Children. When she was finished talking about herself, Lynn directed her questions to Melanie. Chris mostly avoided the shotgun blast of her questions but cringed as he watched Melanie get shredded.

Melanie always said Lynn got worse once their parents retired to California. Her lists of "correct ways to live" and "incorrect ways to live" got longer and more defined, and she got less tolerant of people who didn't follow her rules. Chris hadn't really known her before that, so he mostly considered Lynn a bitch who wanted her sister and her daughter to mirror her own image. He'd seen her turn on the charm in front of strangers, but with Melanie and Amelia she was never satisfied.

Finally, the lights blinked and an adult walked on stage, signaling the start of the show. Melanie leaned back in her seat like she was exhausted. Chris raised his eyebrows at her and she rolled her eyes.

He considered taking her hand, but second-guessed the gesture. When was the last time they'd held hands? They'd sat side-by-side like this plenty of times, mostly on the couch at home, but lately they mostly kept to their respective corners.

Chris's skin heated with panic, suddenly, as he looked around the room packed with mostly parents. The task of going back in time—to the days when he and Melanie cuddled in front of movies on the couch—seemed impossible.

So as they watched the performance in silence, he watched Melanie's hand on her leg so close to his own, mere inches away. Helpless to bridge the gap between them.

CHRIS LEFT EARLY on Monday morning, while she was still in bed. It was unusual enough—he barely left the house, most days—that it crossed her mind he might not plan to come back.

She called into work sick and spent several hours staring at the apartment-beige wall next to their bed, clutching a pillow to her chest.

Staring at a wall putting off decisions was not what her favorite character would do—Diana went on and saved the world after Steve died—but it was all Melanie could manage. After a busy weekend, it had all started to sink in.

For an hour, all she could do was let regret and grief and anger and a confusing mix of all the above wash over her.

Eventually, she got a headache from going without her morning coffee. She hauled herself out of bed and skipped putting on pants—she couldn't be bothered—to go to the kitchen and make coffee.

Chris had left her a note on the kitchen table on the pad she wrote the grocery list on:

Let me know if you've changed your mind.

She paused, standing there by the notepad as it dawned on her that Chris wasn't off contemplating their relationship and where it had gone wrong. He thought, what, that showing up last night made amends for everything else? That sleeping next to each other without touching meant they didn't have problems? He should be begging her for another chance—fighting for them—not responding like it was all in her head.

Melanie opened the junk drawer and found a pen. She scrawled back:

Let me know if you've changed.

She ripped the paper with the force of the period she put at the end and underlined changed three times, which was how she knew she'd gone too far. Her mood flipped entirely from nostalgic to angry in less than a minute.

She crumpled up the piece of paper, straightened it back out to tear it into little pieces, and threw it away. She *hadn't* changed her mind. Just because a thing was hard didn't mean she shouldn't do it.

Melanie got her laptop, made coffee—slowly, using the French press as she stood in the kitchen lost in thought—and sat down with a mug at the tiny kitchen table they never used. She opened her laptop and started scheduling out flights for the Atlanta, Baltimore, Chicago, Seattle and New York conventions over coffee. If only she'd gotten in line in the virtual waiting room for San Diego tickets at the beginning of the year like she'd wanted. At the time it had seemed pointless: Why would *this* year be the year she pursued her bucket list dream of going to the biggest comic convention in the world?

Sometimes even exciting things seemed less exciting when she wanted to share them with someone who didn't care.

"No more of that," she said aloud, speaking to herself. She took a deep inhale of her coffee, slightly bitter and slightly sweet, to snap herself out of it. It was time for Melanie to do what Melanie wanted and hopefully now she could enjoy it because she was not trying to please or modify her enjoyment for stupid Chris.

She took a sip of milky coffee from her tall Superman mug, contemplating the total itinerary cost that popped up on her on-screen calculator.

It was a lot of money, but she'd save on hotels if her circuit friends came through. She could buy a day pass at some cons, rather than planning on full weekends. She could take less time off from work that way. And she could scrimp and get crafty on costumes. She didn't need to buy a lot of merchandise, no matter how tempting it might be. It was about the experience, not the souvenirs.

She'd never been to more than two conventions in a year. Now she was considering a whole spreadsheet of plans. *Unreal.*

She sent a text to Anna, DMs to people she met at a random Sherlocked con she'd gone to two years ago, as well as a girl who was the only other person wearing a costume that involved combat boots and a leather jacket during the height of summer at a con last year.

"I'm so excited you're coming!" Anna was the first to respond to her inquiry about an extra bed at Dragon Con. "Of course you can sleep in my room if you don't mind bunking with me and two others. We'll be four to a room. Also, you should come to San Diego! There are tons of activities outside the con. If you do, we have a pull-out sofa still up for grabs in an official hotel down the street."

Melanie bit her lip. San Diego! The con of all cons. Going had been on her life bucket list since she'd started reading superhero fanfiction as a teenager. People in her old LiveJournal community used to post pictures of fantastic costumes and unreal giveaways there every July.

Last year, she'd obsessively created a Twitter list of people sharing updates on the lines at events and the exclusive merchandise available at San Diego Comic Con. She thought it might come in handy...someday.

She plugged San Diego into her spreadsheet and took off Chicago, just to see. It was doable, financially, if a little tight.

Melanie came up for air from her computer and found herself back in her kitchen. Reality check time. What if her life fell apart this summer? Could she do all this traveling and staying in tight quarters with other people, and deal with a break-up at the same time? Melanie craved frequent time and space to herself.

She stood and went to the fridge for a snack. Chris had gone to the store the day before and bought yogurt. She leaned on the open door for a long time, staring at the yogurt cups and letting the cold air wash over her. He'd accidentally bought at least one of the zero sugar kind she hated, but still. He'd *gone*.

She took the one she didn't like, deciding to get it out of the way first, and closed the refrigerator door. Her problem with Chris was not about what he did or didn't do, it was about how they didn't do anything *together*.

Could she deal with a break-up while still sharing space with her boyfriend? Was there any way around it? Realistically, neither of them could afford to move out before their lease was up. But she was going to have to stay strong. She'd made a decision.

It could only *help* her cause to have excuses to be out of the apartment on weekends.

Melanie pulled up the soundtrack to her favorite musical and by the time she'd eaten the sour yogurt, she'd decided. She was not going to miss her shot at the dream summer she'd always wanted, to sit around and wait on Chris to grow up.

She posted her itinerary on Facebook as proof of her commitment to do it.

San Diego - Jul 22
Seattle - August 21
Atlanta - Sept 5
New York - October 8
Baltimore - October 23

~

From @melly_89:
#SDCC here I come! Finally! Bucket list activated! Thanks to
@miz_anna_doll

From @miz_anna_doll:
@melly_89 Squee I am so excited!

From @melly_89:
@miz_anna_doll Omg SAME

From @miz_anna_doll:
Me, @melly_89 @jezabellegreen @manlybubbles0190 @mtinspace7
@deadpoolsbiggestfannoreally gonna have a great time!

From @manlybubbles0190:
@miz_anna_doll @melly_89 @jezabellegreen @manlybubbles0190
@mtinspace7 bring on the slumber party

From @jezabellegreen:
@manlybubbles0190 @miz_anna_doll @melly_89 @mtinspace7 who's
going to sleep??

From @miz_anna_doll:
@melly_89 PLZ DOCUMENT YOUR COSTUME MAKING
PROCESS IN DETAIL

From @melly_89:
@miz_anna_doll Already started on Instagram!!

From @melly_89:
To close friends only
(close-up picture of red sequins)
Working on my #SDCC cosplay! Gotta be EPIC
From @miz_anna_doll: *heart-eye emojis*

~

"WELL LOOK what the cat dragged in."

Chris rarely went to his company's coworking space. It was full of gadgets and snacks and had free cold brew on nitro and kombucha on tap, but it was also full of people who distracted him. On purpose. Like it was part of their jobs.

People like Jenny, who was chewing on a piece of red licorice as though it was a cigar hanging out of her mouth. She wore a black v-neck t-shirt and ripped jeans with ostentatious brand-name shoes, as she had pretty much every time he'd ever seen her. Jenny always seemed to be putting on a performance, saying lines that nobody would say in real life like she was reading them out of a script. He suspected she spent so much time online she didn't quite know how to act IRL.

"Don't usually expect to see you around these parts," she continued. "To what do we owe the honor? And so early in the day!"

Chris sat down at one of the free desks and started plugging in his gear. He was trying to figure out what to say. He obviously couldn't tell her: *My girlfriend is pissed. I think we're breaking up and I feel like my world is ending.* He might cry and that would be horrifying.

"Just needed a change of scenery," he said finally, like he was one of the clichéd characters in Jenny's play. "Felt like the walls were closing in on me at home."

"Tell me about it." Jenny spun her chair in gentle waves, from one side to the other between her two feet braced on the ground. "Ever since my boyfriend walked out, you could drop a pin in my place. Sometimes I feel like actually talking to the walls."

Chris glanced at her. He wasn't sure he wanted to follow up on that, but it seemed impolite not to. "I didn't know you were going through a breakup," he said. "Sorry."

She shrugged, an exaggerated movement, and screwed up her face. "Thems the breaks I guess. Literally. I'm excited about it, tell you the truth. Gonna try Tinder, like all the kids do. Last time I was on there was before the pictures moved."

"The pictures move?" Chris booted up his computer and plugged in the second monitor, wondering how quickly he could quit talking about his supervisor's love life. Well, *technically* she was his supervisor. He was her direct report. But the company was so flat he worked with people above her on a regular basis. She couldn't get him *fired*.

"Yeah." And then he realized to his horror that she was pulling out her phone. "You can upload a little gif or video clip. Now that you're here, I'm going to ask you later to get a shot of me at my computer. Natural habitat, you know?"

"Yeah," Chris said. She held up her phone and he looked at it politely. There was a short repeating video of a shirtless guy on a mountain bike going down a rocky hill. "He should be wearing a helmet. You probably don't want to date him," he offered with a straight face.

Jenny laughed and turned back to her phone again. "You're right." She swiped left. "Thank you. You probably saved me from some really good, reckless sex," she said, matching his dry tone. She looked around the empty office furtively. "I probably shouldn't have said that. Is that harassment?"

"It's OK, I won't tell," Chris said, standing. "I'm going to get some coffee, you want any?"

"I'm already on my second cup, better catch up." Jenny swiveled back to her own computer. *Thank God.*

Chris stood alone in the mostly stainless-steel kitchen alone and stared at the taps. He hoped that when he went home, everything would be different. *Back to normal. Better.* Any of those things would work. If he knew how to make it happen, he would. But since he seemed to be part of the problem, maybe leaving for a while would be best.

What had he done that was so bad? Sure, he wasn't perfect, but then neither was Melanie. She sometimes committed him to plans with her tyrant of a sister, who was the only member of her family who was still local, without asking—and he went along with it to be supportive. She once went on a detox diet that involved filling their fridge with the most disgusting food he'd ever had the misfortune of smelling. She had, from time to time, literally eaten crackers in bed— reminding him of the inappropriate joke his dad used to make: *I wouldn't throw her out of bed for eating crackers.*

But he thought they both put up with each other because love and companionship balanced out the dumb and smelly stuff. He thought he was *set* in this particular area of his life, like he'd checked the box on a stable relationship and the one deep connection allowed per dude.

The thing Chris was scared of, that he tried to avoid thinking but couldn't stop prodding like it was a hurt tooth, was: *What if she doesn't love me anymore?*

He finally found the motivation to fill a glass and return to his desk in the other room.

Jenny swiveled around immediately, holding her phone. "Will you look at my profile? I want your opinion as a man."

"Can I give my opinion as something else?" Chris collapsed into his own chair and started drinking his coffee like it was liquid courage. It was foamy and almost too smooth, not at all like his coffee at home which he suddenly missed desperately.

Jenny laughed. She held out her phone and he reluctantly took it.

Jenny's profile picture was a picture of her wearing a bikini top and jean shorts. Her hair was down and it was longer than he'd have thought. The next picture was her in a flowy dress, holding what he thought was a mimosa and smiling at someone off-screen.

Her profile text said: "Brunch. PC gaming. Dogs. Tall men. Hmu."

Chris handed it back. "You look cute."

Not a word he'd ever applied to her before, but true.

"Yeah?" Jenny seemed doubtful.

"Definitely."

She also looked nothing like herself, but he was not going to tell her that. The Jenny he knew was obsessed with clean code and UX design. She was a stickler for putting notes in her code to make it easier to fix anything later. Every time she saw a dog on the street, she went all gooey but when asked about getting one she'd shout, "No! Too big of a commitment!" She literally never wore anything but the jeans and black t-shirt, at least in the office. She started drinking after 5, even when they were still working, and once spilled an entire bottle of wine on her keyboard while she was on a Slack video call with him.

"This is great," Jenny said, swiping on her phone. "There are so many options out there!"

Chris shrugged. Lately, he loathed options. He used to come up with five different plans—alternate universes, Melanie called them— for every date. But now he secretly *liked* it when Melanie made plans for both of them without asking. If he had to go out, at least he didn't have to think about what he was doing and second guess going in the first place because he wanted to stay home and sleep.

"Have fun," he told Jenny, and swung around to face his computer. He hoped to get lost in his work so he didn't have to keep thinking about Melanie and when she'd become so unhappy.

~

Chris: (7:09 p.m.) I'm coming home now

Melanie: (7:15 p.m.) OK

Chris: (7:15 p.m.) Do you need anything?

Melanie: (7:15 p.m.) No

Chris: (7:20 p.m.) Have you changed your mind?

Melanie: (7:22 p.m.) No

Chris: (7:22 p.m.) So I'm sleeping on the couch?

Melanie: (7:25 p.m.) We can trade off I guess

Chris: (7:30 p.m.) It's fine, I'll sleep on the couch

~

TUESDAY WAS a beautiful day but her windows didn't open at work.

Melanie's office seemed particularly stuffy. Her job as a data analyst for the district office of a member of Congress meant slow days with a lot of long coffee breaks and conversations in the kitchen. People always took a lunch break, and if they didn't, they left an hour early, at 4 p.m., thanks to government hours.

The stability and routine suited her. But she didn't always like that everyone had a lot of time to chat and ask her what she did on the weekend.

She told them, of course. Melanie didn't like liars so she was certainly not going to be one. But as she stood in the kitchen wearing trousers with an inner hook closure and a button-down shirt she'd ironed after she washed it, she knew that no one suspected she was walking around downtown on Sunday with her ass hanging out of her blue, starred bottoms. "I went to Denver Comic Con," she said, without providing details.

Instead, she warded off questions by asking her own. "Have you ever been?" she asked her coworker Nancy, who framed cross-stitch projects and hung them on her office walls. Nancy laughed way too long before explaining why she'd never go to a con.

"Did you come downtown this weekend and see everyone walking around?" she asked Sam, who lived 40 minutes away in a suburb, and checked at least once a day to make sure his car wasn't stolen out of their downtown parking lot. He went on a rant about trying to park in the city.

"Have you seen the *Avengers* movies?" she asked Penny, the designer intern with a better work ethic than their full-time graphic designer. Penny said she was "more into indie films."

Max, their communications director and the busiest person in the office judging by how she ducked in and out of the kitchen without pausing, asked Melanie if she saw anything politically-themed at the con. "We could use some color on the official feed."

"Sorry," Melanie said. "Nerds are mostly progressive, but in a libertarian way."

Max gave her a decent Vulcan salute. "Live and let live, I guess. Coming to brunch this weekend?"

Melanie shrugged and murmured, "Maybe!"

She wasn't going to Max's standing monthly brunch club. Melanie only joined them when she knew there was something going on that meant she didn't have to talk about her own life.

It was about privacy. She didn't put personal things in her office or wear themed t-shirts on casual Fridays. She didn't follow her coworkers on Instagram or friend them on Facebook.

When she had a bad day, she closed her door.

When it was epically bad, she called in sick. Or worked from home.

She *really* didn't like it when people knew things about her that she didn't tell them herself.

She would have avoided coming into work on Tuesday, but Chris didn't leave that morning and she didn't want to be cooped up with him in their apartment all day. She hadn't talked to him since Sunday. The night before, she'd stayed in the bedroom when she heard him come home. That morning, she'd put her coffee in a thermos and left without so much as glancing into the living room.

They hadn't had much to talk about for a long time. At least they'd stopped pretending now.

Every time Melanie had doubts, she pulled up his text message asking her if she'd changed her mind.

He didn't even try to give her any reason to change her mind. He acted like she would or should or could, and why? Because she was being silly, was probably what he thought. She was hormonal or emotional or other words men use to dismiss women's valid reasons.

Melanie had no reason to want to leave work early that night, so at lunch she closed her office door and sewed sequins for awhile. She didn't have a lot of time to get her San Diego costumes ready and she couldn't possibly go to the con of all cons without a great, new costume.

The rest of the day would be consumed with tackling the new filing software project that the chief of staff kept bugging her about. She spontaneously decided she'd stay late and work on an RFP. Keep herself as busy as possible.

It worked for the next chunk of the day. Around 5 o'clock, she opened a new spreadsheet and titled it *New Apartment*. She researched listings to get a feel for what was out there. It'd been years since she'd apartment hunted alone.

At first, the listings seemed promising, but then almost everything became prohibitively expensive in the fine print. It quickly became overwhelming.

But anything to avoid being squashed in that apartment with the boyfriend she no longer...well. Melanie couldn't quite say, or even think in her mind, that she no longer loved Chris. Her brain shied away from the idea like it was a hot surface. *Here there be painful dragons!* Acknowledging that the person you thought was the love of your life... *wasn't...* was a yawning hole Melanie didn't want to fall into.

She'd get used to the thought. Slowly. By the end of the summer, maybe she'd be using past tense on her relationship.

From @melly_89: Men are the worst. That's it, that's the tweet

From @miz_anna_doll: @melly_89 AGREE

From @melly_89 (unless they're Deadpool. Or Captain America. Or Superman, but not in "Superman Returns" because worst ex ever)

@melly_89: @miz_anna_doll but I bet even superheros can be bros who act like women have different logic than him, like we're a whole other species with less valid emotions

@miz_anna_doll: @melly_89 well at least they have an excuse if they're from a different time period and were frozen in ice for 60 years

@melly_89: @miz_anna_doll fair, it DOES take some kind of other-species logic to wear panty hose and heels all the time like a 1940s woman

@miz_anna_doll: @melly_89 this is why I write about squirrels! They can be badass without being gendered :) ;)

HE THOUGHT ABOUT MAKING DINNER, so that it'd be waiting for Melanie when she got home. It was idea No. 1 on his new Trello board of ways to win her over. But then Chris thought about the effort of coming up with an idea, checking the pantry for ingredients, going to the store for what was missing, probably forgetting some key detail and having to come up with a new plan, putting it all together and not burning it and timing it right and all the rest...and he couldn't do it. He'd started work early and went late and never took a real lunch and he'd had too many days like that lately.

He opened an app instead and tried to predict what delivery food

Melanie would want to eat but failed at that too because thirty minutes later she walked in the door and there was no food, no fresh smells filling the apartment.

She gave him a resigned look when he asked, "Have you eaten yet?"

Then she went to their room and closed the door.

What else was new. It had been like this all week. Chris was pretty close to giving up, because he failed every time he tried, and now he was trying to meet another work deadline so he didn't exactly need anything else on his plate. Emotion management took a lot of time and energy.

He went back to his computer.

Jenny on Slack:

(7:16 p.m.) What do you think of this guy?

(screenshot of a Tinder profile with a guy clearly giving a best man speech)

Jenny on Slack:

(7:16 p.m.) He's cute, right? But what's the deal with this?

(screenshot of a Tinder profile reading: "5 miles away. Likes to play. Dominant. Vanilla need not apply.")

Chris on Slack:

(7:17 p.m.) Are you sure you want to go there?

Jenny on Slack:

(7:18 p.m.) I'm not sure of anything except I'm trying to try new things!

Chris on Slack:

(7:18 p.m.) Idk, this might be TOO new but up to you

Jenny on Slack:

(7:20 p.m.) You might be right

Jenny on Slack:

(7:20 p.m.) Also can you have that Javascript done for tomorrow?

Chris on Slack:

(7:22 p.m.) Working on it now

THE SCREEN BLURRED and Chris rubbed his eyes, hard. Maybe he needed glasses? He stood and walked a circle around the couch, trying to roll some of the tension out of his bowed shoulders. He grabbed a Dr. Pepper from the kitchen. He should probably switch to diet, but that was something to think about later. He sat back down and the code seemed a little clearer, so he went back to work.

4

Four Years Ago

Chris built a pillow fort in his apartment so that they could see the Bat signal on Melanie's cheap plastic alarm clock better. The design was elaborate—it had two rooms and a lobby, and he used all the chairs, cushions and sheets in his apartment to build it.

When he'd shown it to Melanie, after inviting her over for Chinese food and Netflix, he was sweaty and excited. She'd only ever seen a man that flushed when there was a football game playing somewhere nearby.

The idea had been hers, but she'd been joking. The clock had been the first item of hers that she brought to Chris's apartment with the intention of leaving it—a test run that she could say was a joke if he wasn't ready—and when she turned it on and the weak light barely reached his ceiling, she'd shrugged and said it must be designed for a kid's pillow fort.

But he'd built her one. They turned the lights off, crawled inside, and sprawled on the carpet, sharing a throw pillow from the couch. The Bat signal showed up perfectly on the sheet stretched a few feet above them.

When Chris turned his head toward hers, foreheads touching, she could see the bat light reflected in his eyes. "Do you like it?" he whispered. His fingers threaded with hers. It was the most intimate they'd ever been.

She felt like she was looking straight into his soul, illuminated by the children's toy on the floor at their feet. "I love it," she said. "But not as much as I love you."

~

SAN DIEGO - NOW

Melanie had been standing in the hot sun waiting to get into an exhibit five blocks from the convention hall for an hour when a man in a recognizable clown costume cut in front of her. She was sluggish to respond.

The comic convention in San Diego sprawled across multiple convention halls and city streets in the Gaslamp Quarter. She'd seen a glut of humans, most wearing laminated tags on ribbons around their necks and plastic bags emblazoned with advertisements for CW shows or video games, crowded in the blocks in front of convention row. They streamed back and forth from the hotels lining the street, then trickled out into bars and restaurants from there. Everybody walked to get around. Taxis couldn't get down blocked streets. Police were everywhere, guiding traffic and monitoring crosswalks.

The crowd showcased a handful of insanely detailed costumes, but mostly only worn by professional cosplayers surrounded by an entourage. The majority of the regular attendees were dressed in jeans and t-shirts or shorts and tank tops, given the daily temperatures in southern California.

Plenty of local businesses offered an air conditioned Wi-Fi oasis, themed exhibits, themed drinks, or lunch specials. Studios strategically placed "immersive experiences" and real-life "Easter eggs" on street corners blocks away from the convention center. Melanie tried to hit those free exhibits. She was only on her second one and was already thinking about retreating to the A/C in her hotel room.

"Excuse me," she said to the green-and-purple interloper.

She was so far along the path to heat stroke she was too frazzled to even browse her phone, so it took her half a minute to tune in enough to recognize him. "You devil! I didn't recognize you without your leather."

He grinned. "Well, it's July." He wiggled his fingers up and down her body, keeping an appropriate amount of distance. "I see we match today."

"Like you said, it's July." She'd chosen to do the latest movie version of his character's on-screen love interest. Her legs were bare, not counting the fishnets, all the way up to her sequined bootie shorts. Melanie really loved this costume because it was both daring and contained at the same time. She'd decided fishnets were magic. They defied cellulite, somehow making all bare thighs look better than they ever would completely naked.

She put her hand on her hip and twirled the blue-tipped ends of her wig. "Puddin'," she added with a flirtatious smirk at him, because why not?

He threw back his head and gave her an impressive cackle. "Mr. J. approves."

"Can we take your picture?" a mom in the next row of the line asked. Melanie nodded and the woman waved her kids, a boy and a girl wearing matching yellow shirts, over to stand with Melanie and the man whose real name she still didn't know. He put his hand on her shoulder. Melanie cocked her hip and twirled her hair. They both smirked for the camera.

"Tell the super villains thank you," the mom said to her kids, after snagging the picture. They turned in unison and said, "thank you!" before darting away, giggling.

"How did you recognize me?" Melanie asked him.

"Anna told me you were here and then gave me your Instagram

handle so I stalked you down the street until I spotted you," he said. "I needed to get some air so I thought I'd stop by."

"You were in the convention center?" Melanie heard her voice get a little breathless. She'd stood outside the row of convention halls watching as thousands of people moved in and out and stood in lines that wrapped around the outside balconies. It was difficult to be in town this week and not have access to the mythical space—and, well, to the air conditioning.

"I was. It's intense. Very claustrophobic sometimes. You didn't get tickets?"

"I was too late. Anna talked me into coming anyway but I feel totally left out."

"Well, you should definitely come back next year. This is only the second time I've come. Last year, I was completely overwhelmed and lost most of the weekend wandering around in a daze. I saw, like, three panels and none of the big ones." He leaned over and hooked his finger around the bag over her shoulder. "What did you get?" He tried to peer in at her swag.

"The museum down the street is giving out masks and posters." She pulled them out to show off. Melanie didn't quite know why she stood in line for a *Borderlands* mask. *She* didn't play *Borderlands*. Chris did.

"Damn, this is better than anything I've gotten free inside." He held the mask up over his face. "So cool."

What a boy. She should give the mask to him and be rid of the temptation to think about her boyfriend. Ex-boyfriend. "You're just trying to make me feel better."

He laughed. "You're right, I say that to all the girls."

She raised her eyebrows. "Wow, you really need to work on your attitude. That wasn't very realistic."

"We've got a critic over here!"

She laughed. "I'm kidding. Your first laugh was pretty good."

"How long have you been standing in this line?" he asked. He held his hand up over his eyes and peered at the front of the line, still another row of people away.

She checked her phone. "An hour and 10 minutes."

"Damn, I hope it's worth it."

"It's some kind of immersive experience." They both turned to the blue phone booth set up on the corner of the downtown San Diego streets. "And more free swag. I already got a free happy-face cookie."

"Oh, I didn't know there was a free cookie involved." He started looking around.

"Are you going to wait with me?" Melanie would bail if he asked her at this point, to get out of the sun and even though she really wanted to get to the booth and have the "experience" for herself just to know if she'd been wasting her time.

"I don't know, I might need to go find that museum..."

She made a face and tried to look *not abandoned*. She chose to come here on her own. She was having *fun* damnit. She didn't need company.

She had to admit she wanted it though.

"You guys look so cute! Can we get a picture?" Two women passing in a group on the street stopped and pulled out their cell phones.

He turned and put an arm around Melanie, pulling a giant grimace that stretched out his painted lips. Melanie wrapped a lock of blue wig hair around her finger and cocked her hip again.

"Awesome, thank you!" the women called as they move away. "You guys look great."

"Seems like we're meant to be," he said as he dropped his arm and turned back to Melanie. "Standing side-by-side, that is. Guess I better stay."

"And I guess you better tell me your real name, finally." Melanie picked her bag of swag back up off the ground where she dropped it to keep it from messing up the shot. "I can't keep calling you by the name I met you under when you aren't in his outfit."

"No?"

"It feels a little too meta. Not even the same universe."

He laughed. "Fair. The thing is...it's really Matt."

She raised both eyebrows at him.

"Matt Broward." He shrugged.

"OK," Melanie said. "And are you really a lawyer by day and/or a superhero by night?"

"Alas, neither. Media professor by day..."

"And by night?"

He paused and gave her a little side-bow, kicking up one side of his garish mouth. It was surprisingly sexy, for an evil clown. "Guess you'll have to find out."

Melanie bit her lip, not sure she wanted to follow him down this path. It was fairly safe to flirt, wasn't it? Since she didn't really even think there was actual room to get into a lot of trouble here. Everyone she'd met so far at this convention was sleeping in a room with at least three other people. Still, she'd heard rumors. "I've heard things get wild here at night," she said slowly, eyes set ahead at the line and not at him.

Matt cocked his head and shrugged, but she could see he was giving her the same side-eye she was giving him. "Have you?"

"Nerds-gone-wild and all that?"

He laughed again, and it had a touch of embarrassment. She liked that he was maybe a little shy. It was relatable. "I'm going to need at least a drink before I admit to that."

"How many drinks 'til it's more than talk?" Melanie surprised herself. The heat must've been going to her head to blurt out something like that. She'd always liked shy guys, or guys who held back; they made her more aggressive. When she first started texting Chris after meeting him in that grocery store, his responses were so slow and brief that eventually she said, "We should meet for a drink." And he said, "OK, how about 7pm at Union Hall."

Chris used to be really good at taking an opening and running with it.

Melanie tuned back into the conversation, still smiling a little even though the memory was bittersweet.

Matt didn't seem to have noticed her brief mental distance. He grinned, slowly. It was very Heath Ledger, what he was doing as he stood there all tall and gangly with green hair, smirking instead of responding. Very sexy.

At what point should she disclose she technically still had a live-in mostly-ex-boyfriend? Did she even have to?

Maybe the technicality of still having a live-in boyfriend made her reckless. Ordinarily, it took her a solid six months to get over a break-up. At best. She didn't like to date while she was recovering because rebounding was never worth it; at least it never had been. But there was always a first time.

Now, she wasn't sure what the rules were, so she smiled back at Matt in the blazing sun. Enjoying the way it heated her up inside and out.

From @melly_89:
(Picture of Melanie and Matt in costume)
Found my puddin'! @mtinspace7 #sdcc
Liked by @mtinspace7 and 70 others

CHRIS'S VISION went red when he saw a picture of Melanie and some guy in a matching couples costume on her Instagram.

He'd been stalking her on social media in San Diego. Not stalking, really. Casually monitoring. By checking her Instagram account every few minutes. OK, stalking. He wanted to know if she was having a good time. If she was happy. Happy without him.

He was surprised how much he wanted to be there with her, considering he was finally getting some sleep now that he was in their empty bed and able to keep his own hours. And considering that for the past few months, even the thought of travel had been exhausting to him.

Melanie had always wanted to go to San Diego Comic Con. He tried to get her tickets one year, logging on right when they went on sale, but never made it out of the virtual waiting room.

He always imagined they'd go together. He wanted to see her glee and hold her hand while she explored—trailing her while she darted from booth to booth.

Now she was there hanging out with some other guy. They looked so right together, in their matching costumes, it hurt.

After he saw the post, Chris stomped around their apartment, having a quiet tantrum. He threw a tissue box. He slapped the wall. He drank a glass of water because there was nothing else to drink.

He was impotent in this situation and it frustrated the hell out of him.

She'd put a list—a printed list—of "rules" on the fridge before she left:

- Negotiate who gets the bed early in the day
- Buy and eat your own food + do your own dishes
- Alternate who takes out the trash every other week
- Keep common spaces clean (except couch may be left made-up as a bed unless we have company)
- No committing each other to events without asking

Chris was beginning to understand what she really wanted: She wanted him to be who he was when they met. But Chris wasn't sure he still knew how to be that guy. He'd lost some of the components that made him that Chris, as if his hardware deteriorated with time. He didn't notice when it happened, but Melanie's announcement made him confront the facts.

He hadn't been functioning at 100 percent for a while.

Over the last few days, he'd been swinging wildly between anger, because Melanie didn't understand he was tired and confused and didn't mean to stop being the boyfriend he used to be, and the understanding that of course Melanie didn't want to be with someone depressed and exhausted. He couldn't find a way to fix either of those things.

His Trello board of ideas to win her back was woefully empty: It included things like "make dinner" and "initiate sex" and "get groceries."

There must be something in this apartment that would give him the clue he needed to get their relationship back on track. Chris started with Melanie's "memory box"—a box in their hall closet of momentos from their relationship—pulling out old comic con tickets and printed photos, like a Polaroid they took at some party.

She'd given him three months.

If nothing else, he still had it in him to buy himself a little time to get them back on track. He must.

Matt, Anna, Roger, Tim and a couple of other people Melanie didn't know were sitting at a table tucked in the corner of a busy bar on Fifth Avenue that was filled with a wide range of people—a few people still in costume, a few in shorts and baseball caps, and a bunch dressed up to party with celebrities.

Melanie wasn't cool enough to have any celebrity party invitations, but Anna was, and had offered to bring her along as her plus-one. So Melanie went to her hotel room and showered and changed into the low-cut pantsuit she'd bought after she saw it worn on British TV. She was poised and elegant and ready to run into someone like Michael B. Jordan. *Omg, if only.*

Even though it was ridiculously unlikely, a small thrill ran through Melanie at the thought that she *could* hook up with Michael B. Jordan now if she wanted. She was free, wasn't she?

She pushed aside the niggling thought that it was only sort of true. She'd figure out the loopholes when she needed them.

Matt stood and pulled out a chair when Melanie approached the table, like he was watching for her. He wore dark jeans and a Henley that clung to him in a way that made it obvious he wasn't wearing fake muscles under his costumes. "Good thing you're here. We've had to save this chair multiple times from interlopers," he said, gesturing around at the busy restaurant.

"Folx," she said seriously, scanning the table and trying to be gender-inclusive, mainly for Roger, but also because she didn't know the two people at the end dressed up as anime characters. "I want you to know you are all heroes to me, every one of you. Thanks for the chair."

They all laughed and Anna provided Melanie with introductions to people she was never going to remember because they were too far away to make conversation in the loud space.

Matt moved his chair closer to hers once she sat and filled her in on what had happened so far: Anna made it into Hall H to see Kristen Bell, the cocktail special was called Space Force 'Tini but tasted delicious, and Matt had a plus-one to a nostalgia party later featuring the cast of a TV show she still hadn't watched yet, if she was interested.

"Oh wow, are you sure?" Melanie answered without looking directly at him, because they were so close her lips would practically meet his if she turned. What was the etiquette for this? Was accepting a date to an exclusive party like letting the man pay for dinner? Was something expected of her in the unwritten dating code if she went with him? What if she met a celebrity there, then did she *really* owe Matt?

"Of course," he said, lightly, as if none of this crossed his mind. "Who else would I want to go with?"

She smiled automatically because it was really nice to feel wanted. Across the table, Anna was deep in conversation with Tim about something on her phone. Melanie hadn't yet had the chance to get the download from her about what she knew about Matt.

Still, she was in San Diego to have fun and see what she could see outside of the convention hall. And just because she was dressed as Melanie, not a character, didn't mean she couldn't step outside of her careful bubble. So she said, "Then I'd really love to go. It sounds amazing."

Matt smiled in response. "I'm glad I don't have to go alone. There will be lots of people there who think they're too good for me."

"Smart to bring another loser along then." Melanie quirked her lips at him to let him know she was joking.

"At the very least, there will be a lot of free food and booze. That's the main reason I go to these parties."

"So don't eat too much here, is that what I'm hearing?"

"Exactly." His breath tickled her ear a bit as he leaned even closer. She wasn't sure she liked the way he was getting in her space, but she was also not sure what to do about it. Was it her residual ideas about "being in a relationship" and loyalty to Chris that were making her hesitate over Matt...or was she picking up red flags somewhere else?

She and Chris hadn't actually had a conversation about the rules or boundaries of their new existence. They'd barely talked. He'd been working from coffee shops or his co-working space and sleeping on the couch. She'd been staying at work late and eating out or with friends. The weekends were the most difficult—navigating breakfast in the kitchen around the same time and not always having plans to run off to—but Melanie had been spending most of her free time working on costumes, including one she didn't finish in time for San Diego and that probably wasn't going to be ready for Seattle either (she couldn't get the leather right). And Chris could literally put on his noise-cancelling headphones and spend hours gaming at his computer. They'd been working around each other, tensely and in silence.

Anyway, she was glad to get away this weekend.

The celebratory mood of the crowd in the restaurant was infectious. Somehow Melanie knew without eavesdropping that every conversation in here was deeply, deeply geeky. They might be talking about anything from a blockbuster movie to a queer, indie manga but they were all geeking out over something. She adored it. She looked around the table of friends and strangers and knew she was among her people.

"I'm so glad I came," she said, leaning into Matt's ear. She brushed up against his shoulder as she did it. The sensation of a man that close to her gave Melanie a little zing. She hadn't been touched in a long time; she'd been specifically avoiding it at home.

He grinned back at her. "I'm glad you came, too."

"How many times have you been again?" she asked.

"This is only my second time. I loved it so much last year I had to do it again." He shrugged. "I can really only afford two cons a year. So I go to the one close to me and this one."

So they lived near each other. *Interesting.*

"Do you make art or write or anything or are you..."

"Just a fan?" He laughed. "Yeah, I'm just a fan. I mean, I'm a gamer and I've seen all the *Star Wars* movies and shows a million times. But I don't make anything, not even my own costumes."

"I make some of my costumes, but otherwise I'm just a fan, too. Unless you count the reviews and how-tos I write on Instagram."

"I guess you could count all those comments I leave on reddit..."

She chuckled. "I find that most geeks are really creative people when it comes right down to it. We're all expressing ourselves somehow."

"You seem to have a theory for everything."

Melanie withdrew into herself briefly. Her voice sounded small: "Is that a bad thing?"

"No, not at all. I like it." He pulled out his phone. "Tell me how to find you on Instagram."

She did, and gained a new follower who she followed back.

Melanie glanced around the table. Everyone was on their phone, some of them leaning close together in groups to watch a video or read a Twitter thread. "We're a bunch of socially awkward geeks, for sure," she said to Matt.

"Nah. We're just technologically-forward," he volleyed back. She'd already gotten two Instagram notifications that @mtinspace7 liked her pictures. She needed to retroactively tag him in the selfie she'd posted earlier.

They all had another round and then people started bailing for parties. Everyone seemed to have a different place to go and Melanie was grateful she got to tag along somewhere. Matt's party was later in the evening, so they exchanged numbers and she joined Anna at the AMC party.

The party was themed for a show she hadn't been watching, and a little more corporate than fan-driven, with posters for AMC shows everywhere and people in actual suits trying to deliver a presentation while everyone ignored them and talked. But they were offered free appetizers the minute they walked in the door of the bar, and the star of the show stood by the open bar. Just. Stood. There. Waiting for a drink like a normal person.

"Omigod," Melanie said, frozen in place. Anna dragged her over to him and asked if they could take a picture.

"This is Melanie's first San Diego Comic Con," Anna offered as reasoning. He said yes, and joked he had to with that logic.

Melanie immediately posted the selfie on Instagram and Matt commented: "You're having more fun there :("

"That might be the highlight of the night, so don't set your expectations too high," Anna warned her.

Melanie was surprised and a little bummed to be warned off her high. Of the two of them, Anna seemed like the one with constantly high expectations—and the one who usually saw them pay off. For example: She decided to start posting her own comics on her blog one day and a year later had a book deal. It was not a big seller or anything, and she maybe only got it because she already had connections, but it allowed her to afford going to more comic conventions and got her into cool parties like this.

"You mean this party isn't just chock-full of celebrities?" Melanie asked, distracted because she couldn't stop admiring the picture on Instagram, clearly her best post of the year.

"Mostly starving artists. Like me." Anna shrugged, taking her drink from the bartender.

"I've got it," Melanie said, tipping for both of them. They turned their backs to the bar and scoped out the party. "Do you think of yourself as a starving artist?"

"Maybe not *starving*. But only because it's not my full-time job," Anna said. Then she went off on a tangent about one of the educational panels she sat on at the convention. Melanie didn't get to see any panels, so even a boring one sounded fascinating, but she listened politely to Anna's complaint that there was nothing original about their presentation and panels at smaller cons had to try harder.

"Enough about *me*," Anna finally interrupted herself. "What's going on with you and *Matt*?"

A flush crept up Melanie's lower back, where she always felt her embarrassment first. Even though she wanted to talk to Anna about Matt, she didn't like that Anna knew there was something to talk about. She hated when other people knew things about her that she hadn't meant to reveal. It meant she was being way too obvious. "I wanted to ask you about him..."

"He's cute. Good cosplay."

"How do you know him?"

"Hm." Anna made a vague gesture. "From...around? I think we met in Denver last year?"

"Is he, like, known for anything?"

She frowned. "I don't think so. I mean, I know he volunteers sometimes. You know, stands in the back and keeps time for the panels and that kind of thing. Raises the 'five more minutes' sign for the moderators? I think he was a volunteer supervisor last year in...maybe D.C.? I'm sorry, they all start to blend together at some point. I'd have to look through my Instagram feed. Maybe he's in one of the pictures."

"OK. So, good at cosplay and responsible, you think?" Melanie ticked the qualities off on one hand. "I guess that's a promising start."

Anna laughed. "And flirty. With *you*."

Melanie tipped her head in acknowledgement. She couldn't deny it. And even though she wished Matt was a little more discreet, for her sense of privacy, she was also thrilled by the overt attention.

"What's happening with the boyfriend?" Anna asked it casually, while she was bringing her drink to her mouth.

A sense of guilt tiptoed up Melanie's spine. "Um we're...on a break." She winced immediately, because that was obviously the most famous and famously loaded line from *Friends* she could possibly use.

"You do you, girl. Take advantage of the time apart." Anna raised her eyebrows. "What happens at comic con stays at comic con."

"Is that true?" Melanie checked the room. The bar was crowded and loud but that didn't mean no one was listening. She went for it, anyway. "How does anyone hook up...we're all three deep in hotel rooms."

Anna laughed. "Ask Roger and Tim."

Melanie blinked, eyes wide. "What? Seriously?"

"They get creative somehow. It's like a con-only situation. Roger has some kind of open relationship back home." Anna waved at someone in the crowd. "I'll be right back."

Melanie, who was not as extroverted as Anna, surveyed the crowd uneasily. She knew no one here besides the friend she came with. Anna was already deep in conversation with two other people, her back to Melanie. Melanie stood holding her drink with her free hand propping up her elbow, trying to appear like she was standing there alone by choice.

Everyone at this party must be *connected* somehow—connected enough to have an invitation, anyway. But these Hollywood types were not *her* people.

She pulled out her phone again, to give herself something to do. She was racking up a lot of likes on Instagram, including one from

Chris. That he knew where she was and that she was doing something amazing but that he didn't know the full story made her something she didn't want to examine too closely. He might as well be anyone, not the one person she used to update throughout her day.

She eyed Anna, who showed no signs of returning, before she texted Matt back.

> Melanie: (9:09 p.m.) Your party doesn't have celebrities?

> Matt: (9:10 p.m.) Literally sitting in a corner trying to disappear

> Melanie: (9:10 p.m.) Same. At least you're sitting

> Matt: (9:10 p.m.) Want to find a bar to sit at together?

Melanie glanced around, trying not to look uncomfortable. She should stick it out at the party for more than five minutes, but it really didn't seem like her scene. She noticed Anna had been swept away somewhere. She couldn't even see her.

> Melanie: (9:12 p.m.) Let me find Anna and see if she'd mind

Anna didn't mind—"go get some," she hissed, taking Melanie's half-empty drink—so Melanie met Matt at a brewery on a quieter street a couple blocks up from the con mania.

There were fewer people obviously from the convention and more people who might be locals or hapless tourists who didn't research the dates they were booking. The windows were all open and the garage doors rolled up. There was a California breeze coming into the brewery that wiped away the smell of yeast Melanie usually hated.

"I don't mean to be choosy when I'm getting in as somebody's plus-one, but I hope your party is better than Anna's," she said, sitting on the barstool next to Matt.

"About that..." He pivoted toward her. "It doesn't start 'til 11 so we have some time to kill."

"Damn. I did not drink enough coffee today for this kind of party-ing. Do they do this all three nights?"

"Four nights." He grinned. "Thursday through Sunday."

For some reason, Melanie noticed his grin more deeply than she had the rest of the night, probably because she was looking directly at him this time, and her gaze dropped involuntarily to his lips. She instantly blushed and jerked her eyes away, but it was too late. He definitely noticed.

"Any ideas what we do for the next hour and a half?" Something about the way he said it—not sly, not suggestive, but patient and undemanding—went straight to Melanie's overly-sensitive lady parts.

"Um," she managed.

"Not to be too forward, because this doesn't commit you to anything, but my hotel room is empty right now." He paused and ran his long fingers around the rim of his pint glass. "We could take a crowler back and chill for a bit."

"Is it close?" Melanie fell back on practical questions because she wasn't sure what she wanted to do.

"As close as yours. We're staying in the same hotel." His lips flipped again into a small grin and damnit she was focused on his mouth again.

"Well then," she said, not sure what would come out of her mouth until she finished: "Let's go."

He put one foot on the floor, tipped back his head and chugged the rest of his beer. He was pulling his wallet out of his back pocket with his other hand at the same time. "What beer do you want to take with us?"

She lifted one hand and dropped it over the laminated menu on the counter, finger first. It landed on a New England IPA. "This one," she said. She didn't care about beer and she particularly didn't care about beer right that moment.

"Good choice," he replied, and ordered a large can to go.

And then they were walking down the street in the rapidly-cooling night air. Heading for a hotel room. Together. Alone.

Melanie slowed her steps. She needed to be sure about this, not carried away by California and comic con and feeling more free than she had in five years. She paused on a street corner and turned her face up to Matt. He looked great in the street light. She stepped into his space and he opened his arms to her.

It was the closest they'd been since they met. He felt good; he smelled good. The ingredients were all right.

She kissed him. That magnetic mouth made it easy. His face was completely smooth; he must have shaved before he came out. His tongue tasted like grass from the beer. He was very warm.

She liked it all.

Simultaneously, her stomach clenched from the wrongness of the moment. She was cheating. She was cheating on Chris because she'd been too scared to have the conversation with him that she needed to have before she could run around kissing other men.

Melanie stepped back from Matt. The way he frowned at her, she knew he could tell something was wrong. "It's not you," she blurted, then winced at the cliché. Heat and then ice filled her veins, leaving her clammy.

"You face is as white as the character you were wearing earlier," he told her. His voice was solemn, maybe slightly disappointed, but not judgmental.

"I'm sorry." Melanie thought she might be sick. She took a deep breath in through her nose, held it, then breathed out through her mouth. She started to say something diplomatic and then closed her mouth with a click.

She opened it again and was honest: "I just realized there's a conversation I need to have with someone before I can do this."

Understanding swept across Matt's face, replacing the worried lines in his forehead. "Ah," he said.

"I'm sorry."

"There's no need to apologize." He held up the beer. "Do you still want to...we don't have to..."

"No, I'm sorry. I need to. I need to have that talk right now." Setting a course of action for herself brought Melanie back into her body. She was back on the street corner, and the air was cool but not cold and her fingers existed again. It was not the end of the world.

"Then I'll walk with you to the hotel," he suggested. "Or not?"

Melanie smiled, grateful. "Thank you. If you don't mind if we don't talk?"

He shook his head and gestured for her to walk ahead, all in silence. What a great guy she'd managed to stumble across in the middle of her very messy life circumstances.

Melanie walked back to the hotel with him mutely beside her, and tried to play out her conversation with Chris. She thought she knew him well enough by now to predict his responses.

But really, she had no idea what was going on in his head.

5

———————

Four Years Ago

Baltimore Comic Con was Melanie and Chris's first big trip together and he'd agreed to her idea to go, even though she worried he'd feel like he was tagging along on the cross-country trip. Doing her a favor, like when she went with him to a sports bar.

But he'd joked, "I like seeing you in action in the field."

Walking into a con alone, facing all those thousands of strangers in a massive convention hall or hotel, was still daunting every time. But he'd asked questions and held her hand and asked strangers to take pictures.

Showing someone around geektopia gave her confidence and made exploring the cons more fun than overwhelming. They found cool merch together and raced each other to recognize and shout out obscure costumes. He was better at characters from video games; she was better with TV. They ate hot dogs standing in a corner, like they were at a ball game, and tried the convention beer even though it was inevitably terrible (to him; she thought all beer was terrible).

Falling in love with Chris was all wrapped up in what at the time she thought was him falling in love with her secret hobby. So few people in Melanie's real life knew she spent her down time working on costumes—sewing, thrift store shopping, testing makeup—or how many posters she had hanging in her bedroom. He only teased her a little about how many girls in sexy outfits she had pinned on her bedroom walls.

After the second day of the con, when they got back to their hotel room and she was still wearing her skintight leather catsuit costume, he'd lifted her by the hips onto the minifridge in their Best Western room.

"Your ass in this costume has been driving me mad all day," he said, rubbing his hard cock between her legs. Her pleather catsuit was cheap and the material thin; the seam of his jeans alone gave her goosebumps in all the right places.

She threw her head back and a mass of fake red hair slithered down her back. The sensuousness of the hair, much longer and fuller than her own, made Melanie less inhibited than normal. Sexy. Free to want what she wanted.

With her back arched, her breasts strained against the front of her suit and his eyes fell to the zipper that ran from her chest all the way down to her crotch. He ran his fingers, lightly, over her breast under the plastic material. Her nipple peaked beneath it and the material was so tight it shifted slightly, rubbing against her and making her sigh gently. He put his hand to her face and she took a finger into her mouth, sucking it.

He started to unzip her, a long, slow pull that revealed so much skin so quickly. When her boob popped out, he put his whole mouth wetly over her small breast, sucking on her in return.

It was his standard move—he knew how sensitive her nipples are—but somehow fresh because of the circumstances, because he was holding the edge of the suit away from her sensitive skin with his other hand to keep the zipper from snagging her.

He dragged his tongue farther down the slit of skin created by her zipper.

The suit made a squeaky noise as he spread her legs farther and put his tongue between them. They both laughed. His access wasn't ideal so they wrestled the suit off, peeling her out of it carefully because it was thin and easy to rip, and then the wig eventually fell off and she had to pause to pull off the wig cap and shake out her short brown hair because she was self-conscious about it being all matted.

Then it was just Melanie and Chris naked in the hotel bed together. But that was OK, because they'd shared a fantasy and somehow it brought them closer, made them more *them*.

~

SAN DIEGO - NOW

Melanie typed and erased several versions of a "we need to talk" message to Chris before she finally called him.

"Hey Mel," he answered. She was pacing in the bedroom of the hotel room, stepping over other people's things—a shirt, a blow dryer, a green scaled aqua-queen costume Anna brought even though she wouldn't wear it while she was working—as she walked.

"Hi," she said. Then stopped. Plunging into this conversation felt exactly like diving head first into the unknown.

"Where are you?" He sounded vaguely suspicious. What did he think, that she'd put him on speaker phone at a party?

"San Diego. At my hotel. Um, I didn't wake you did I? I forgot it's later there."

"Nah. I was just playing a game. Not a multiplayer."

He probably wouldn't have answered if he was in the middle of a game with friends. Melanie rolled her eyes. The anger helped brace her to push forward. "I wanted to talk to you about what's going on with us."

"OK," he said. Not helping at all, as usual.

Melanie cleared her throat, although she didn't need to. "I know we haven't really talked...about anything. In a while. And I probably wasn't that clear when I said I wanted some space. But I wanted to see if, well, if we broke up."

She cringed at making it an "if" rather than a statement, like she'd meant to. But there, she'd finally said it. She held her breath.

There was a long pause.

"Do you *want* to break up now?" he asked. She only now remembered saying that she didn't want to before.

"I mean...breaking up was never really the goal," she said slowly. "But it might be necessary. I just don't think we're really working together anymore. Really. Do you?"

She realized as she'd been pacing the hotel room that she'd walked into the bathroom. She picked at a drop of foundation matted on the sink.

"Not at the moment. I'm not sure how that would work with you halfway across the country."

She gritted her teeth. "We had problems before I was halfway across the country, Chris." She said it patiently. Mostly.

"I guess."

Melanie rolled her eyes. She blew off a really nice and sexy guy to have this conversation and Chris was making it so difficult. "Really? You guess? You can't even say for sure?"

He paused again. "OK, we had problems. They weren't all my fault."

She held the phone away from her mouth while she took a deep breath and blew it out forcefully. "OK," she finally said. Calmly, she thought.

She thought about his good qualities, to keep her anger in check. He usually let her know if he was not going to come home on time—except he was always home so did that really count?—and he was kind to animals and service people and he never mocked her for talking to her mom too long on the phone. He taught her to drive a manual transmission and made it possible to afford a nicer apartment. And when they were together, she could be the person her costumes brought out of her. He'd always seen her, no matter what she wore.

Her eyes started to well.

OK, don't get carried away, Melanie.

He also never folded his laundry and he slept in his socks. And forgot to take out the trash. And didn't like the same things she did.

"I guess it doesn't matter now whose fault it is if you've given up." Chris sounded bitter.

She swallowed. "Given up is not quite how I'd put it."

"How would you put it, then?" He sounded genuinely curious.

"Resigned. To the inevitable."

She could almost hear him nodding through the phone. "Got it," he said. "I guess I am resigned, too, then."

Silence for another long moment before he said: "OK, so we're broken up."

It seemed easier for him to say it than it was for her.

"OK," Melanie repeated. It was too fast, suddenly. Too easy after years of holding on tight. "We're broken up."

There was another pause over the line and she realized that was it, that was the whole conversation and now one of them was going to be the first to say goodbye. She should do it because she wanted to be first. But she couldn't open her mouth.

Even though she'd be flying home to their shared apartment in a few days, Melanie's heart screamed she would never see Chris again if she hung up now. And she was not ready for that, after years of seeing him every day. Of touching him frequently. Of discussing everything with him.

"So, what are you wearing?" Chris asked.

"I..." Melanie was confused by the question. Her mind went blank and she looked at herself in the mirror, puzzled. "I'm not in costume. I just came from a party."

"So what did you wear to the party? Can I see it?"

"I guess?" Melanie wasn't used to refusing Chris. It'd been so long since he made any specific requests beyond "OK if I stay up another hour playing games?" or "what about McDonald's for dinner?"

She pulled her phone away from her face and glared it for at least half a minute. Was this some kind of trick? But what could the end goal possibly be? They were broken up. Officially. She owed him at least some consideration. If he wanted to see her outfit, that was not a difficult request.

He switched to FaceTime and suddenly she was glaring at Chris's face. He slowly, without breaking eye contact with her, leaned over and brought a can of beer to his lips. He took a sip.

She switched over to FaceTime and held her arm out as far as it would go to show him her outfit.

"You look hot."

Small spike of pleasure. She couldn't help it. "Thank you?"

She brought the phone back to her face. He was wearing a backward baseball cap and no shirt. This was unusual attire for him since normally it was all t-shirts and basketball shorts—or no pants and only his boxer shorts—when he didn't have to go anywhere. Maybe he'd run out of laundry since she didn't do it this week.

He smirked at her through the screen. "We're broken up now; I have no ulterior motives for telling you that is a great outfit." Like he knew what she was thinking. The way he used to just know.

"But it's weird."

"Why?"

She paused. The weirdness of this conversation was that it wasn't weird at all. It was easy. Teasing. Kind. The way they used to talk. "I don't know why. It just feels weird."

"You shouldn't dress so nice if you don't want to hear that you are hot."

She opened her mouth to snap at him for telling her what to do, then closed it again because he was clearly joking. She fiddled with the band of fabric around her neck.

"Are you wearing anything under that?" he asked.

What?

She blinked at his face on her phone. She couldn't be more surprised if Chris was a complete stranger asking that question. "Seriously?"

"What? You want to play a little, I can tell." His voice went deeper for a second, flirty. Then he grinned, settling back onto their couch at home. Without seeing it on screen, she could see him prop his bare feet up on the ottoman, probably by his can of beer. Which, she was sure, was not on a coaster. "After all, aren't you in San Diego to play?"

"Yes..." *but not with you*, she thought. Her heartbeat quickened as though her blood was flowing a little faster beneath her skin. Her nerve endings lit up with the craving to be touched.

Not touched in general. Touched by her boyfriend.

"What are you doing?" she finally asked.

He shrugged, his limbs loose like a weight had been lifted. For a second, she thought he was going to say "enjoying my freedom" and her eyes got hot around the edges. Was he going to be cruel by showing her how good it felt to not be her boyfriend anymore? Would he taunt her with desire and then yank it away because it was no longer hers to feel?

She didn't know what to expect. She barely knew this Chris anymore.

"Talking to you," he said instead. "Trying to get you to enjoy it, too."

She studied him as closely as she could through the screen. Was this some kind of dare or joke to him? She didn't get any weird vibes, though. He seemed...spontaneous and playful. More the way he was when they first met.

She could hang up. Maybe she even should. She should also hate the easy confidence he seemed to have that she wouldn't do that.

But she didn't. Her inability to predict what Chris was going to do seemed a little...exciting.

"What do you want me to do?" she asked finally, still wary but also curious.

He smiled, acknowledging that she was not going to make it easy for him. Then the smile turned into something more carnal, the turn of his lips letting her know he was thinking about her skin as much as she was.

"Take off your top," he said simply.

Was she really doing this? Melanie scanned the empty hotel room and thought about the risks. There was almost zero chance the others came back before midnight. And it was not like Chris was some stranger who was going to take screenshots to post on the internet. He'd seen her naked breasts before—even on camera a few times.

She propped the phone up on the dresser so she could get at the zipper high on the nape of her neck. She pulled her arms out of her top so that she was only wearing the pants part of the pantsuit, letting the top fall around her hips.

She stood in front of the phone, letting him see her naked chest. It didn't even feel that weird, more like she'd traveled back in time somehow, maybe a year or two, to when this would have been normal.

"Cup your tits, the way I would," he directed her. His voice was even but she could tell he was sitting forward now, not relaxed on the couch. Interested.

She put her palms under each breast and pressed them together toward her chin, giving herself more cleavage. Wanting him to see and want.

"Touch your nipples."

She obeyed.

"How does that feel?"

"Not the same," she said. She remembered the first few times she and Chris had sex—his obsession with her breasts, her incoherence every time he sucked on her skin there. The enjoyment she got from watching him adore her.

"If I was there, I would run my tongue from your nipple straight up your neck," he said. The shot of pleasure went straight down her core.

"I'd like that," she said. Her voice was already wobbly.

"I know you would," he replied. His voice had gone intent. "Then I'd push you down onto that bed behind you and rub myself on your breasts so you could feel how hard I am."

She sat down, a little faster than she intended. "Are you hard?"

"I am so hard. Do you want to see?"

She pressed her lips together. But her desire to keep going pushed her anxiety out of the way. "Yes."

He tilted the camera down so she could see the bulge in his shorts.

"Tell me how wet you are right now."

She let go of her breasts and got one hand down her pants. "Pretty wet." In fairness, she had a head start earlier this evening.

Ha, *head* start. But what about Chris? What has he been up to that put him in this headspace? She wondered if he'd been watching porn all day with her out of the house. Maybe that was what had gotten into him.

The thought was almost enough to make her hesitate. But she really didn't care how they got here; her own fingers dancing sensation across her skin.

"*Pretty*?" he repeated.

"Very," she amended.

"I want to see you spread your legs and touch yourself. But first, if I was there, I would peel that suit off you so you were wearing nothing but your thong and—are you wearing heels?"

"Booties with a heel."

"Mm."

"And I..." she paused to lick her lips. She was nervous. She could picture herself touching Chris, because she'd done it so many times, but describing it was a whole other task. "I would take you out of your shorts and let the head rub over my chest, over my breasts."

"Show me your underwear," he said softly. The phone was too small to really look into his eyes, but she could see they were steady on her. Wanting her. Or wanting to see more of her, which right now felt like the same thing.

She slid the zipper the rest of the way down her back and stood back up slightly to let the black pantsuit slide to the floor. She kept an eye on where her clothes were, in case the outside door on the other side of the bathroom opened unexpectedly. She could get back into them pretty quickly. Somehow the element of danger made the bite of her desire sharper.

"I like that pair," Chris said of her red lace thong. "Put your fingers underneath it and touch yourself."

So she did. She leaned back, her other hand bracing against the bed behind her, and closed her eyes. She could imagine Chris touching her like this, maybe taking his time in a way she won't because she was too eager for release now.

"I'd tease you a little," he said, reading her mind. Knowing what she liked after all these years. "I'd slide a finger inside just to the first knuckle, then back out. Then touch you where you want me to. Just once."

She groaned. "Come on, Chris."

He laughed lightly. She could see the movement of his arm off the screen and knew he was touching himself, too.

"Then I'd slide two fingers all the way in without warning. Because I know you're wet enough to take it."

She bit her lower lip hard, clenching her internal muscles against the phantom fingers.

"Open your legs wider," he said quietly. So she did, letting herself fall back and spreading herself out for him. She put her free hand to her nipple. She liked when she would arch her back into Chris's mouth and let him work his way up over the curve of her breast to her neck, which was even more sensitive than her breasts, making her gasp. She imagined him doing that now.

"I'd put my lips to your core and suck lightly, until you moaned, then come back up to nibble on your neck some more."

She drew circles around her clit, over and over, the pressure building rapidly. She wanted the imaginary Chris to spend more time with his mouth down there, but she didn't protest his narration.

"Then I'd line myself up and enter you just a little. Teasing you again."

She clenched her eyes closed and moaned again. "Chris..." He knew. He knew she liked being teased before her entered her. She liked when he positioned himself over her and lined up so she could feel the slight pressure at her entrance and then gazed down at her and waited for her to beg. While she touched herself, circling her clit, she imagined him penetrating her and the mental picture got her further than her touch alone: That first thrust that caught her by surprise even when she knew it was coming. Those times—infrequent though they might be—when the angle was right and every thrust touched the right place.

"Then all the way inside, all the sudden, deep and hard."

"Fuck yes," she whimpered, touching herself the way she needed. Clenching her muscles at the idea of him deep inside her.

"Then I'd alternate. Shallow thrusts with deep ones."

She was getting close. "Keep talking," she told him, her toes curled around the end of the bed.

"I'd blow into your ear and bite your neck."

She heard herself make a high-pitched noise.

"And reach down between us and touch you right where your hand is now while I was deep inside you."

She came then, gasping and arching up from the force of it. "Omigod," she said, collapsing back onto the bed, her legs still splayed. She probably looked ridiculous from the angle Chris was at, but he'd seen worse. She didn't care.

She couldn't help grinning helplessly at the ceiling. She slowly pushed herself up and grabbed the phone before flopping back down on her stomach, holding the phone in front of her face.

"Did you come too?" she asked.

He laughed and nodded, reaching across himself, probably to toss a tissue into the trash can under the end table.

She could see her own toes still curling behind her in the tiny screen showing her own satisfied face. What on earth was happening and why did it feel so good?

"We're still broken up though, right?" She was smiling as she said it. She couldn't stop it.

"Right," he replied. He was smiling, too.

"OK. Thanks."

She ended the call and stared up at the ceiling for several minutes with her head blank in nothing short of astonishment.

Well...that was unexpected.

Matt: (9:49 p.m.) I had a fun night hanging out with you and hope to see you tomorrow. Let me know if you need anything at all

@miz_anna_doll:
San Diego, California
(picture of Anna with a large group of people mugging for the camera)
Cast party! #SDCC #Afterhours

Anna: (11:23 p.m.) Omg you skipped the party?? I hope you and Matt are getting into the good kind of trouble, I'll text you before I'm headed back JIC

CHRIS WASN'T GOING to be able to keep up this pace. He was working 10 hour days, still, but trying to avoid the apartment for Melanie's sake and also avoid the coworking space because of Jenny. So he was working in coffee shops, wedging his legs under tiny tables and fighting over outlets like some college student.

He'd thought it might get better at home after San Diego, and the night Melanie came home, tired and sunburnt from California, he'd tried.

"Can we share the bed tonight?" He'd thought it was a pretty smooth opening. Practical, yet suggestive. Open to interpretation if she wanted the opening.

Melanie's expression said different. "Why?"

Chris had started to backpedal, trying to carve out an exit plan. "The couch isn't very comfortable and it's a big bed. I'm just...tired."

She'd sighed deeply. "I can sleep on the couch tonight then."

"No, because I get up before you. Anyway you hate sleeping on the couch."

"I can't sleep with you."

"Come on, Melanie," he'd said, getting irritated despite his resolve. "We've slept together in the same bed, just slept, for years. This isn't some kind of rom-com movie where we can't resist each other."

Even as he said the words, he called himself an idiot because that's exactly what he was hoping for—that lying side by side, she wouldn't be able to resist the pull of their past.

"I don't want to wake up curled up with you and I'm not going to build a pillow wall between us." Melanie crossed her arms and glared at him, giving him "mom" vibes that were definitely not sexy.

What he wanted to say was, "let me hold you until we figure out how to talk to each other again." But instead, Chris had given up. "Fine, I'll sleep on the couch."

Now, back at the coffee shop, his phone buzzed.

Mom: (7:05 a.m.) Did you eat breakfast? How about this one? (has:attachment)

In a moment of weakness, he'd told his mom that he and Melanie had broken up. She kept insinuating Melanie wasn't taking care of him—something about not having dinner on the table, which was so old-fashioned and sexist of her—and Chris finally told her Melanie's job wasn't taking care of him anymore because they were over.

Now she kept sending him apartment listings.

He was not ready to pick a new apartment yet, but he dutifully opened them and found some reason to reply to her why it wasn't perfect. OK, so she wasn't wrong to think he was incapable of doing this basic thing that needs doing by himself. Women ran Chris's life and it was a good thing because he wasn't sure he was capable of running it himself.

But every time he thought about moving, Chris remembered the *Borderlands* mask Melanie brought him back from San Diego. Clearly she still considered him, even when they were far apart. She must still care about him a little.

Maybe it was not too late.

But for every moment of hope, there was also despair because he didn't know how to convince her to give them another chance.

He had no game and no plan. Now he had analysis paralysis and it was exhausting. So he put it all in a box and distracted himself as much as possible.

He sent his mother a picture of his bagel and coffee.

Chris: (7:10 a.m.) I'll look at it later, thanks

The coffee shop he usually went to was literally below their workspace, so Chris could park in the lot rather than paying for a meter. He always sat at the booth nearest the window, to the side of it so he didn't get too much glare on his screen. It was hard doing his best work with only one screen, but better than being distracted by guilt or having to give Tinder advice.

Dani, the morning barista, knew his order now. She'd tried to get him to branch out from his plain bagel to an everything bagel once or twice. He was pretty sure she was flirting with him. But he'd barely interacted with any people besides Melanie for months so he might be reading too much into normal human conversation.

The scratchy Slack notification sound interrupted him when he'd almost gotten in a flow.

Jenny on Slack:

(7:22 a.m.) Are you working on the Goski.com project?

Chris on Slack:

(7:23 a.m.) Roger

Jenny on Slack:

(7:23 a.m.) Are you in the office?

Chris on Slack:

(7:24 a.m.) Coffee shop. Why, aren't you?

Jenny on Slack:

(7:30 a.m.) Nightmare date last night. I'm working from home.

Chris on Slack:

(7:30 a.m.) Are you OK?

Jenny on Slack:

(7:31 a.m.) Just shaken up, I'm OK. No physical danger or anything

Chris on Slack:

(7:35 a.m.) Emotional danger?

Jenny on Slack:

(7:40 a.m.) I think I'm going to take a break from dating.

Chris on Slack:

(7:41 a.m.) Sounds like a good idea. Maybe try Hinge next. I've heard better things

Chris on Slack:

(7:41 a.m.) When you're ready

Chris on Slack:

(7:42 a.m.) I'll even look at your profile again

Jenny on Slack:

(7:45 a.m.) Thanks, Chris.

"Do you need a refill?" Chris raised his head and there was Dani, out from behind the bar.

"Oh, yeah, thanks so much." Chris had to squint because the sun was in his eyes, so he smiled and got a better view of her face when she leaned down to the table, blocking it. She was wearing a grey denim apron that shouldn't look good on anyone, but on her it had a wholesome, farmgirl vibe. She was blond and her cheeks were round and pink in a healthy way. She seemed like the kind of girl who would dress as something goofy for Halloween, like a banana or library card.

"Do you want me to bring over the cream?" She smiled, watching him and not the coffee as she refilled his cup from a thermos. Definitely not normal service. Definitely flirting.

"Oh, no, no, I'll get it. Thanks Dani." He kept his smile polite until she left. He couldn't remember the last time someone flirted with him. Was an alert sent out when he became single? Of course, that fact that he never went out or socialized could also be an explanation.

Working in the coffee shop was really not working for Chris. He had so much to get done on this project and he'd already wasted an hour there.

He watched Dani go to another table with the coffee. Was he missing an opportunity to move on? He was clearly in denial about Melanie. Their relationship was already in past tense; he just hadn't gotten used to it yet.

But he didn't want newness, he wanted a relationship that was established and reliable. He wanted ordering takeout to be their Friday night default. He wanted to roll over in the middle of the night and throw his leg over her hips. He wanted someone to care about and didn't want to go through the tedious process of fitting someone new into his life. That sounded so exhausting. Constantly thinking about how to put his best self forward; changing his life to accommodate someone new—did that used to seem *fun*?

Of course, maybe if he'd thought a bit more about being his best self over the past year, Melanie wouldn't be leaving him.

But it was so tiring trying to figure out what she wanted all the time. It was never easy with Melanie; it was never a direct conversation; it was always little hints and things like a grocery list she thought were "obvious" on the front table.

He used to have more brain space available to think about all this. He used to have time to look at Melanie and think, wow, how can I show her how beautiful I think she is? Or, how can I prove to her that playing video games is a fun activity to share? Or, what should I pick up on my way home from work to make her smile? None of that came naturally anymore.

Chris rubbed his hand up the back of his neck, where he was starting to feel the strain of bowing over his laptop. These tables weren't exactly ergonomically friendly. They were *slightly* lower than was comfortable as a work surface.

Chris brought up Slack again.

Chris on Slack:

(8:01 a.m.) Can we talk about my workload sometime?

Jenny on Slack:

(8:11 a.m.) Of course. Are we running you ragged?

Chris on Slack:

(8:12 a.m.) Only a little bit.

Chris on Slack:

(8:12 a.m.) I just think I need more regular hours again

Jenny on Slack:

(8:15 a.m.) So you don't want to hear that HQ wants you to fly out for a week to talk about making you a manager?

Chris on Slack:

(8:15 a.m.) ...

Chris on Slack:

(8:15 a.m.) Since when?

Jenny on Slack:

(8:15 a.m.) Since i just checked my email and they asked for my sign-off

Jenny on Slack:

(8:16 a.m.) It's not all up to me, you have my recommendation no matter what

Chris on Slack:

(8:20 a.m.) They want me in Seattle? When?

Jenny on Slack:

(8:21 a.m.) Next week

Chris on Slack:

(8:25 a.m.) OK I'll do it

6

Three Years Ago

Melanie wore the leotard that did triple-duty on multiple costumes, along with the thigh-high boots she wore with pretty much every costume she could, but otherwise she wasn't wearing anything unusual. Her own hair was down, around her shoulders.

It was clear later, watching, that her smile was shy, that she was too aware of the camera and embarrassed about what they were doing. It was his idea, one of his random nighttime ramblings when they'd been talking about trying something new. She'd asked if she could wear a costume.

"Sure," he'd said. "Wear your boots maybe?"

And she'd gotten so excited he asked for a specific costume item that she'd spontaneously agreed.

He'd never done this before, either, so he was clumsy about how to position them. They decided, after some discussion they should have done before starting to record, to try it from behind. Melanie, standing, leaned over and braced her arms on the bed and spread her legs. Chris pushed the bottom of her leotard to the side so he could get one finger inside her, then another.

Blocking the frame was not their strong suit. When they watched it later, splitting a bottle of wine for courage and holding their hands over their faces, at one point Melanie's head was completely off screen.

But then, surprising both of them, she started saying the filthiest things. She used to practice, in her head, at work sometimes or in the shower, saying the dirtiest things she could think of without giggling about them. Aroused and in costume, Melanie was completely uninhibited. Granted, they'd been drinking—but she knew for sure Chris would take everything she gave him and take good care of it.

And Chris had slapped her ass as he got even harder inside her. She screamed when she came, maybe performing a little, and enjoyed the entire process from idea to sharing the embarrassment about their creation.

She'd enjoyed *them*.

MELANIE WAS busy creating her next costumes with a week to go before Seattle. Spending her evenings and weekends browsing thrift stores and watching YouTube videos with sewing tips, she might be getting a little carried away. She'd started two more costumes besides the one she was already struggling to complete. A girl liked to have options. Melanie was going for broke this season—but hopefully not *literally*. She kept track of her expenses in a spreadsheet, as well as everything she was saving by not going out for coffee or on dates. Eating out too much was her biggest problem; she was still trying to avoid being home. Moving out was still looming ahead of her, and all the expenses that went with it. She was trying not to think about it.

She'd let herself have this summer to play. Then she'd go back to worrying about real life.

She also got really into browsing staged cosplay photos on Instagram and reddit. It was a rabbit hole of eco-warrior villains wrapped in real plants and flying heroes staged somehow standing in mid-air.

A whole new level of professional cosplay that Melanie suddenly wanted to reach.

Chris had some photography experience. But she didn't want to ask him to help.

They'd gone back to passively avoiding each other. When she got back from San Diego, the laundry hamper was overflowing and he hadn't done dishes since she left. It was like she came running home hoping to maintain the fantasy only to slam head-first into reality.

She tersely informed him she didn't plan on doing his house-keeping anymore, since they'd broken up.

"I didn't ask you to," was all he said. She removed the hamper from her room and stacked all his dishes to the side of the sink—and left them there.

She was *not* surprised the reality didn't live up to their FaceTime sex. She had not gotten her hopes up high enough to be disappointed.

OK, she had. And she was.

For maybe 24 hours, she thought he might have flipped a switch to go back to the Chris she used to know and love. Of course he hadn't. She didn't even know if that switch existed, but if it did, it was clear Chris didn't plan on using it.

Anyway, it was too late. She was changing and moving on. The old Chris might not even fit into Melanie's new life.

She started sending Matt direct messages on Instagram of the coolest cosplay pictures. They tried to theorize how the photos got made. Did they use a burst shutter and take a million pictures while the guy in costume jumped, trying to keep his feet flat in mid-air? They ultimately gave up on figuring it out.

Matt: (8:44 p.m.) Ever thought of doing my counterpart?

Melanie: (8:45 p.m.) (grimace face emoji) Her outfit is basically a red scarf and nothing else to hide behind.

> Matt: (8:46 p.m.) But you have a sai to stick 'em with if they get fresh.

Melanie, lying in bed as she read the message, laughed to herself. Men never quite seemed to understand body image issues. But that was OK. It was especially OK if he assumed her body was perfect.

Maybe he was right, maybe she *should* do the bad girl counterpart to his red devil hero. She could do a version with pants. Maybe for Atlanta, where all the events took place in air-conditioned hotels.

As she tucked herself into bed that night, she thought about costumed characters having sex—with all the challenges of skintight leather and peekaboo skin. She tried to be quiet when she touched herself so that Chris didn't think her moans were an invitation, but at the last minute before she came, Chris was who she thought about. She imagined Chris sliding into her room, dressed as a black-caped hero. With a mask and long sash. Holding her down with his sword at her neck.

Damn it. She felt terrible after she came. Why could her vagina not cooperate with her head?

If she wanted to sleep her way through an entire comic convention, now, she could. There was nothing stopping her but her own fears.

Of course, she'd never done anything that sexually adventurous in her life. Melanie was still Melanie.

> Melanie: (9:15 p.m.) Do you think cosplay is kinky? Like in a sexual way?

> Anna: (9:59 p.m.) It is whatever you want it to be!

Cosplay was just play to Melanie, the kind of playing she might have done back when she was six or seven. She vaguely remembered not thinking first about what other people thought before she climbed a tree or leapt off a swing. Sometimes, when she put on a costume, she had that sense of freedom again.

Fact. Sadly, even if Melanie was just playing, she couldn't stop some anonymous man on the Internet from seeing it as a proposition for him.

She poured all her frustration—both sexual and generally with her living situation—into her new costume over the days between cons. It might be her best yet. She practiced the makeup several times and splurged on the pre-made shoes.

Deal with everything else later. That was her mantra as she sewed and glued and then re-did her work because she was not actually very good at crafts.

At work, no one knew about her alternate life as a cosplayer. No one knew about her break-up with Chris, either. There, she could zone out on numbers and Excel and talking about the latest Netflix binge. And if Melanie had to have two secrets, at least one of them brought her joy.

~

MELANIE REFUSED to tell him what flight she was on.

"We have rules," she insisted, pointing at the dumb list on the fridge. "You do your thing, I do mine. Just because we're both going to be in Seattle doesn't mean we need to go together."

It was like they talked and no noise came out, for all that they understood each other. "I don't get you," Chris said, folding his arms over his chest as he sat at the kitchen table. "I thought you wanted to do things together."

"A) it's too late," Melanie said, and Chris threw up his hands because not only could he not believe she'd written them off without giving him even a *chance*, but because she was making another annoying list about it.

"And B) this is not *together*," she continued. "You are working and

I am—this is my thing, Chris. I am trying to find my own thing because you and I together is not working and I need my own thing!" Her voice was high-pitched and bordering on hysterical by the time she reached the end of the sentence.

At least she was not tiptoeing around, leaving the house without saying goodbye, eating in the bedroom after work and completely ignoring him. At least she was telling him what she really *thought*.

"I agreed to go because you were going to be there!" Chris insisted. "I knew it was Seattle Comic Con weekend!"

"You agreed to go because you never say no to those people," Melanie snapped back, sounding a little like his mother. Chris cringed. "That's not fair," he finally said, gazing into his cereal bowl like a child. What was wrong with him that he couldn't explain this to her and discuss whatever their problem was like grown-ups.

"Nothing! About this! Is fair!" Melanie yelled back and slammed the door on her way out to work. At least he wasn't the only immature one.

Chris collapsed dramatically out of his chair onto the floor after she left and laid his cheek against the cool kitchen tiles. He was counting his attempts at making up with Melanie as one to infinity at this point. He'd given up on tracking it on his Trello board. And trying to have sex with her wasn't working anymore. He was running out of ideas.

Mom: (7:55 p.m.) Did you look at the apartment?

Chris: (8:05 p.m.) How could I not when you literally made me an appointment

Mom: (8:05 p.m.) (shrugging woman emoji) I didn't think you'd go otherwise!

Chris: (8:10 p.m.) You were probably right

Mom: (8:10 p.m.) So did you like it?

Chris: (8:14 p.m.) It was fine

Mom: (8:15 p.m.) Did you take pictures?

Chris: (8:15 p.m.) No

Mom: (8:15 p.m.) Are you going to take it?

Chris: (8:18 p.m.) Maybe

Mom:(8:20 p.m.) Oh honey, if you're holding out hope I'm not sure it's healthy

Mom: (8:20 p.m.) She's clearly moving on and you don't want to look pathetic

Chris: (8:20 p.m.) Gee thanks mom

Mom: (8:21 p.m.) Well I see her Instagram photos where she's all dressed up and out partying! She's not staying home moping every night like you

Chris: (8:23 p.m.) How do you know I'm home moping every night?

Mom: (8:23 p.m.) Well you keep answering me don't you?

She went to Max's Ladies Brunch Club the day before her flight to Seattle, mostly to avoid Chris. Lately it was like she couldn't get away from him. Not only did they have to share space at home, now they'd have to share Seattle.

Brunch was a rotating group of women who Max invited to get together one Saturday a month because, she said, "the world needs more female friendships."

Melanie tried not to resent ending up stuck in the corner of the booth where she had to ask two people to move if she needed to go to the bathroom. She barely sipped her mimosa, hoping to avoid having to make a nuisance of herself.

"It's the *Great British Baking Show* in the U.S. but the *Great British Bake-Off* in the U.K.," Penny was explaining. "I use a VPN and stream it before it airs here."

"I don't know what a VPN is, I just know I liked it better before Mary Berry left," said Nancy. "She really knew her stuff."

Everyone was a super fan of something.

Being geeky was more acceptable these days, but there were unwritten levels of acceptance. Watching superhero movies was normal, and even going to conventions was OK as long as you were doing it partly to be ironic. But cosplay at conventions was too much. Dressing in drag for a *Rocky Horror Picture Show* singalong would prompt some gossip. Writing fanfic on AO3 would get some puzzled smirks and jokes about needing "to get out more."

"I know a girl on TikTok who is re-making all the *Bake-Off* challenges," said Penny. Maybe Penny was actually the "girl she knew on TikTok" and she was afraid to admit it. Was it possible Penny was also a secret uber-fan? *Maybe we're both in hiding.*

"I don't know what a TikTok is but I'm certainly not going to start making puff pastry from scratch!" said Nancy. "Thank God for frozen food."

Melanie met Penny's eyes for a moment and they both smiled. Melanie had seen Penny's Instagram, where she shared what seemed like every second of her life—work and personal, like there was no difference. Maybe Melanie was a generation behind on understanding nothing was truly secret.

"What about you, Melanie?" Max asked. "I've seen you sewing in your office lately. What are you working on?"

Melanie's face got hot. "Oh," she said, unable to respond quickly because her organs were tying themselves into knots.

She hadn't been as secretive as she thought. Maybe people knew about her cosplay already and weren't saying anything. Her full name wasn't on her social media but her face was; it wouldn't be that hard for someone social media-native like Penny to figure it out.

"I'm just working on...a costume," she said, finally. Everyone was watching her expectantly. Max nodded encouragingly.

"For Halloween?" asked Nancy.

Oh god, now she had to decide if she was going to lie to save herself the inevitable judgment. "Yes?" she said, because she probably would wear one of her costumes for Halloween this year. She took a deep breath. "It's a comic book costume."

"I never read any of those!" Nancy said. "My son has so many in boxes in our attic. He claims they're worth money but I don't know what anyone would pay for old paper."

The attention moved on from Melanie, thankfully. But she was left beating herself up mentally for getting so embarrassed and tongue-tied. Why couldn't she own her hobby? Sometimes she was not sure why she tried so hard to edit what other people saw.

～

@melly_89:
People at work don't know that I'm a cosplaying super-fan type geek. Is that bad? (thinking face emoji)

@miz_anna_doll:
@melly_89: It's your choice! If it bothers you, let you freak flag fly

@manlybubbles0190:
@melly_89 @miz_anna_doll Anna's right but I would also add that some people who are different in various ways can't "pass" and it might behoove those who can to help normalize it

@miz_anna_doll:
@manlybubbles0190 @melly_89 good point!! Different workplaces can make it more difficult though

@mtinspace7:
@miz_anna_doll @manlybubbles0190 @melly_89 I think there's room for different personalities, too. Introverts don't necessarily have to bear the freak flag for everyone else, it's a bigger burden for them than extroverts

@manlybubbles0190:
@melly_89 @miz_anna_doll @mtinspace7 It's a fair point. But remember some introverted people can't "pass" either

@melly_89:
@manlybubbles0190 @miz_anna_doll @mtinspace7 Thank you all, this is really good food for thought!

~

OF COURSE CHRIS would end up at an arcade bar and unable to actually play any games.

The bar had terrible beer—even a good brand didn't taste right, maybe because of the ancient translucent plastic red cups—and everything was generally so sticky even *he* noticed. But the games were legit. Original PacMan, Space Invaders, Galaga, Tron.

The games were packed in so tightly he had trouble keeping Jenny and her date in sight, much less hear anything they said. Jenny specifically told him, "Tell me afterward if I say anything stupid."

The way she was giggling, he assumed everything she was saying was stupid. He'd never heard her giggle before and the guy she was with didn't seem that funny.

He was only here because Jenny tricked him. She told him on Slack that he should "get out more" and invited him to join her at this arcade at 7. Then it was all "I need help" and "I'm on a date" and "you're the only person I trust to tell me the truth if I'm bombing this."

Unbelievable.

He would have turned around and left, but she was kind of right that he needed to get out more. At least this outing gave him a good reason to shower.

Jenny seemed to be asking her date a lot of questions and he was talking and talking. He was explaining games to her as if Jenny couldn't program a game like Donkey Kong in her sleep.

Jenny kept tilting her chin to the side in "listening face." Chris couldn't figure out why she didn't interrupt the guy, or at least stop egging him on. No way she was having fun.

On a shooter game, the guy literally took Jenny's plastic gun from her and demonstrated how she should hold it.

Jenny covertly glanced up and caught Chris's eye. Chris mimed shooting himself in the head. She bit her lip to hide a smile, but she was not giggling any more.

Finally, finally, the two of them started wandering back to the seating area of the bar. The guy was suggesting another drink.

"I have to work tomorrow, so I think I should call it a night," Jenny said. Her head was down and she fiddled with the wallet she pulled out of her purse. It was blue plastic and Chris was pretty sure it once had a chain on it that attached to her pants. It matched the lanyard she wore around her neck that attached to her cell phone. But she was not wearing either tonight; she had on a flowy skirt and flats instead of her usual high-top shoes.

Chris sat down in a booth near enough to hear them and started rolling his cup between his hands. Sounded like his agony was almost over.

"I'm going to hear from you later, right?"

"Um, sure," she said.

"Then you should give me your real number so we don't have to talk through the app."

There was a pause. The back of Chris's neck itched to turn around and look at them. He stared hard at his empty cup.

"Actually, I don't think so," Jenny said. Her voice had changed in pitch. She sounded more like she did on Slack calls with the team. "I think I'm good."

"Seriously? I came all the way downtown for this."

Chris rolled his eyes. Next this guy would complain about the parking. He hoped Jenny told him off for being a suburban asshole.

Her voice hard, she said, "And?" *Thatta girl.*

"And you can pay for the beer."

Chris did turn around then, in time to see the guy walking away as he shoved his arms through his jacket sleeves.

Jenny slumped down in the seat across from him in the booth. "Well, that was a disaster."

"I thought you handled it beautifully."

"He never asked me a single question about myself."

"I noticed."

"I think I need another drink."

Chris sat up straight, because he couldn't save Jenny from bad dates but he could definitely save her from more bad beer. "Not here you don't."

He paid for both their tabs and when they stepped outside, it was pouring. Denver rarely got rain, but when it did, it got buckets all at once.

The entrance to the bar was a tiny door in a brick wall on the street. There was not much space to huddle without getting wet or blocking entry. But neither of them brought an umbrella.

Jenny barely seemed to notice. She folded her arms around herself because she didn't have a jacket, either, and peered down the street both ways. "I don't know what I'm doing wrong," she said.

"Jenny," Chris began, not sure how to navigate the crossover between their work dynamic and this new thing where they seemed to be friends. He suspected there was a line he shouldn't cross and he would rather not find it. "You aren't really acting like yourself. Do you really want to end up with someone you have to fake it for the rest of your life?"

Jenny turned and gazed at him like he was stupid. "What's the alternative? Ending up alone the rest of my life? I'm not going to find someone by being myself."

"Well if you're yourself...you might find someone more *like* you?" Chris twisted his face up into what he hoped was an innocent, non-confrontational expression.

"How are two weirdos who are better on the internet than face to face supposed to find each other, much less get together?" Jenny demanded. She turned back to the closed door, then pulled out her phone and opened Tinder, the glow of the red flame bright in the gloom. She refused to look at him. "I'm tired of chatting with people on reddit I'll never meet in real life. I'm tired of tech bois who end up with supermodels and not the people sitting next to them at the computer desk." He didn't know Jenny's ex, but he assumed she was talking about a specific example.

She held her phone to her chest and turned like she was going to walk out into the rain, then rocked back on her heels. She stared hard out at the street. "So, I'm trying out dating normies. What else am I going to do." Her back to him, her shoulders slumped, making her look much smaller than her usual outsized personality did.

Chris should have the resources to fix this problem and didn't. Jenny was pretty cute and really talented. If he had more male friends —or any friends, really—he would totally introduce her to them.

"I'm sorry," he said. "Melanie and her friends always say it's a numbers game. You just...gotta keep trying."

It was weak. So weak. He cringed saying it. Dating was probably harder for girls than guys—or at least he'd heard way worse stories about dates from them than he ever had from a dude—but there was no way Jenny hated the idea of dating again any more than Chris did.

Maybe he should get jazzed up about all the new options, but he didn't want to date anyone but Melanie.

It wasn't that he was too comfortable to find someone new, it was that reaching a level of comfort in a relationship took a lot of work. Getting past the point where they both pretended to be someone slightly better than themselves took time and commitment. He knew all of Melanie's weirdness now, and she knew all of his, and they didn't have to fake perfection with each other. He didn't want to do all that again with someone new. He wanted to get back to that place with Melanie and no one else. He supposed it was sunk cost, a little, but he really believed in what he and Melanie had built. Tearing it down was unthinkable.

Jenny made a face and stuffed her phone back in her purse, then pulled it back out again immediately. "At what point when you're getting no results do you just...stop trying? Don't answer that. Listen, I think I'm going to get an Uber and go home. But you should stay and play games. On me."

Chris shook his head. "Nah, I'm going to go home too."

"Come on, do it for me so I can live vicariously believing you're actually enjoying yourself."

Chris was pretty sure he wouldn't enjoy himself playing arcade games alone while drinking terrible beer. His sweats and computer were calling to him. "Jenny. I have *work* to do."

"Wow." She turned to him. Her frenetic motion stopped for a moment. "You really *do* work too much."

Chris threw up his hands in frustration. Someone save him from women who see all his problems but offer no solutions.

"Look," Jenny said, and her voice had turned into work-mode again. "I'm going to give you some advice I literally just got yesterday from my online therapist. She's great, by the way. You should see one. But she told me to stop asking permission to have a healthier life."

Chris's attention was caught by this. It appealed to him somewhere deep in where he assumed was his soul, but he wasn't sure why. "What does that mean?"

"It means don't ask me if you can take a break to go for a walk or make lunch; tell me you are, dumbass! And if I'm a dick about it, tell me so. Or find a new job because I can't change the entire culture of the workplace and that toxic shit will ruin your life."

He smiled slightly, wishing this Jenny was the one he'd seen on the date. It would have ended a lot earlier, but at least they would have missed the rain.

"Thanks, Jenny." He opened his arms a little, trying to both look like he was offering a hug and not like he was offering a hug simultaneously, in an effort to not make it weird if she didn't want one. Jenny stepped in and gave him a quick, brisk one, turning her face away from his chest.

"Appreciate you, Chris," she said. "You're a good one."

Chris grimaced and watched a car pull up out on the street. "Tell my girlfriend that," he mumbled.

7

Three Years Ago

They kept having this dumb fight. Melanie would point out Chris was 28 and didn't have any friends with wives or with serious, live-in girlfriends. She called it "immature," like she was afraid his friends defined who he was.

"We're just so *different*," she'd usually end up saying at some point during those fights, and it made him want to throw up his hands and walk away.

He didn't this time, though. "Why don't you move in with me and maybe we can start a trend," he suggested.

Melanie stopped and stared at him, like that wasn't what she'd been hinting at all this time. "Really? Are you sure?"

Chris shrugged. He hadn't really thought about it before, but he and Melanie had been dating over a year—almost two years—and it was not like they were rushing anything. "Yes."

She hesitated. He couldn't believe it. He knew she wanted to but she was pretending she didn't. "Your apartment might be too small for both of us."

Ah. Chris got this hint faster. "Then we'll find something for both of us."

Melanie smiled and it was like hitting the jackpot. He thought then that he'd happily keep bushwhacking forever through Melanie's secret hopes and dreams to find the one he could fulfill, in order to make her smile like that.

Every time Chris figured out what she wanted, he won a prize.

~

Seattle - **now**

Seattle's comic con was a more traditional convention in that it took place in one convention center right downtown near Pike Place Market. There was a trend toward regular people wearing costumes —running the full gamut from makeshift to amazing— on the streets. There was also a notable "weirdness" in the pop-ups near the convention center, like palm readers and people who made personalized felt ornaments.

The first panel Melanie attended was about diversity—or the lack of it—among convention-going fans. The panelists bucked the trend but the audience did not.

Melanie leaned over and commented on this in an undertone to Anna during the panel and got a dirty look from the white guy dressed as a space cowboy on her left.

This particular character's wannabes all seemed to be dicks, in Melanie's experience.

One of the panelists, a Black woman dressed as a badass space hero who talked about accessibility as "more than a physical issue," raced over to Melanie and Anna after the panel. "Your costume is amazing! I never see her done anymore."

"Oh, thank you," Melanie said, theatrically doffing her top hat. "This show is one of my all-time favorites and she's one of the only ones I hadn't done from it."

The taller woman laughed. "I love that. Hi, I'm Emily. Do you make your own costumes?"

"I do now." Melanie shrugged, but she was inwardly proud of herself. "Self-taught."

"O.M.G.," Emily said, spelling it out. "Those buttons. Thrift store find?"

"Yep!" Melanie grinned back. She'd bought way too many buttons that didn't work before she found these ones. She was still not great at recognizing perfection when she saw it. Ha, metaphor for her entire life.

"How long have you been making them?"

"A couple years, but I just got really serious about it this year. Like you should see the evolution. My originals were barely recognizable. And very unflattering." She warmed to the conversation, loving to talk about her costumes.

"Do you have pictures of the different stages?" Emily leaned forward.

"Um, sure..." Melanie reached for her phone.

"That's perfect! You should be on our panel about costume-making!" Emily announced, like Melanie had passed a test she didn't know she was taking. "We just had someone drop out. It's tomorrow, what do you think?"

The other woman was moving too fast for Melanie, who thought her eyes were going to pop out. "Um..."

"She'd be great for that!" declared Anna, who had been on more panels than Melanie could count. She put her hand on Melanie's back and pressed, like this was an opportunity she needed to physically step up to.

"Well..." Melanie hesitated, not sure how to say "no." Not sure if she should. "What would you want me to speak to? I can really only talk about budgeting and, basically, bootstrapping costumes. And how much time it takes. Like, every lunch hour and happy hour time."

"That's perfect!" Emily said again, enthusiasm rolling off her. She pulled out her phone and it dinged, so Melanie assumed she was recording herself speaking: "Sacrificing for your art! Making art accessible to the masses! It's the perfect balance of artisan and thrift. That's what I'll put on the new description."

And that was how Melanie ended up sitting in her hotel room—she caved and agreed to share with Chris, as she couldn't handle crashing with another group of mostly strangers—with her computer late that afternoon instead of at happy hour with friends.

She pulled together a PowerPoint of photos documenting some of her worst costumes—mostly major wig fails—transitioning to some of the ones she was most proud of. She included a slide about the trouble she'd been having lately, her albatross costume, because she wanted to be transparent and, hell, maybe she'd get some tips out of it. She jotted down as many thoughts as she could about costuming, pulled data points from her spreadsheets, and made an outline. Then she tried to brainstorm every question she thought could possibly be asked and prepared good answers. She hated feeling like she was on the spot.

By 7 p.m., Melanie, staring at her messy document full of unorganized notes, got restless. It was quiet in the hotel room and she was miles away from the central business district—closer to Chris's office —but she thought she could hear the phantom sounds of partying from the street. She checked her phone.

Matt: (7:09 p.m.) You joining us later?

From Roger @manlybubbles0190
Seattle, Washington
(picture of Matt, Anna and Roger in front of a Starbucks)
Fuel to party all day, party all niiiiiight #EmeraldCityComicCon

It was like her friends were flowing in a fast current while she was watching them from a sluggish boat. When she first started going to conventions, it was something she shared with Chris and she wasn't really looking for new friends. Then, when he stopped going, Melanie's dread of talking to strangers slowed her involvement. Then she met Anna, who knew everyone, and sort of cruised along by attaching to her. And now Melanie was sitting there, still in the boat she'd climbed into five years ago, watching the party happen on the other side of the stream. Or some other tortured metaphor.

The click of the door interrupted her thoughts. She put down her phone as Chris walked through the door, wearing a laptop messenger bag across one shoulder and carrying a coffee even though it was nearly 8 p.m.

"Hey," he said.

"Hey," she said.

They looked at each other for a moment. She internally debated asking him about his day. But if he wasn't going to ask her, she didn't want to be the only one putting work in.

"No costume?" he asked.

She hesitated. "I took it off already."

"Can I see it?" Chris put down his bag and coffee on the dresser across from the desk where she was sitting.

She paused and met his gaze. It wasn't that they weren't talking on the trip; he asked her if she wanted him to grab her coffee from the continental breakfast that morning before he'd left for a day of meetings. It was just that he'd never showed interest outside of their routine.

"OK," she said, because she didn't know how else to respond without starting an argument. She picked up her phone and scrolled through it for one of the best pictures of her in a top hat, leotard and fishnets from earlier in the day.

She handed her phone to Chris and he looked at it closely without saying anything. Then he handed it back. "You got a text," he said, turning away.

She looked at her screen and pulled the text down from the notification panel.

Matt: (7:55 p.m.) Come out and play, I promise not to kiss you this time

Melanie considered throwing the phone across the room. *Don't feel bad.* They were broken up. She kept getting sucked into thinking Chris was going to give her what she'd been waiting for, for at least the whole past year. And he was not. He was not giving her anything but breadcrumbs, making her hope there was still something there of substance.

"Hey," Chris said, as he started to unpack his shoulder bag, his back to her. "I looked at some apartments online today and there was one I really liked so I think I'm going to sign a lease. I'll keep paying my half of our place through October."

Melanie stared hard at his back. It didn't change, it was still Chris's back, his shoulder blades flexing through the fabric as he moved his arms.

Chris was already moving on—faster than Melanie was, in fact.

A cold fear started at her core and spread outward. The walls of the hotel room seemed too close and the room too empty and too crowded at once. She imagined going home to an empty apartment. She'd never lived in that apartment without Chris; they picked it out together. They drank cheap champagne after they moved in and christened all the rooms with sex. Different positions for every room.

The memory was as distant now as the ones Facebook's algorithm popped up in her daily feed.

"OK," she said. Her voice was small.

He tossed a glance at her. "This is what you wanted, right?"

Melanie ran a hand down her t-shirt, wishing she were still in costume. Then she would know how to react—decisively, not torn by the two competing emotions of fear and determination. "Yes," she finally said. Even to herself, she sounded uncertain. But Chris nodded and accepted it without arguing.

"Are you still using the desk? I have some work to do." He paused. "Unless you wanted to go out?"

Melanie gathered up her computer and notes in a messy stack and backed away from the desk. "I'm going out with my friends. I'll get out of your way."

But when Melanie went into the bathroom to check her makeup, she started to cry.

She stood there looking at herself in the mirror. She didn't see a badass, one of the characters she imitated. She was just Melanie of the broken relationship and emptying bank account.

And she didn't want to party. She wanted to crawl into bed.

She couldn't help thinking about good times with Chris in hotel rooms—like Baltimore, or the first time they visited his mother and Melanie was so panicked about whether they'd be allowed to share a room in her house that Chris said, "let's get our own hotel room." Then his mother caved and let them sleep together under her roof the next time they came to visit.

Chris used to do things like that: Listen to Melanie's fears—she had a lot of them—and come up with solutions that he made look easy. For Melanie, who had a lot of worries and self-doubts in her head constantly, being with Chris was like having a bodyguard always clearing the path in front of her. Now everything was so hard. She had to choose her own path and deal with all her worries about the choices she made. And there was no one to walk that path with her.

When she came out of the bathroom, Chris was at the desk. He looked up at her and she said, "You know what? I changed my mind. I'm going to call it a night."

She put her earbuds in and crawled into bed, facing the wall away from him, without waiting for him to answer. Music playing on her phone, eventually she drifted to sleep.

Anna: (9:15 p.m.) You cannot possibly be any more prepared, come out and play!

Matt: (10:20 p.m.) Hey what happened to you? I was looking forward to hanging out (sobbing emoji)

Anna: (11:03 p.m.) You OK?

Missed call from Anna (11:30 p.m.)

Anna: (12:11 a.m.) Text me if you want to have breakfast tomorrow!!! I can do 7 am

From @miz_anna_doll:
Seattle, Washington
(selfie of Anna with Emily)
Went to an AMAZING panel today with @emilyinarush who would say we need more diversity in #fandom than accepting fake green makeup #cosplay #emeraldcitycomiccon
(Liked by @manlybubbles0190 and 108 others)

@emilyinarush:
Come to our how-to panel tomorrow on cosplay! We'll talk costumes on a budget, tricks to picking the accessories that matter and how to pick your best look @emeraldcitycon

@miz_anna_doll:
@emilyinarush Hoping to be there, can't wait to see @melly_89 share her best cosplay tricks! @manlybubbles0190 @mtinspace7

@manlybubbles019:
@miz_anna_doll @emilyinarush @mtinspace7 @melly_89 is so dedicated she couldn't even come out to play tonight (sobbing emoji)

Jenny on Slack:

(9:05 p.m.) How is it? Did you set boundaries??

Chris on Slack:

(9:08 p.m.) I'm trying, Jenny, I'm trying

Nick on Slack:

(9:15 p.m.) Hi Chris, hope you're enjoying Seattle.
Hope to see you here more often. Jerry and I would
like to meet with you tomorrow at 10 a.m. in the
office. Can you make it?

Chris on Slack:

(9:16 p.m.) Absolutely.

SEATTLE HEADQUARTERS WAS like the Denver workspace on steroids, because the company owned the whole building. There was a full kitchen on every floor and a lot of "rest areas" scattered between desks, like bean bag chairs placed in nooks and random diner booths with good lighting and grounded outlets.

Chris's bosses, Nick and Jerry, met him in one of the booths. It was not private; they were sitting in the middle of a busy floor buzzing with flannel-clad employees on computers. Nick offered him a cookie with the company brand frosted onto it.

"Oh, thanks," Chris said, taking the wrapped cookie. He held it, uncertain if he should go ahead and eat it in front of them. It seemed like a weird test. He decided not to open it and opened his laptop instead, to show that he was ready to get down to business.

"The wrapper dissolves in water," Nick told him. "Sorry we don't have those in Denver, yet. We're working on it."

"That's one reason we wanted to talk to you."

Chris paused. "To talk about wrappers?"

"To talk about innovation. And growing the Denver office so that we can launch more cool initiatives there."

Chris nodded. "It's been very busy."

"Understatement!" Jerry cut in. Chris smiled, feeling like they were on the same page. Maybe they were going to reorganize? Maybe they'd seen that the workflow wasn't working and were going to hire more people so Chris would get some relief.

"And you've been overdelivering every time," Nick added. "We've noticed."

"That's why we wanted to talk to you," Jerry continued. "Since we see you can handle a lot on your plate, we want to reward you by adding more to it."

They laughed. Chris closed his laptop. He had worked so hard to get to this level in his career but he knew there were plenty of other jobs out there. It was a matter of finding the energy to make a change.

Nick opened his own computer, as though Chris had given him a signal. "We're proposing a substantial promotion, including a raise and new title."

He turned it around and showed Chris. Talk about understatement. *Substantial* was right.

"Here's the thing, though. We want you in Seattle." Jerry crossed his arms. "You can manage Denver better from here, where our resources are concentrated."

Chris opened his mouth, prepared to reject the idea by saying "my life is in Denver," or something like that. He closed it again. Without Melanie, what did he really have in Denver now but a job? Seattle would be closer to his own family.

"Good, you'd consider it," Nick said, correctly interpreting Chris's body language.

"I guess I would," Chris said, surprising himself because his stomach didn't agree with his words. "But I'd have to have a more flexible schedule," he added, half thinking they'd change their minds. "I want to be project-based, not on a shift."

"Done," Jerry said, without hesitating. Nick nodded.

Chris tried not to look too shocked.

"Chris, why don't you think about what else you would want and let us know," Jerry suggested. "You're one of our top-performers. You're not going to be aiming too high with anything on your wishlist.

We'd really like to get you here and have more of a chance to pick your brain."

Nick and Jerry didn't believe in long meetings, so they took off after that, leaving Chris with a "starting point document" in his e-mail and the cookie in its disposable wrapper. They wanted to reward him for the long hours and sweating over the details.

His hard work over the last few years was paying off. But as he thought about taking the promotion and leaving Denver, he wondered if he'd been putting his efforts into the wrong project all along.

~

MELANIE MET ANNA FOR BREAKFAST, even though she was shorting herself on time to prepare for the panel. The coffee shop was on the top floor of a stack of shops near Pike's Place Market. It was cramped quarters, full of people already at 7 a.m., and after they ordered, they had to wait for their food while watching for someone to vacate a table.

She told Anna what Chris said about moving out. Anna went off on a tangent about some guy she dated for a few years who broke up with her by text message that lasted until after they picked up their coffee orders at the counter.

"Basically, my philosophy is to make sure you're getting what you want out of a relationship upfront because they always end," she concluded, dumping cream in her coffee until it was almost white.

Melanie eyed Anna, who was dressed as a cartoon character with pigtails. "You'd never know you were such a cynic."

Anna shrugged, her pigtails wagging. "I'm just saying. Channel your inner magic cynic," she suggested, gesturing at Melanie's new outfit. She really went all out for this con: *Two* new costumes. She should have reserved one, but she brought them both just in case and this morning when she woke up, she felt so emo she couldn't resist wearing all dark colors and a cape to wrap around herself.

"I'm trying," Melanie sighed. Anna lunged for a table as two people got up to leave and Melanie followed in her wake.

"Do we need to get you laid?" Anna asked, sitting down.

Melanie flipped her hood up and glanced around at all the people nearby.

"Don't be like that!" Anna exclaimed, equally loudly. "Sex with someone else is a time-honored, organic method of getting over an ex. It works for a reason. Chemistry. You have to get his—what's his name? Chris?—Chris's hormones out of your system. But don't sleep with Matt," she added, almost as an afterthought.

"Wait, why not?" Melanie jerked, completely giving away her thoughts about doing just that.

Anna's forehead scrunched up, like she was skeptical that Melanie didn't get this. "Because you guys might have an actual thing and you're not ready for that yet. You need a strings-free rebound. *Then* you go for Matt. I didn't know how fun he was until last night. But he's also got some substance, you know? I like him for you."

Melanie got up to get their food when their number was called. Anna unwrapped her egg sandwich but she held her croissant without taking a bite; she didn't have an appetite. She sighed. "So I'm supposed to just hope for some kind of idealistic rebound?"

Anna waved around the cafe, almost hitting someone dressed as a toy block with her arm. "Look around. Pick someone. Go after him. These geeks are here for the taking, trust me."

"Do you know that from personal experience?" She balanced her sandwich on top of her coffee cup and started fiddling with the pastry. She couldn't even think about long-term right now, when her last long-term option ended in a complete flame-out.

Anna laughed, putting jam on her croissant. "Maybe. Back in the day. Nerd sex is objectively the best sex. I don't know what you were doing with a non-nerd in the first place."

He didn't seem like a non-nerd when Melanie met him. She crossed her arms over her chest and leaned back from the table, taking a furtive sweep of the room. There was a superhero with his cowl off in the corner carrying a few too many pounds for his tight spandex suit. And another whose package was a little too defined under his external underwear. She looked away quickly, not wanting anyone to see her scoping them out.

Did she want the ideal fantasy or did she just want sex or did she want neither? The one thing she definitely *didn't* want was to keep accepting whatever came along. That was how she'd ended up with Chris—they met by accident and dating seemed to work, because they both liked movies and pizza and sex, and then moving in together made sense because splitting rent was so much easier, and now it seemed they were both waking up to the reality that they didn't make very many conscious choices about what they wanted their relationship to be, besides easy.

No more falling into things just because they were available.

"I don't know," Melanie said. "I'm not sure I'm ready for all that."

"Are you scared or just uncomfortable? You want to change your life," Anna said, chewing. She caught a giant dribble of purple jam on one finger and licked it off. "Challenge yourself."

The problem was, Melanie had never been good with performing under pressure. She couldn't figure out what she wanted on a deadline. Her stomach started hurting and she couldn't even finish the rest of her breakfast.

~

From @melly_89:
Downtown Seattle
(selfie of Melanie with her hooded cape over her head)
I'm speaking on a panel about #cosplay in 15 minutes! Tune in live at www.emeraldcitycomiccon.com
Liked by @miz_anna_doll and 79 others
@miz_anna_doll: (three heart emojis)
@mtinspace7: You rock! Celebrate tonight?

CHRIS HAD DECIDED to give up.

He was clearly not what Melanie wanted. She'd made that very clear, despite his best efforts at reform: he'd been taking out the trash and doing his own dishes and here he is, following her across the country, sort of.

And now he had a completely unexpected offer from his bosses, Nick and Jerry, that would make it possible for him to move on without feeling like he'd been left behind.

But it bothered him that he didn't understand what Melanie *did* want.

So he took a long lunch and bought a day pass to the convention. Melanie was really too easy to track down using social media—he'd warned her about it before—so he found the event where she was speaking, or at least found the room number and its location on a map. He got lost in the convention hall trying to get there, but that seemed to be how convention halls were made: To get people lost.

He entered the room after the speakers began, getting a stern look from one of the people at the door in a red shirt that read "volunteer." Chris hurriedly ducked into a seat in the back, keeping his hoodie pulled up around his head and his chin down.

He was not here *for* Melanie; he was here to understand her.

The woman speaking at the front of the room was talking about cosplay being "a Pisces thing." She went on and on about only picking a new costume when there was a full moon, and Chris watched Melanie, who looked like she was disappearing into her hooded outfit. He knew she had opinions about creativity—how it was not a matter of "the muse" or the moon but a matter of acknowledging your inner child—but she said nothing.

Come on, Melanie, he silently urged her. *What would your character do?*

Melanie's shyness was a way of life. For most of their relationship, he'd made reservations that required a phone call and sometimes even ordered for her at restaurants. She depended on him to compensate for her.

But she'd always been different in costume. Like it gave her a map to follow for how to interact with the world. In costume, he'd seen Melanie speak her mind, tell off someone cutting in line, and get up to ask a question into a microphone at a convention panel. The costumes made her, somehow, more able to use her voice. More herself.

That was why he'd loved taking Melanie to cons.

So he was holding his breath to see that Melanie again. She was the real reason he was here. He saw that Melanie the morning a few weeks ago when she told him off while wearing her red, blue and gold-starred outfit. But he hadn't seen her in awhile—she didn't come out for him much anymore. Maybe, if he was in a relationship with *that* Melanie more often, he'd actually know what to do to fix this.

MELANIE WAS STILL ASKING herself the question: *What does Melanie want?* as she took her seat on the panel in front of a sparsely-populated room in a back hall of the convention center.

She was also, unfortunately, in a pretty grumpy mood. Between uncertainty about her future *and* certainty that Chris was blithely moving on from his role in their relationship ending without bothering to take responsibility for any of it, she was really channeling the character she was dressed as today.

Most of the panelists talked about achieving grand visions of cosplay and the nuances of things like makeup brands and Instagram sponsors.

Melanie talked about choosing between time and money when putting together a costume and choosing what character to dress as based on how complicated their costume was to put together. She became impatient with everyone else on the panel, even though she knew they'd all been doing this longer than she has. But their costumes seemed so out-of-reach. One woman was even dressed in a skin-tight blue body wrap covered in what looked like jewels that Melanie had about 50 questions about, beginning with *HOW*.

A guy in the middle of the crowd dressed in a pretty terrible video game costume raised his hand and asked if he could become an influencer if he was on a budget.

"I'm sure you can," Melanie answered. "But why."

She didn't bother to couch her response in something gentle and she felt the response ripple a bit through the others down the long table where she was seated.

"Well...I guess because I dress up to be noticed," he replied.

Her character wouldn't care that her ideas conflicted with the popular line of thought. So Melanie shrugged. "Dressing up is its own reward for me. If you're making the best costume you can despite limited resources, people won't notice that you were on a budget doing it. They'll just notice the costume. That's the reward."

The other women on the panel giggled to diffuse the tension and Emily asked the crowd, "Does anyone have an opinion on Hot Topic versus HerUniverse?"

A guy who was not wearing a costume—unless he was dressed as "standard geek" in his blue superhero t-shirt—raised his hand next and said, "This is a follow-up for the girl in the hooded costume. This is an obvious question, I guess, but why do you think you like cosplay so much if it's not about getting Instagram followers or getting con-famous or something?"

Melanie paused. The whole room was looking at her. She wished she had a brilliant answer. "It's a chance to be someone else," she said.

She tried to think of something to add but she had nothing. The room was silent, expectant. She raised both hands and shrugged. "I don't always like myself," she admitted, speaking quietly. The mic picked her up anyway. "The cosplay gives me a chance to enjoy who I am, even if I'm being...someone different."

Someone clapped. Emily quickly picked up the applause and

then so did a few other people in the room. It ended quickly, and Melanie didn't know how to react so she kept hiding behind her smile. She wanted to duck behind the curtain framing the stage. She'd revealed way more than she intended to a room full of strangers.

The guy not wearing a costume came up to her afterward and said, "I might actually try costumes after that speech."

"Oh." Her face would never be cool again. "It wasn't exactly a speech." Except he was right: It kind of was. She got up on her soapbox in public, in front of strangers who made all kinds of judgements about her. Who *was* she right now?

"I don't know this character," he said, gesturing at Melanie's purple cape.

Melanie waved that off as an easy lapse in knowledge. Not everyone liked cartoons. "She's from a kids' show."

"Well, whoever you're being right now, the person underneath it all actually seems pretty cool."

Melanie eyed him. Ordinarily, she would smile involuntarily, automatically thank him, and turn back to gathering up her things. But she was in such an unruly mood that she stopped and looked at him for a moment. He was kind of skinny and pale, but also tall and dark haired with wide-rimmed, square glasses that made him look a little like a Kansas farmboy-turned-reporter.

"Do you want to go get a drink and talk some more about cosplay?" she asked.

He only looked surprised for a split second before he said yes.

On her way out with him, Melanie caught Anna giving her two thumbs up.

Anna: (2:13 p.m.) Make good choices! Send me an SOS if you need me to interrupt and/or send in reinforcements

Matt: (2:15 p.m.) Where'd you go! Loved your panel. Are you coming out with us tonight?

Emily: (2:33 p.m.) You were fantastic, thank you so much for joining us! Let's talk more soon

Roger: (3:49 p.m.) Girlfriend, I keep seeing you pop up in Stories from that panel today. So proud. (fire emoji)

Anna: (4:04 p.m.) Ummm you're not dead in the bay rn are you?

Anna: (4:05 p.m.) You better be at drinks tonight or I WILL call the police

THE BREWERY LOOKED like it'd been on the corner since Seattle's founding. The wood was dark and so was the beer. The menu was mostly pub food and even the appetizers seemed heavy and rich. Melanie was not totally loving it, but it was David's choice.

"So what would you dress as if you took up cosplay?" she asked, turning her glass in circles of condensation on the table.

He pushed the glasses up the bridge of his nose and laughed a little. "I don't know. What do you think?"

"Clark Kent is the obvious answer."

He laughed louder, ducking his head as he put his elbow on the table. "Really?"

"Oh come on. No false modesty." Melanie rolled her eyes a little, because her costumed persona had a hold on her today, along with her character's confidence to react however she felt in the moment. Also, she was hungry and nothing sounded good on this menu. She stole one of David's sweet potato fries.

"I'll take that as a compliment." He was hiding behind his foamy drink.

"No one's ever told you that you look like Clark Kent?"

"My girlfriend thinks I look like Harry Styles."

"Ah..." Melanie paused, absorbing that statement. Rewriting their interaction in her head. "I can see that. A little bit."

"Oh, sorry. That wasn't a, like, subtle reference to my girlfriend in order to keep you from making a move."

She smiled a little, appreciating his directness. It put her on firmer ground. "Good, because...I wasn't thinking of making a move."

He gave her a bashful little grin back. "That's too bad."

What? Melanie narrowed her eyes at him. "Says the guy with a girlfriend?"

He raised both hands defensively. "We're in an open relationship."

Great. She rolled her eyes. "Oh, one of those."

He raised his eyebrows so high he had to fix his glasses again. He sat up a little straighter, as if *this* subject made him more comfortable than talking about his looks. "What does *that* mean?"

"It just seems like that usually means, you know, one person wants to sleep with other people and the other person has to pretend they're OK with it." She'd had this conversation with Chris once, when they were watching some movie. Chris had agreed with her, saying, "There's a reason why it's called 'having a partner.'" He'd said one girlfriend was more than enough for him.

David sat back in the booth without breaking her gaze, totally calm. She was starting to suspect he'd reeled her in with his shy persona and this was the real David. "Is that the only version you've seen?"

Melanie shrugged. "I mean, I guess I've only met one side of the couple at a time and I've learned to be skeptical about the other perspective."

"Ahhh." Something blinked in his eyes.

"What?"

"Well...would you like to meet both of us? She's, I mean she's nearby. You can talk to her and get both sides."

Melanie frowned at him, trying to read his too-cute gestures and assess how quickly she got to this point in the conversation. "What do you mean 'nearby'?"

"I mean, she's at the convention too."

"Is this some kind of set up?" Melanie's voice was sharper than she intended, but this was too fast. She'd been looking for new opportunities, but she didn't plan on something quite like this. Did she owe it to herself to hear him out? Or should she run as fast as she could?

He shifted on the bench seat and shoved his glasses up again but didn't deny it. "It's nothing planned," he said finally. "It's more an opportune moment. Maybe. Depending on what you're into."

"What I'm..." Melanie paused, hearing her voice keep going up in pitch. "What do you mean?"

He pulled his phone out and put it on the table between them. It was dressed in a library card case. "I'm probably not explaining this well. Is it OK if I invite Laura to join us?" He raised both hands again. "No pressure."

Melanie eyed the phone like it was going to make this decision independently. It continued to look cute and unassuming. She picked up her still-full pint glass and took a big gulp. She was unhappy with her life and looking for change; she needed to be open to all possibilities.

"OK," she agreed. She kept drinking her beer, even though it tasted like wet bread.

Melanie had finished her beer by the time Laura arrived and found it funny that such an unconventional couple had such conventional names. David ordered her another beer when he ordered one for Laura, who was wearing an old-school superhero costume with ears and a shorter cape than Melanie's own. Laura slid into the booth beside him. They didn't kiss, but she put her hand on his thigh and they sat so close it was obvious they were continuing to touch under the table.

"So why didn't you come to the panel?" Melanie asked. She

gestured at Laura's costume. "I guess maybe you don't need any advice. That's really good."

Laura smiled, her lips shiny red beneath her mask. "Thanks. I bought it, I didn't make it. And I only have the one because I kind of busted the bank on it."

"You actually would have found Melanie's talk helpful, she's all about crafting costumes on a budget," David told her.

"And you made this?"

Melanie touched the fabric of her cape. It was like she was on a double date without a plus one, all the sudden. *Not fun.* "Yeah. I mean, it's not perfect."

"Oh stop," Laura interrupted. "You look so great. I love how the cape drapes. And the color really works for you."

This subject, at least, was one she knew. "Yours is great too. What fabric is that, do you know?"

Laura flipped the dark fabric over her shoulder on the open side of the booth. "Oh I don't know. I'm sorry, I buy off the rack to avoid the details."

Melanie shrugged and smiled. Laura was obviously trying to make her feel more comfortable. And this conversation put her on more familiar ground. "So why haven't you gotten this guy to wear a costume yet?"

Laura smiled, putting her hand on David's arm. "He likes to look more than participate."

Maybe Melanie's cape was too heavy in this badly ventilated bar. Laura kept looking at her with her hand on David's arm and David was looking at her too and she was overheated. If she was really a cartoon character, she would shrink into a smaller and smaller drawing of herself.

"Don't be nervous," Laura said. She reached across the table and put her other hand on Melanie's. "David said I'd find you intriguing and he was right. I'm totally turned on. But how do *you* feel?"

"Um." Melanie tried to come up with an answer. Embarrassed?

Confused? "Intrigued," she finally said. "Yeah, that seems accurate. But also uncertain. I've never done this, exactly."

Laura gestured between herself and David. "This? Or..." She pointed at herself. "This?"

Melanie laughed a little, which sounded weird when she heard it because she didn't really find it funny. Was this really happening? It was like she stepped outside her normal, boring life and fell down a rabbit hole of opportunity she wasn't sure she was ready for. "Neither."

"Well there's always a first. But...there doesn't have to be, either." Laura looked at David and they smiled at each other, then turned encouraging looks on Melanie. They looked like suburban parents at a PTA meeting. It made Melanie want to get a good grade. "Why don't we walk around for awhile, get to know each other better?"

Melanie cleared her throat and glanced out at the crowd, trying to stabilize herself. Everything looked as normal out there as a group of people in costume could. Uncomfortable, but not scared.

Anna told her to challenge herself.

She looked back at David and Laura. "Well...I'm willing to investigate further?"

They both smiled. It was a little Stepford-y but it made Melanie laugh. She didn't have to do anything she didn't want to. It was nice to be wanted.

The two of them exchanged another look. David put his hand up for the waitress.

They walked down the street, making a loop past the gum wall under the market. The walking and fresh air helped clear Melanie's airy head and upset stomach. Laura popped some gum into her mouth, chewed vigorously, and then David used it to attach a parking ticket stub to the wall.

Melanie thought it was kind of gross—thousands of people's spit preserved in an alley—but she took a picture of them with Laura's phone, posed with their pop art. Laura did a Vanna White pose and, as she did, the wind obligingly picked up to spread her cape around her. It was a great shot.

They came across a tiny store where a woman sitting outside at a table was selling crystals and reading palms. "It's not as precise as a horoscope, but if you're looking for answer to life's big questions, you've come to the right place," she said, standing to gesture at the three of them expectantly.

"I'll do it," Laura volunteered, stepping toward the table. But David didn't let go of her hand; he was looking at Melanie.

"You look like a woman with some questions," he said in a low voice. Melanie glanced at him. She thought the whole concept was silly; if answers were written on her hand, she would be doing a lot better at passing life's tests. "Give it a shot. On us."

Laura grinned, going along with him. "Yes, go on, Melanie. Couldn't hurt, right?"

Melanie thought about resisting, but it seemed like a silly reason to take a stand. So she stepped forward and took a seat in the chair pulled up to the woman's table. When she sat, she felt dizzy for a moment. She put out her left hand. "Does it matter which one?" she asked.

"It does. But this will be fine." The woman took Melanie's hand in both of hers, spreading her palm. Her fingers were cold but dry.

"Hm," she said. Her voice was business-like, not at all like a witch in a movie. "The most interesting thing I see here is that your love line is split but parallel."

"What does that mean?" Melanie looked down at her hand, which looked the same as ever. Pale and narrow, with a mess of lines running all over it.

"It could mean a lot of things. Two lines can mean two loves. But both are deep, very deep, so great loves, not love affairs. And very close together. Your two loves are intertwined."

The woman looked up at Melanie, looking intently into her face. Too intently. Melanie braced herself, sensing something coming that she wouldn't like. "Are you in love now?" she asked.

Melanie's eyebrows shot up. The presence of David and Laura behind her urged her to respond quickly, but she didn't want to lie. "Um." She struggled. *Should I know for sure I don't love Chris anymore, considering I'm in the middle of breaking up with him?* "I don't think so?"

The woman's expression didn't change, but her eyes seemed to understand something. "You'll make up your mind soon," she promised. "A love line like that doesn't stay indecisive very long."

How does this woman, out of anyone, sense that she doesn't know her own mind? Melanie took her hand back. She was done. She stumbled back from the table and David caught her elbow. Laura stepped forward to pay.

"*You* could use a crystal to clean your aura," the woman said to Laura, sitting back down to plug the credit card reader into her phone.

"Just the palm reading for now, thanks," Laura said. She glanced back at Melanie and David and widened her eyes beneath her mask.

"That was weird, huh?" Laura said briskly, once they were walking away. She said it like she was washing her hands of the whole episode, not like she was opening a conversation. Melanie didn't really believe in signs, but she still wished she were talking to someone who knew her history and why that woman's comment left her shaken.

Was Chris her first great love? Did she only have one more chance to get it right?

"It was silly," she said aloud. She suddenly had a very strong need to get back to her real life. "Listen, guys, I think I'm going to run back to my hotel."

They paused on the corner, Melanie facing Laura and David. They both looked disappointed.

"But you should come out for drinks with me and my friends later," Melanie added. "I think you'll like them. Very geeky, of course. Most of them will be in costume from just leaving the convention."

Laura and David looked at each other and had another one of

those silent conversations partners are good at. Melanie and Chris used to do that, as well.

"We'd love that," Laura said. "And, listen, all this foreplay is nice but if you want to join us in our hotel room later...the invitation remains open."

Melanie barely ignored the temptation to look around furtively to see if anyone else heard that. They were standing on a busy street surrounded by normal people who, she assumed, didn't discuss threesomes randomly in public.

"I'll keep that in mind," she finally said. Then she walked away. For once, not taking an opportunity was the right decision for her.

8

Two Years Ago

When you've shared a bed with someone as long as Chris and Melanie had shared a bed, you start to get annoyed when they don't cut their toenails. Or didn't shower that day.

But Melanie tried to be understanding. Chris just took a new job—it allowed him to work remotely, yey!—and he was getting used to his schedule. Things would level out soon. So he worked on a special project through dinner most of the week. "It's a sign of confidence that they already chose me for a team like this," he'd said. So he had to catch up on his regular work over the weekend and that meant he couldn't go to the convention with her for the first time in four years.

It all gave Melanie more time to work on her costume.

She was wearing green tights and a long, red wig. She walked out into the living room, ready to go, and Chris barely glanced up from his computer.

"I'm leaving," she said, trying to imbue the words with the obvious fact that he should get up and see her to the door. That he should kiss her and say he wished he was going. That he should prioritize her in that small way if he's not going to in the big one.

He kept typing. "One sec. OK." He hopped up and hurried over to her. "You look great." He kissed her on the forehead and was turning away as Melanie reached for him. "I'll see you later. Have fun."

Melanie hesitated. She felt like saying, "forget it, I don't want to go without you," and flopping onto the sofa. But no, she thought. She would go and she would make new friends—if she could manage to talk to anyone—and she wouldn't come back all day. He would miss her more that way.

She hoped, anyway.

~

SEATTLE - **now**

When Melanie got back to the hotel room, she was tired but satisfied. When she closed the door behind her, she realized Chris was in their room and immediately wished she was alone. He didn't see her in her costume before he left that morning and she dreaded seeing him *not* look at her. But she needed to change before she went back out with her friends that night and Chris had to pack for his flight back home. Melanie didn't go back home until tomorrow.

Chris was sitting on his bed. He wore joggers and a t-shirt and had a bag of chips next to him. There was a basketball game on the TV at low volume and he had his laptop on his lap. He looked over his shoulder at her and smiled. It seemed genuine, and for a moment Melanie was transported into the past. To when shared smiles were easy and not a ploy to hide their problems behind.

"I watched your panel," he said.

Melanie stared at him, completely unable to grasp the meaning of the words. The costume panel must have streamed online. Why did he bother?

"It's cool that you've gotten so into costume design," he added.

Why am I so irritated? Am I allowed?

She decided that she was.

"Don't," she said. She looked up at Chris and his face was blank with surprise. "Don't watch me online when you're not involved in my life. Don't act interested when we barely talk. This is why we broke up. You *don't know me* anymore. Stop pretending like you do."

Chris looked like a kicked puppy for a moment. Melanie reminded herself she was practicing speaking up for herself. It was too late for Chris to act like he cared about her life. If he really cared, he would have come to the convention with her, not watched like a creeper online.

She went into the bathroom and slammed the door. She hoped he had to go to the airport before she came out.

CHRIS BOUGHT Wi-Fi on the flight home, rather than sit and listen to his own brain. Nothing about the trip had gone right. Professionally, it had been a success. But the rest of his life was falling apart. He was all tied up in his own thoughts, unable to sort out what he should be feeling and why.

He messaged Jenny to ask about the online therapy she'd mentioned. Jenny, who never seemed to sleep or be offline, responded right away.

Something about being mid-air reminded him he was hanging in between real life and the reality he wanted. Like maybe it was possible for things to get better. So he clicked the button to sign up.

Hi Chris,
My name is Anna Marie Kendell and I am a licensed therapist.
Thanks for signing up.
Welcome to the online counseling room, which will be our private and secure place to communicate. You can enter this room from any Internet-connected device wherever you are.
To help us get started, can you please tell me what brought you here? Just write a few short sentences about the challenges you're experi-

encing or what you would like to talk about and we will go from there.
Looking forward to working with you,
Anna Marie Kendell (MSW, LCSW)

Hi Dr. Kendell,
A friend thinks I'm struggling with burn out and I'm not sure what to do.
Chris

Chris,
Thanks for sharing. Tell me more about why your friend thinks you're struggling with burn out. Is this impacting your daily life or relationships? In order to help, I need to know how the problem is showing up in your life. Do you want to set up a video appointment to talk about it?
Anna Marie Kendell (MSW, LCSW)

From @miz_anna_doll:
Seattle Convention Center
(picture of Anna's squirrel book on a table with sharpies and a fuzzy, stuffed squirrel)
Spoke on a panel for librarians today about the power of anthropomorphism to get kids reading more! #bookstagram
Liked by @melly_89 and 117 others

From @melly_89:
Seattle, Washington
(close-up picture of a palm)
Got my palm read today and basically came away thinking I better live it up before my life line ends. Or is that my head line that ends abruptly? #yolo

Liked by @miz_anna_doll and 56 others
@miz_anna_doll: Omg I want to do that, take meeeee
@lauraloowho: That woman was so weird!!!!

From @jezabellegreen
Seattle Convention Center
(picture of Tim and 2 other men in matching costumes)
I don't always wear my panties in public but when I do they're kelly
green
Liked by @miz_anna_doll and 32 others
@manlybubbles0190: Diva
Reply to @manlybubbles0190: Not everyone's afraid to shine

~

ANNA WAS GIGGLING UNCONTROLLABLY when Melanie got to the table.
"So then I end up with Neil at a bar that night talking about Terry's
books and arguing about George R.R. Martin and the whole time I'm
just thinking, omigod I should have changed my underwear!"

The bar was not near the convention center, so there was no one
in costume there and it felt less friendly as a result. Everyone looked
like normies, wearing street clothes, and suddenly Melanie wasn't
sure she fit in without their uniforms. She might look like everybody
else, wearing jeans and a long-sleeve t-shirt, but she had never
figured out how to "play" normal-life Melanie and be a geek at the
same time. Listening to Anna and the others discuss geek life while
wearing real clothes was jarring.

She sat down between Roger and Tim, who had left a chair
between them at the table. They must have been fighting, because
neither of them turned her direction, and there seemed to be a cold
spot where she sat, as if they were ignoring it. So now she was accidentally stuck in between people who didn't want to talk or even look
her direction. Terrific.

Melanie spent a lot of time telling herself she only missed having a generic boyfriend. But for the first time in awhile, she realized that she specifically missed Chris. Not the Chris she'd go home to after this, but the Chris he'd been at other times to her. The Chris who had shared so many moments with her, and then told stories about them better than she did. The Chris who would spend half an hour diagramming how time travel worked in *Terminator: Salvation* to prove it didn't make sense. The Chris who would only tease her about her shyness in private and always covered for her in public. Chris had been the bridge between real life Melanie and geek Melanie. He was one of the only people in her life—maybe the only person—who knew both of them.

Chris would find this conversation a drag. And they would exchange glances and both know what the other was thinking. And that would make it better. And then they could leave together.

Instead, Melanie sat there, pretending she knew who everyone was talking about. Even Matt, sitting across from Melanie, looked intent on Anna's story. He'd barely looked up and nodded at her when she came in.

"You really had drinks with Neil?" he asked. "But what did he think about George R. R. Martin? Are we ever getting the next book?"

"Can we grab this extra chair?" a man wearing a long tunic top was asking, his hands on the empty chair at the other end of the table.

"Oh I invited a couple more people, we need that," Melanie said quickly. "Sorry."

He raised his hands and walked away. The others looked at Melanie.

"I met a couple people at my panel earlier," Melanie told the table. "They seemed fun so I invited them tonight."

Anna's eyebrows raised, probably because she thought Melanie was planning on sleeping with David when she left the panel with him, but she said, "Great! The more geeks the merrier!"

"Or the geekier," Matt offered.

"Which is merrier," Anna responded.

Laura and David arrived as they were ordering a second round of drinks. Laura, out of her cowl, still had red hair IRL, and she was pretty but not as intimidating as she'd looked in the mask. She had freckles.

"We brought stickers for the table," Laura said, and David spilled a small bag full of sticker art across the table. They were metallic-toned caricatures based on a variety of shows. "Didn't want to come empty-handed."

"Ooh!" Everyone reached for their favorite character. No duels immediately arose so Laura and David must have chosen well.

"Are these from that table somewhere in D through F?" Anna asked. "I saw these earlier and wanted to buy all of them but I couldn't decide so I just bought nothing."

Laura and David started asking Anna about her work, once they learned she was an exhibiting artist. Melanie was glad she invited people who fit into the group, but a little hurt that Laura and David barely looked at her. She thought they'd been interested in her specifically. Was she a warm body and now they'd moved on? Was it because she wasn't as interesting out of her costume?

Eventually, Roger got up and went to the bathroom and Tim turned to her. "I'm sorry you ended up in the middle," he said.

"Literally," Melanie agreed. "What's up?"

"They just never commit to anything," Tim said. He was wearing a v-neck sweater and used his hands a lot to talk. He was keeping his voice low, like he was sharing secrets, but Melanie knew Tim was the type to spill tea to anyone who would listen. She suspected everyone else already knew what was going on between them and Tim was eager to fill someone in. "I knew that, going into it, but somewhere along the way..." He shrugged. "I'm a fool, I know."

"You're human," Melanie replied. "Is it love?"

Tim smiled, but it only quirked one side of his lips. "What is love?"

Melanie hesitated, because she was not sure if she was actually supposed to answer that—or what her answer would be if she was.

What did she know about love? She thought she'd found a love that was going to last—but was five years that ended like *this* really a love story?

"I have *feelings* for them, but they're not holding up their end of our agreement. It takes both things," Tim said. He turned away from Melanie again when Roger came back to the table.

Roger leaned over to her next. Their voice was too high to really whisper when they asked, "Has my lover given you any messages for me?"

"Not your anything," Tim sing-songed without looking at them.

Melanie looked at Roger and offered her most sympathetic look. "Sorry."

Roger waved at their server and pointed at his empty margarita glass. "Lots of salt," they said, loudly, over the other conversations.

Tim snorted from Melanie's other side.

"I'm sorry, darling," Roger said to Melanie, their eyes on Tim. They didn't actually seem that sorry; they even seemed to be enjoying the drama a little bit. "Very indiscreet of us."

Melanie was a little annoyed with both of them. If this were a show, she'd be the Mary Sue hated by fandom because she was written in exclusively for their use as a prop. Mary Sues usually had nothing going on in their own lives.

"It's OK," she announced, while bringing her glass to her mouth. "I'm still living with the boyfriend I broke up with. Your drama is nothing compared to my life."

Roger and Tim both turned in their seats to look at her. Unfortunately, so did Matt and Laura.

Melanie took a long sip of her gin drink. She pulled her phone out and started scrolling Instagram to make it clear she was not sharing anything else with the table. What was wrong with her? Normally, Melanie was so good at keeping herself to herself.

Her phone buzzed and a text popped up.

Matt: (8:14 p.m.) Do you want to get out of here?

Melanie raised her eyes. Matt was on his phone, across the table. She scanned everyone else. Anna was talking to Roger. Tim was talking to David and Laura. Cari and Isabelle and Emily were huddled at the other end of the table looking at something on an iPad.

> Melanie: (8:15 p.m.) Yeah let's ditch

> Matt: (8:16 p.m.) Take your stuff with you to the bathroom and just go outside, I'll make excuses and follow you

> Melanie: (8:16 p.m.) I need to pay

> Matt: (8:16 p.m.) I got it

> Melanie: (8:16 p.m.) As you wish (laughing emoji)

Matt met her out front a few minutes later. "Were you quoting *The Princess Bride* to me?"

Melanie handed him her purse while she put her jacket on. "Inconceivable! It's just nice of you to do all the work while I pull an Irish goodbye." She paused. "Is that phrase culturally offensive?"

Matt shrugged. "I'm not Irish so...no?"

She took her purse back. "What do I owe you for the drink?"

"Let's go get another one and you can pay for it."

"Sounds like a plan."

They walked down the street, idly looking in windows of bars seeing if one called them in. The night was misty and cool for summer. They were near the water, so the rain smelled slightly salty.

"It was getting a little claustrophobic in there," Matt offered, gesturing at what they left behind.

"Yeah...I mean, I love them all," Melanie offered as a disclaimer. "But I'm more of a one-on-one person, generally. Crowds all day and then another crowd at night gets a little intense for me."

"Me too. Anyway, I've been wanting to catch up with you."

Melanie glanced at him. Was he going to bring it up? They should definitely talk about it. "Yeah..."

"Have you been avoiding me?"

Melanie shook her head. "No. I mean, if I have it's not personal. I've been kind of all over the place. You heard what I said in there?"

Matt nodded slowly. "Yeah. Is that what San Diego was about, too?"

Melanie sighed. There was really no unwinding Chris from her decisions, even now. She paused on a street corner, not sure if she wanted to cross. The next block looked darker, with fewer bars and restaurants. "Yes."

"But the two of you are broken up? You just live together?"

Melanie nodded. There was more to it than could be summarized in two sentences, but those were the facts. She looked up at Matt as he moved out of the way of two other people crossing the street. They stood there, too close together, as the light changed again.

"It's complicated...but we are officially broken up, yes."

Matt's eyes dropped for a second to her lips. Melanie's breath caught. She looked at his mouth. His lips were a little more pink, more full, than she was used to. How many hundreds of times had she kissed Chris like this, spontaneously, out in public? That was what she was thinking of now—the past—even on the cusp of kissing someone new.

Melanie stepped back, away from Matt. Anna was right. Kissing him should mean something besides moving on from Chris.

"But I'm not ready to start anything new yet," she admitted. The honesty released some of the weight on her heart.

"I get it," Matt said. His voice was a little disappointed. No, resigned. This was the second time she'd done this to him and she was frustrated with herself for putting him in this position.

"I'm sorry," she said, looking down at her hands. She wished she could snap her fingers and make her feelings something else. Things were over with Chris; why couldn't she start looking for something new?

"Don't be sorry. You're just being honest. Timing is super important, unfortunately for me." No promise to "wait until she was ready," she noticed. Which was fair. This wasn't a Netflix Original romance. Matt turned and looked at the bar they were standing next to. "Maybe we should check this place out?"

Melanie hesitated, because she was not sure what they were going to talk about over drinks. Now that romance was off the table, they were out of other conversational options.

"We could text everyone to come join us," Matt offered. "I left it open ended. Told them we were scoping out other bars."

Relieved, Melanie smiled. "That'd be great," she said, and watched him pull out his phone. Her eyes unexpectedly filled with tears and she looked out into the street, blinking until they went away. She wished Chris was here, and yet she also didn't because the Chris she was imagining being here with her was the Chris from three or four years ago, when they were intent on going to every Mexican restaurant in town in order to rank their burritos. The Chris who, on their third date, parked and came into her apartment and then said, "I guess I better head out..." as if they weren't obviously going to have sex. The Chris she used to make dinner with every Sunday night while they alternated whose playlist they pulled up on Spotify. That's not the Chris she broke up with. That's the Chris she would watch sleeping at night, in love with his existence and terrified he might somehow disappear.

Stop. No more of this. She was moving on.

Melanie pulled her phone out of her purse and spontaneously texted Emily: "Do you have any more opportunities on panels coming up? Interested in doing more of that type of work."

She took a deep breath. No more falling into things or accepting what she got as the best she could do. She needed to get better at figuring out and asking for what she wanted. No more letting life happen to her.

〜

From @manlybubbles0190
Seattle, Washington
(picture of two cocktails, from above)
Drinks with geeks #afterparty
Liked by @miz_anna_doll and 32 others
@jezabellegreen: So basic
Reply to @jezabellegreen: I believe yours was the pink one

Chris: (9:53 p.m.) Hey letting you know I'm back home. You didn't leave a grocery list, did you want me to go to the store tomorrow? Let me know what you need.

Anna: (8:45 p.m.) Ummm plz fill me in on the Matt situation asap I thought you were LEAVING with him leaving with him

Anna: (9:12 p.m.) P.S. your friends Laura and David are WILD

Melanie: (9:13 p.m.) What do you mean?

Anna: 97:20 p.m.) Did you know they write fanfiction?? I looked it up on A03 and it's all NC-17 stuff. Like elf orgies and threesomes

Melanie: (9:20 p.m.) Lol. Somehow I'm not surprised

9

Six Months Ago

"Where do you want to travel this summer?" Melanie was curled up on the other end of the couch with her computer. Chris was staring at the TV because he finally closed his own computer and his eyes couldn't handle anything else. He tried to turn his head to her and realized it was too much effort.

"I don't know," he said. "Where were you thinking?"

"Hmmm I'm looking at my spreadsheet. We've talked about Costa Rica before. Did you ever look up surf camps? Or wildlife tours?"

"No." A creeping sense of unease weighed down his chest. He didn't want to open his computer or look at his phone. He did not want to think about or make any more decisions today.

"Or what about Cuba? We talked about that before. We'd have to change all our money before we went and we might not have Internet there."

Chris closed his eyes. So many decisions. "What about a staycation year," he suggested. He pushed himself up off the couch because he had to go to the bathroom. "I don't really want to go anywhere."

"Really?" Melanie sounded disappointed but Chris kept walking, disappearing into the bedroom with some relief at being away from her gaze.

He ended up flopping down on the bed face-first. By the time he woke up, Melanie wasn't asking about vacation plans anymore.

Denver - now

Every time Chris ducked his head under the water for that first lap across the pool, the cool relief that no one could reach him washed over him. No phone strapped to his arm. No music filling his head. Only the sound of breathing and the rhythm of his own body moving through the water. Angling his hand so it cut the water. Keeping his legs together as they kicked.

He was not very good at swimming laps, but he did it in high school and decided to pick it back up because he didn't have to tell Melanie what he was doing. If he started running again, she'd know and she'd be waiting for him to give it up. She didn't trust him anymore, on anything. Or maybe didn't trust the hope that she could trust him? He hoped she still cared, at least.

He also hoped he wouldn't give up on himself. She might be right, the imaginary Melanie judging him in his head. He'd only been swimming every weekday for six days. His new routine had plenty of time to fail yet. He didn't quite trust himself not to fall back on what was easy: Sitting at his computer constantly waiting for something to break or someone to need him.

When he'd questions in Seattle about work culture and what was acceptable, every answer had emphasized flexibility. Nick and Jerry hadn't flinched when he asked questions about managing his own time—something Chris hadn't been taking advantage of at all.

Now, every time he told his team on Slack he wouldn't be reachable for an hour, he hesitated before he hit send.

So far, no one had acted like it was weird. Jenny sent him a thumbs up emoji every time.

He was actually more productive at work during the other hours. He was getting more done, which meant he was signing off earlier. When he had some down time after work the night before, he wasn't so exhausted when he woke up in the morning.. And he was actually sleeping again, despite the awful couch. He even went to the store on Sunday and bought himself ingredients to make dinner, rather than chips and frozen pizza.

"I forgot I could feel good," he texted his therapist through the chat room that morning.

"You've made a lot of progress already. Let's talk about techniques to make sure you're able to keep that up," Dr. Kendell responded.

What Chris really wanted to talk about were techniques for getting his old life back. Now that he had a little more energy every day, he was realizing how much he let slip away: Melanie. Friends. Hobbies. He wished reversing course was as easy as following a new routine. But there was no swimming backward.

He pushed air out forcefully as he turned his head, then took a breath and turned his face into the water again. He swam hard, probably too hard considering how little exercise he'd gotten for the past few months. His shoulders had been aching for the past week. But they'd get used to it. And if he couldn't go back, Chris would get used to a new life. As he got used to listening to himself again and trusting his own decisions, he'd find a way to build one, slowly.

Even if it didn't include Melanie.

~

Jenny: (2:20 p.m.) I deleted Tinder again

Chris: (2:30 p.m.) How do you feel?

Jenny: (2:30 p.m.) Like I should give up and get a cat

Chris: (2:31 p.m.) Don't get a cat. Get a dog. A big one. Guys love seeing a girl with a giant dog.

Jenny: (2:32 p.m.) Have you SEEN me? I could literally ride a giant dog like a horse

Chris: (2:33 p.m.) I'm telling you.

Jenny: (2:35 p.m.) I'm a failure

Chris: (2:36 p.m.) Everybody's a failure at dating, some of us are just slower at failing than others

Jenny: (2:37 p.m.) Still won't talk to you huh?

Chris: (2:38 p.m.) Based on how she ignores me I am not even sure my voice still works

~

From @mtinspace7:
Wichita, Kansas
(close-up photo of insignia)
Thought I might branch out beyond for Atlanta but wow has this costume ever been hard to find
Liked by @melly_89 and 125 others
@melly_89: Omg! So excited to see this
@miz_anna_doll: Yessssss

~

MELANIE WAS WORKING on her apartment spreadsheet while hiding in her bedroom on Sunday night. She gave herself five minutes to work on her costume spreadsheet for every 15 she spent looking at apartments online. She'd started a list of ones she needed to find time to visit in person and she had fields for must-haves: one bedroom, parking, hardwood floors, dishwasher. She was trying to be realistic about paying rent on a single income, so she gave up the idea of an in-unit washer/dryer.

Chris had always paid for more of their apartment because he made more than she did. In exchange, he got their one dedicated parking space. And, well, Melanie always did most of the chores although that hadn't technically been part of their agreement.

She was beginning to think she'd have to move to a suburb, because she couldn't afford downtown alone. It'd make her commute worse, but maybe she could get something with more room that was at least clean.

She went out to the kitchen when she couldn't ignore her stomach any longer only to find Chris was cooking.

Actually cooking, like he planned it out and put on an apron to do it, rather than stumbling into throwing together more ingredients than he originally thought his pizza or ramen required. He had steaks on one cutting board and vegetables on another one. The oven beeped that it was at temperature as Melanie stepped into the kitchen.

He was wearing the apron she gave him three years ago that almost made him look like he was wearing a costume. On his birthday that year, Chris wore it while cooking naked. She remembered joking that the "real" crusader's butt couldn't possibly look any better. Melanie's eyes dropped involuntarily to his bottom, which was now modestly clad in sweats. The curve of muscle was still obvious in the loose pants.

Chris tossed her a glance. She jerked her eyes away.

"Do you want some food?" he asked, rubbing salt on the steaks. "I have plenty."

Melanie looked around the kitchen, which was pretty much taken up by Chris's project. She might be able to microwave something.

"Or I can get out of your way," Chris added, picking up on her hesitation. He looked over his shoulder at her again.

"No, you're fine," Melanie responded automatically, because she was not that vindictive that she was going to kick Chris out of the room in the middle of a project. Of course Chris was allowed to use the kitchen he also paid for. "I'm just pretty hungry. Not sure I want to wait."

Chris flipped a steak over in one big hand. "Suit yourself. But I know you love my steak."

Melanie winced a little at the double entendre. Chris smiled and went back to rubbing his meat like he knew what she was thinking and liked it.

She was aware that she was still attracted to Chris. It didn't mean anything; Chris was an attractive person and she was hormonal. And it would be so easy to fall back into bed with someone she'd slept with so many times before. But she also knew she didn't want to—no, couldn't—act on the attraction because that would send a false signal to both of them. So, with all that in mind, she was not certain if it would imply something more if she admitted that, yes, she absolutely wanted to eat Chris's steak.

She and Chris had barely spoken for the past week. Melanie had decided the only way she could deal with her sadness was by drawing a hard line between the two of them. No more working together on daily tasks, like groceries or dinner. No casual conversation about the neighbors' music or what work was like that day. But by accepting a meal, she'd be accepting a favor from him, shifting the power dynamic back in his direction. It was like opening up a door to him and letting vulnerability leak back into their relationship.

"OK, sure," she said finally, thinking more about how tired she was of camping out in their bedroom. But she would not sit here like a lump accepting whatever Chris wanted to give her. "Can I help?"

"You can cut up the carrots and take the ends off the peas if you want."

Melanie slid behind him, avoiding touching him or the cast iron skillet that was heating on the stove, and picked up the second cutting board so she can move it a little further away from Chris, who somehow smelled freshly-showered even though she'd been blocking the bathroom most of the day.

"You haven't cooked in awhile," she said, hoping she said it in a neutral way. They hadn't had any blow-ups since Seattle. Over the past week, he hadn't even tried to start a conversation in the morning or at night when they couldn't avoid sharing the kitchen. On Monday, when Melanie got groceries after work, he silently came out to help her get her bags out of her car.

He didn't seem to take it as an accusation. "I know. I missed it."

Chris put the steaks in the hot cast iron pan and started searing them. He set a timer on his phone for each side.

"This OK?" he asked, as the sound of one of his dinner-making playlists hit the Bluetooth speaker on the table.

"Sure." Melanie wasn't going to argue about music. She was very deliberately trying not to be petty. It was totally backward that she was irritated that Chris was acting like everything was normal when Melanie desperately needed reminders that it wasn't. But, she kept reminding herself, normal was better than fighting. And after all, they had nothing to fight over anymore.

She had to keep telling herself that.

Chris put the cast iron pan in the preheated oven. He set another timer on his phone.

"Wine?" Chris asked, taking a bottle down from the rack on the fridge.

"Sure," Melanie said again, not sure what else to say. She kept chopping.

He poured them both glasses of red—surprising, since Chris was more of a beer-drinker.

"Thanks," she said, pausing her task to take a sip. "Did you buy this?"

"I bought it at Trader Joe's over the weekend."

Melanie nodded and went back to chopping. The last time they made dinner together, Chris abandoned the task in the middle because he got pinged on Slack for work.

"Are you even supposed to be working right now?" she'd asked him.

"If I don't do it now, I'll get a call from Nick or Jerry later," he'd said.

Nick and Jerry were the co-founders. They didn't really seem to do much for the company anymore besides micromanage the staff and insist all the snacks came in recyclable material. And, apparently, demand their employees make last-minute trips to Seattle.

Melanie personally didn't think it would be the end of the world to tell Nick or Jerry you expected not to work on your time off, but she hadn't said anything. Chris's response to her comments in the past had veered wildly between sighing in defeat and agreeing the expectations were unfair and scowling back with a sharp, "You work for the government. When was the last time you stayed past 5 o'clock?"

Now, she eyed his phone on the counter like it might erupt any moment, bracing herself for interruption. This time, she planned to eat alone and not be disappointed. It would almost be better if it happened now, for Chris to bail on this moment of togetherness and provide a tangible reminder why they're not together anymore.

Chris started washing the cutting board he used for the steak. She watched him out of the corner of her eye, the muscles in his back moving under the black t-shirt. Their nearness in the small kitchen made her uncomfortable. Like chopping vegetables was one small step away from having sex.

She wished a number of things in that moment—that they were at the beginning of their relationship instead of the end; that breaking up a relationship somehow cut off all emotions for that person; that she could ask him about his meetings in Seattle without it dredging up all their problems.

Melanie debated whether she should ask about his day or tell him about her horrible apartment hunt. Small talk was risky. He was not bringing up anything either. He was not interested in talking about their lives. Or maybe he was merely thinking about other things. Chris was always good at being oblivious to the elephant in the room.

The elephant, in this case, being their history and entire relationship.

She carried the chopped vegetables on the chopping board over to the Wok on the stove, on Chris's other side. He turned around as she got there and crashed into her, sending the vegetables sprawling.

"Shit," they both said.

"It's OK. Look, some of them ended up in the Wok," Melanie said, dumping the ones that managed to stay on the board into the pan.

Chris stood up from picking up some of the ones on the floor. He was smiling down at her and he was much too close. He smelled really...fresh. She lowered her eyes and noticed he had a splotch of grey on the hem of his black t-shirt.

Chris followed her eyes. "I guess I'm not so good at laundry," he admitted.

Guilt that she abandoned him to figure out something on his own was immediately followed by anger over a burden she shouldn't be responsible to bear.

He looked back up from his shirt and met her eyes. "I'll learn," he added quickly, like he read her mind.

She hated this response because her emotions read it as "sweet."

She was definitely not ready to be friends.

She stepped back from Chris, and her face must have showed how unsettled she was, because he put his hand on her arm. "You OK?"

Melanie shook him off. She looked at his face and he looked like she'd slapped him.

"I won't fall into this trap of thinking everything's OK," Melanie said. "I don't want to go back to pretending and being in denial and overlooking things. I won't do it."

Chris looked down at his handful of vegetables. It drove Melanie crazy that he looked like she hurt *his* feelings. It was *his* fault they were in this mess. Melanie had wanted to keep on loving him forever and *he* forced her to not let herself by being distant and unavailable and forgetful and annoying.

She wished she could skip the hard part, jump to the part where she enjoyed sleeping with someone else or liked cooking alone with her ear buds in. But she was in the shitty part right now and she knew from experience that there was no fast forward. Someone told her once it took at least half as long as the relationship lasted to get over someone. It had been true for Melanie in the past, but she'd never been with someone as long as Chris. She could have years to go before she was ready to move on. And she couldn't even get that process started while she was standing here letting Chris hold her back.

She needed to get away from him. The sooner, the better. She dropped the cutting board in the sink and went over to the cupboard where they kept the cereal and protein bars. She could sense Chris watching her, but didn't look at him. She couldn't meet his eyes right now. Something might happen. She might cry. She grabbed a box and took it with her back to the bedroom, where she pulled out her phone and scrolled back to January in her texts with Chris. She needed a reminder of how bad it was.

The texts were a litany of Melanie's "did you scoop the snow?" and "I took the trash out again" and "Can you Venmo me your half of the rent so the check doesn't bounce?"

His responses to each of them were one word: "Soon." "Thanks." "Sure."

She needed to take her cues from Chris, the Chris she broke up with, and learn to be polite without giving away any emotion.

MELANIE DISAPPEARED into the back of the apartment, saying, "I'm not that hungry," without looking back at him.

Chris's phone timer went off and he got the steaks out of the oven. He covered them with aluminum foil to rest, moving automatically. He turned off the oven and the music, because it was starting to annoy him.

After the roller coaster of this evening, he wasn't hungry anymore either. He and Melanie had coasted up to the top for a few minutes and looked out over a view of their relationship that was lit up with hope and possibility. And then came crashing down, under the dark clouds, into the reality that Melanie wasn't open to reconsidering her decision.

Sometimes it was easier to start new than start over. But Melanie didn't seem open to either option. And Chris couldn't seem to let go. If he was honest with himself, he didn't want to.

He looked down at the dinner he'd hoped would be an olive branch. He couldn't give up. Because he saw something in Melanie's eyes when she looked at him. If nothing else, she remembered what they use to be like together.

She missed it.

It'd take time to convince Melanie the work they've already put into their relationship was worth the work they needed to get it back.

But with the end of summer and the end of their lease looming, it was time he didn't have.

It was time for something dramatic.

10

Atlanta - now

Melanie didn't finish a new costume.

She regretted it because she'd never seen so many
people in costume in one place in her life. Dragon Con was the real
cosplay convention. Unlike most cons, it took place in a series of
hotels with shuttles constantly running between them. So the air
conditioning was constantly on high and nobody wearing elaborate
cosplay had to worry about melting.

For the variety, she and Anna traded costumes on the first day
there. It was almost like having a brand new outfit.

Melanie was staying at the Hilton with Anna, Roger, Matt and
Cari. Roger and Matt volunteered to take the pull-out couch and
floor, alternating nights.

Melanie also texted Laura and invited her and David to join the
group at happy hour. She finally told Anna the whole story and
Anna, unphased by the threesome part, only responded, "I'm so
happy you're making your own convention friends!"

"You won't even need me next year," she added. She was smiling
but Melanie leaned over and hugged her.

"You are the master here, although I think we're trying to retire that word. But I will still be a padawan for many years."

Anna laughed. "Omigosh. We should do *those* costumes next summer."

"I like the sound of that." *Next summer.* What would next summer look like in her life? She'd be living alone again. But at least she'd still have this. She looked around the hotel lobby at all the colorful costumes—the tall furred space pilot in the corner and the giant, red-and-gold robot standing outside the glass doors—representing people dressed in whatever made them happy.

She loved this.

Melanie had worried, when it was dark and late at night and she was alone in her apartment, even with Chris out in the living room, that she was only going to conventions to get away from her life. *Am I a second-tier fan, attending not because of pure love but as an escape? Because I love looking like someone else, feeling like someone else?*

But, standing in that Atlanta hotel lobby with Anna and waiting for the rest of her friends, she realized maybe that was what she had in common with everyone here. Because wasn't *escaping* what super-human characters and strategy games and even threesomes were all about: Creating a different world, and by doing so creating community? By building a world they preferred, geeks found each other.

Matt was the first to arrive, playing up his drunk pirate as he wobbled up to her grinning. She didn't want Matt to be an escape, but more importantly, she didn't want sex with *anyone* to be for the sake of escape. Sex, to her, was about building a connection. And she couldn't build a new connection without clearing space for it. She was a little disappointed to realize that meant she couldn't sleep with him or anyone else this weekend, but knew it was the right decision.

"Parlez?" Matt slurred, then straightened. "OK, that's the extent of my French."

Maybe a little making out would be OK. Melanie could really use an escape from all the hormones, the ones that kept making her want to sleep with her ex.

She grabbed Matt by the lapel and smirked at him, that idea on her mind. He pulled his phone out of his jacket to take a picture.

"You are looking feisty tonight," he observed.

Melanie laughed. "We'll see. The night is young..."

Anna teased Matt about his mainstream character choice, calling it "dangerously stereotypical, dude."

"Where's the costume you posted on Instagram?" she demanded.

"I could only find a t-shirt with his logo! It just didn't look right."

"Melanie and I can help you. Did you bring it with you?"

"No, I left it back in Kansas."

"Bring it to New York or Baltimore."

"I'll try. I can't make it to Baltimore though. Too expensive. New York is my last con for the season."

"No!" Melanie and Anna gasped together.

Matt ducked his head and nodded. "I know, I'm sorry. Let's make New York a real blow-out though."

"In that case...where's the happy couple?" Anna looked at Melanie, wriggling her darkened eyebrows. She meant Laura and David.

"Roger and Tim?" Matt asked, faux innocently.

Anna laughed loudly. It was incongruous with her emo outfit. Roger, who was wearing a fantastic gender-bent costume and standing nearby talking to Emily and someone in an outfit that looked like flames, glanced over. Anna lowered her voice, "No. Tim didn't come."

Matt leaned in, the beads in his wig swinging. "How do we feel about this?"

Melanie checked her phone to see if David or Laura had texted. She had a text from Chris.

Chris: (7:11 p.m.) You're at the Hilton, right?

She frowned and tucked her phone back in her boot without

answering, because she didn't think she needed to update Chris on her whereabouts anymore.

Then a man in a black armored suit and cowl walked through the front doors and it was Chris.

It took Melanie a few minutes to place him, but her subconscious knew before her mind sent the identification to her emotions and her whole body tensed. His walk was familiar. She knew that chin.

She cycled in quick succession through multiple stages of shock: Disbelief; denial; anger; planning how to get out of what was about to happen.

She finally settled on a pervasive level of discomfort as she watched him walk up to her and her group of friends. Matt and Anna, who were standing in front of Melanie, turned toward him expectantly.

"Great costume, man," Matt said before Melanie could speak.

Roger reappeared amid their group and agreed. "Very manly," they murmured, clearly checking Chris out from behind.

"Thank you. You, too." Chris smoothed a hand down his plastic chest. He looked at Melanie, his head moving stiffly. "Hey Melanie."

"Hey," she said. *Hey? HEY? What the hell is he doing here?* Melanie was hot from embarrassment and didn't want to make a scene. She looked at Anna, but Anna's face was blank because she'd never met Chris.

"Hi everyone!" David and Laura walked up, together as always. Laura was wearing a grey jumpsuit with a "no ghosts" patch on the arm, although the top zipper was rolled down toward her belly with some serious side-boob showing. The others greeted them and formed a larger circle, with Chris a member. David and Laura told him hello. Anna, Matt and Roger looked at Melanie, waiting for an introduction.

"Everybody, this is Chris," Melanie finally said. She watched Anna's face as realization dawned. It gave Melanie some small satisfaction to share the horror. But it was very small. She had no idea what to say next. She didn't think there was a Miss Manners etiquette guide for your ex-boyfriend unexpectedly showing up wearing a surprisingly realistic costume.

"Chris..." She went around the circle and named everyone, taking bitter pleasure in the fact that he was probably overwhelmed by all the new faces.

"Are you joining us for happy hour?" Matt, oblivious, continued to be too nice to her stalker ex-boyfriend. "We were just going next door." He waved with a pirate-like flair, his sleeve flouncing.

"Yeah, that'd be great," Chris said. He looked at Melanie again, as if waiting for her to chime in. To welcome him among *her* friends when he was the uninvited guest. She said nothing, along for the ride on a slow-moving train wreck.

Matt led the way toward the bar and Chris was swept up in their crowd. Like he was one of them. Melanie followed the chatty crowd as if she was in a cloud, floating above them with wooden legs.

"Did you know he was coming?" Anna hissed in Melanie's ear as they trailed behind the others.

Melanie shook her head. Words were trapped in her head, suffocating her with everything unsaid in this moment. This was exactly how Chris has made her feel for the past year. It wasn't fair. This was *her* group, *her* activity, *her* trip.

"He's unusually tall and broad for a nerd," Anna added, giving Chris sidelong looks as he walked ahead of them with Matt and David.

Anna checking out her boyfriend—ex-boyfriend—knocked her out of her numb state. Melanie stopped dead, letting the group go on without them, and looked at Anna in desperation, grabbing her forearm. "Anna! What am I supposed to do?"

Her friend returned her clasp, grabbing Melanie's own forearm. Anna's white makeup and dark contacts made her look very serious.

"His actions don't reflect on you and his decisions are not your problem," she said in a low voice. "Don't take him on as a project just because he invaded your space."

Melanie squeezed Anna's arm in gratitude because she was right and that was exactly what she needed to hear. It was *not* Melanie's job to make this go smoothly for Chris. He could drown in his own idiotic gesture.

~

From @melly_89's Story, reshared:
From @miz_anna_doll:
Hilton Atlanta Downtown Hotel
(picture of Melanie and Anna)
Redux! #dragoncon
Comment from @melly_89: Fierce (fire emoji)

From @jezabellegreen:
(picture of a whiskey rocks glass and a hardback graphic novel)
Missing friends at #DragonCon. Don't have too much fun without me!
Comment from @melly_89: Wish you were here!! (woman crying gif)

From @mtinspace7:
Hilton Atlanta Downtown Hotel
(picture of Matt and Melanie)
A dishonest man you can always trust to be dishonest. #dragoncon
Comment from @melly_89: (laughing emoji)
Viewed by @gamerchris_1989 and 45 others

~

HE WAS AN IDIOT.

If this were one of Melanie's rom-coms, he'd have some kind of sidekick character cheering him on in making a grand gesture. Not Jenny, who was bitter about romance in general. But like a happily married brother—that Chris didn't have—who would extol the fulfillment of long-term relationships and the sacrifices of one's general ideology required by such a commitment.

The thing was, though, in those movies no one ever talked about how long grand gestures take. Or how slow, slow, *slow* the process was of trying to pull one off.

Finding a costume sized for a tall man, for example, took several tries before he finally decided he was going to have to pay much more than the $150 he had estimated in order to look decent. And he wanted to look more than decent, he wanted to look breath-taking. Preferably like someone who could sweep a girl off her feet without opening his mouth—since he still had no idea what to say when he finally landed in Atlanta.

It was Melanie in Seattle telling him to stop faking it that inspired the plan. That was when he realized, *oh, I've got to up my game so she'll up hers.*

That realization might have been new, but therapy and time to think, away from work and mostly underwater, have made him understand that he hasn't known where he stood with Melanie for a long time. More than a year, at least. They haven't been checking in with each other for a long time.

Sometimes she'd say everything was fine, but he knew there was something she was not saying. Like when they'd go for ice cream and he'd pick the closer shop, because it was the most convenient, and when they got there she'd "mention" that the other place that was farther had Whiskey Brickle, but when he asked if she wanted to get back in the car and go there, she'd say no and look away.

But then when, a few months ago, she said she wanted space, suddenly it seemed like their relationship was the Whiskey Brickle and he was supposed to know she wanted *that* without her really asking for it.

Chris was not good with words or metaphors and this was why he was hoping he could just show up in costume as one of Melanie's favorite male characters and not have to explain that he was *trying.*

Because if nothing else, he knew how Melanie felt about costumes and he could meet her there. He could show up.

He didn't know how to fix everything, but he thought they could fix it. He thought they used to be Whiskey Brickle together and he missed that. He wanted it back.

He hoped Melanie missed it too, and if she didn't, then he hoped he could remind her. Like showing her what her favorite ice cream tasted like again. With a grand gesture. Because trying to be subtle and slow clearly hadn't been working.

But when he walked into that hotel and saw Melanie's face, hoped drained out of him.

She was dressed as a villain—he didn't know what version she was but he recognized the girl clown—and she looked hot. And happy.

Until, that is, she saw him.

She was with a bunch of other people and Chris wanted to turn around and make a run for it. He paused. Everything was super-heated in this suit. As expensive as it was, it was still mostly plastic. He wanted to take the cowl off because he couldn't breathe but he took a slow sip of A/C to calm down.

Remember why you're here. No one ever said it would be easy.

Except, OK, so he *did* think it would be easy. That was why he paid the $400 for the costume, plus the practically last-minute flight and hotel and cab fare which totaled up put him over $1000 for this grand gesture. And that was nothing if it worked, but it was an expensive mistake if it failed within the first five minutes.

But thinking about that was not helping him calm down.

Melanie was staring at him, giving him no clues about how she felt. Chris forced himself to move forward. He tried to walk like his character would. A superhero who operated mostly in the shadows wouldn't be caught dead in broad daylight in a fancy hotel lobby wearing his costume, but if it somehow happened, he definitely would march instead of stumble toward the woman he loved. He would keep his head up. He would...

Chris was interrupted by one of the guys with Melanie complimenting his costume.

"Thanks," he managed. At least not everyone thought he looked stupid. Maybe the costume was worth it.

He glanced at Melanie, who still hadn't greeted him or smiled or acknowledged that they *live together* or have dated for more than four years. Or even that she knew him.

"Hey Melanie," he said.

"Hey," she said. "Everybody, this is Chris."

The guy who liked Chris's costume held out his hand. "Hi, I'm Matt."

One of the women did that thing where she turned her shoulder to him and might as well be turning her back to him. She stepped a little closer to Melanie, protectively, like he was here to attack her or something.

He was not *the bad guy*. He wondered what Melanie had told them about him. He started to feel a little resentful and tried to remember his goal. He was trying to convince Melanie to give them another chance.

"Joining us for drinks?" Matt asked. Chris nodded and fell into step with the other man to give himself a reprieve, because Matt seemed cool and since he was a guy he was probably not trying to figure out Chris's story or guess what Chris's ulterior motive was or whatever. Walking with him gave him a breather to refocus.

His motives were *pure*. It wasn't like he was here because he *liked* wearing a silly costume and making strained small talk with strangers.

The conversation in the bar revolved around something called a Mary Sue and the male gaze. Even Matt and two others, Roger and David, joined in debating the feminism or lack thereof in recent comics that Chris has never heard of.

He was trying really hard to hold his tongue, which meant that he was being weirdly silent. He could tell Mel was uncomfortable with his presence, which meant his plan was going off the rails, but he wasn't sure how to save it.

In his vision of how this would go, she was *happy* to see him here. Happy that he made an effort.

He hoped he hadn't made a huge misstep. Again.

"Well, what about the characters you dress as," Matt said finally, turning to Melanie. "When you dress as a sexy character, is it because she's an empowered character or are you just perpetuating the male gaze?"

Chris looked at Melanie, because if he asked her something like that she'd probably pitch a fit. Instead, she smiled at Matt.

"Well, start with the fact that there are so few key female characters in the canon," she said. Of course Melanie had a lot to say about this. "You know, ones who are not just 'the girlfriend' or 'the victim.' I at least choose the ones I dress as according to whether they have agency."

"But is it agency to have to wear skin-tight leather?" Laura added. She'd had at least three gin and tonics that Chris had seen. She raised her hands. "Just to play devil's advocate."

"The other problem, from a pragmatic perspective, is that gender-bending costumes are so much harder to do. I am not sure I have the skill." Melanie's voice dropped, like it did when she was self-conscious. Chris wished he were in a position to talk her back up, but he was afraid it would be patronizing.

One of the other women, whose name Chris has forgotten, jumped in: "That should be the next topic for our panel!"

"I would *love* to be, like, a girl god. With a hammer." Melanie grinned.

"You would look great," Chris mumbled. Matt said it at the same time. Melanie glanced at them, sitting next to each other, and then away. It was awkward. Matt leaned away from Chris slightly.

Chris looked a little closer and realized this guy Matt might be the same guy he'd seen getting way too close to Melanie on her Instagram. It was hard to tell under the outfit but he was pretty sure. *Terrific.*

"I would put real money behind this proposition," said Roger, who was holding a flowered umbrella. Chris knew that outfit. He and Melanie had watched the one perfect season of that show at least three times since they met.

Chris wondered if Melanie's had sex with anyone since they broke up. Like this guy sitting next to him, for instance. This was something he should have considered before getting on a plane.

What was he thinking coming here? This was a disaster. She clearly didn't have the doubts about breaking up with him that he'd sensed. He'd thought that look in her eyes in the kitchen the other week was saying, *Chris, try harder to win me back.* But he'd been wrong a lot lately.

He needed to come up with an exit strategy. But everyone was acting like they were settled in.

"How about a bar crawl?" he blurted out. "You know, check out a new scene?"

There was a dramatic pause in conversation as everyone looked at each other, checking for consensus either for or against the new guy's idea.

"That sounds great. New bar!" Laura said. *Thank god.* The drunk girl came through for him.

There was a lot of bustling and gathering in order to get everyone together to leave. With this many costumes and swag totes involved, it was clearly a process. Chris really didn't get the appeal of this kind of thing; it seemed so commercial, everyone out to own or look like the latest popular theme.

When he first went to cons with Melanie, he loved the childlike, nerdy gleam she got in her eyes when she held plastic toys or glossy books. But eventually it was overwhelmed, for him, by the massive crowds of greedy eyes and hands reaching into wallets.

Even Mel fit right into that crowd sometimes.

They waited to cross the street at a light in a claustrophobic crowd of other people in costumes. Laura was waving her hands in overly broad gestures to get her point across about some hero's relationship to Peter Pan syndrome or something. Chris stepped to the side because he didn't have great peripheral vision in this cowl and he couldn't see whether her waving hands were coming at his face.

A little kid wearing a superhero shirt was in a car waiting at the light and pointing at a guy on the corner with them who was wearing an incredibly life-like costume of the same hero.

Some woman next to him who could be dressed as generic movie girlfriend or could just have long, blonde hair was FaceTiming or talking to her screen while holding it at an angle above her head. Chris only used his Instagram to follow Melanie, so he had no idea what the latest trends were.

This was surreal.

The little kid was suddenly out of his car and in the turning lane without an adult and a car was flying toward them while hitting the brakes. Chris's feet in their enormous plastic shoes were moving through quicksand as he stepped into the street and grabbed the kid, stepping back on the curb before the car came to a screeching stop right before they would have collided.

"Omigod," someone said into the sudden silence.

The parents left their car, doors open and blocking traffic, as they came running toward Chris, who awkwardly bent at the waist because he couldn't kneel in his costume. Then he had to endure the literal pain in his neck as he looked into the kid's face. "You OK?" he asked the little boy, who looked maybe 8. His eyes were huge and dark, reality catching up with whatever compelled him out of that car.

The kid put both his hands on top of his own head and reverently whispered the name of his costume.

"That's right," Chris said, and grinned because the kid seemed fine. He should probably be a *little* scared so he didn't ever hop out of a vehicle by himself again, but at least he wasn't crying. "You should never jump out of a moving car again, OK?"

The kid nodded solemnly.

His parents scooped him up and started examining him head to toe for marks. Cars were honking and people were gawking. It was becoming a scene.

"Thank you so much," the woman said to Chris, then repeated it twice, her eyes as huge and dark as her son's. "I can't believe that happened. The child locks should have been on."

He shrugged. "It's OK. Everything's fine. He's OK right?"

"He's OK. He's OK," the man repeated over and over, holding the kid up high by his elbows as though he wanted to turn him upside down to see if something important fell off.

The driver of the other car was standing there, looking like he was going to throw up. "He's OK?" he repeated.

"He's OK," Chris said.

"The police are here," someone said, and then they were, directing the crowd and asking for statements. The crowd scattered, like they were at a rave that got raided.

Chris's dad was a cop so he knew how long this process was going to take. He started shifting his weight from foot to foot, his feet already aching from the lack of arch support. The rest of Melanie's group had already drifted away. He looked for Melanie, as the officer in front of him pulled out his notebook. She was talking to her friend Anna, standing on the sidewalk and turning her phone over and over in her hands. She didn't look up.

At least half an hour later, Melanie brought him a plastic water bottle while he was sitting on the curb waiting to be dismissed. It was nice of her and knowing she thought about him gave Chris a second wind even though she handed it to him and didn't stick around.

Eventually, the cops released him and he thought about texting Melanie to see where she ended up, but he was so exhausted that he decided to go back to his hotel. He messaged to let her know.

His hotel was far from the convention center because everything else was sold out, and not only did it take forever to get there, but he had to endure his driver talking about how weird it was to see a man in a costume when he drove up to get him.

"You should change your picture on the app, you going to go around dressed like that," the driver kept saying.

It was a relief to take off the costume and shower off the weird, sticky black residue before he finally fell into bed.

Melanie texted him back a link to Instagram that he opened while lying on his stomach, barely lifting his head off the pillow.

It was a video of him grabbing the kid out of the street. It already had 75K views. The caption read: "Costumed hero saves child at Atlanta Dragon Con."

> Melanie: (9:51 p.m.) Instagram famous (yellow neutral face emoji)

He groaned because he didn't have the energy to try to decipher how she felt or figure out whether this helped his game plan or not. He texted back a shrug.

He fell asleep within minutes but woke up several times that night and checked to see whether Melanie had texted again. He couldn't resist clicking on the Instagram video every time he saw she hadn't. The views and likes kept ticking up all night.

> Jenny: (11:45 p.m.) OK so I downloaded Hinge. I'm already talking to somebody! I have good feelings about this one

> Unknown number: (7:15 a.m.) Hi, this is Liz Nubert from Fox 5 Atlanta. We'd love to have you on to talk about the Instagram video Costumed Hero Saves Kid at Atlanta Comic Con. Please text or give me a call at your convenience!

Jenny: (7:20 a.m.) I know you're not working today but plz plz check Slack, Jack is being an idiot as usual

Jenny: (7:21 a.m.) I'm sorry ignore me, don't work! Be free!

Unknown number: (8:14 a.m.) Hi, this is Melanie's friend Emily! Please wear your costume again today so we can highlight your heroism on Instagram! It would be great for the convention + a great draw if you come to my panel at 2pm (Mel will be there). Please come??

He HAD to hand it to Melanie's friend Emily—she knew how to provide an incentive.

He texted her back: "Ok" and he bet it set off a flurry of other texts between Emily and Melanie and Melanie's other friends.

He was proved right when he returned from the bathroom to a text from Melanie.

Melanie: (8:31 a.m.) Are you really going to dress up and come to Emily's panel today?

He typed and erased several texts before he responded.

Chris: (8:42 a.m.) I will if you want me to.

Period? No period. He backspaced that and hit send.

She didn't respond immediately, so he decided to shave. His hotel was lightyears away from the convention center and he had to get moving if he was even going to make it there in time for this panel.

When he came back to his phone, he had a new text.

> Melanie: (8:50 a.m.) Emily really wants you there
> and it's a nice thing to do.

WITH a period?!?!

He sat down on the edge of the bed wearing his towel around his waist and contemplated this. She clearly didn't want to owe him anything, that much was obvious. But he was not hearing her deny that she wanted him to come. OK, fine, he'd be the direct one.

> Chris: (8:56 a.m.) So you want me to come?

He rolled his eyes as he stared at his phone's small screen. He hated this kind of thing. He didn't know why Melanie couldn't pick up the phone and tell him what she wanted. But he had to be patient. He had to work on his listening skills. He had to let the grand gesture work its theoretical magic.

He waited, trying to decide if putting on his costume before eating was better or if he would be able to get a coffee cup under the nose of that cowl. No way he was going to sit downstairs at the continental breakfast wearing that suit, miles from the convention area where at least, in context, he might look half-way sane. But considering how long it took him to put the costume on the first time, he wasn't sure he could risk going down to breakfast first. Maybe grab food on the way out to the Uber? This was complicated.

> Melanie: (9:27 a.m.) Yes. Don't be late.

It was chilly but definitive, so he'd take it. Chris whistled to himself as he went to reverse-engineer putting on his outfit.

~

> Anna: (7:31 a.m.) Are you still going to the Women
> of Dark Horse panel this morning?

Melanie: (7:31 a.m.) I can't, now I have to meet Chris and babysit

Anna: (7:21 a.m.) What!

Anna: (7:22 a.m.) Why?

Melanie: (7:22 a.m.) Emily wants him at her panel. I have to make sure he makes it

Melanie: (7:23 a.m.) He's all con famous now

Anna: (7:23 a.m.) That doesn't make him not a dick. Famous people are famously dicks

Melanie: (7:24 a.m.) I know

Anna: (7:24 a.m.) What about your schedule? I saw your spreadsheet last night

Melanie: (7:25 a.m.) Gonna be a bust I think.

Anna: (7:26 a.m.) I think you should let him fend for himself

Melanie: (7:27 a.m.) I would but I don't want to disappoint Emily (sobbing emoji) Her panel is at 2pm if you want to come or can get away from your table

Anna: (7:28 a.m.) I'll try

Anna: (7:29 a.m.) I have to go sign some books but I'm really sorry this sucks

Melanie: (7:30 a.m.) Thanks. Kick some ass!

Melanie: (7:31 a.m.) But not children ass

Melanie: (7:31 a.m.) You know what I mean

Anna: (7:39 a.m.) (3 laughing emoji)

"So that's the boyfriend?"

They were at the coffee shop on the ground floor of the hotel. It was a chain, so it was not good coffee, but Melanie stayed up too late last night and she was thankful for it.

She looked at Matt over the rim of her paper cup for a moment as she continued taking a long sip. She spent her evening drinking too many Moscow Mules after she saw Chris's rescue going viral on Instagram, then crying too much, quietly in bed beside the sleeping Anna, when she got back to the hotel room. But she didn't want to cancel on Matt, so she'd gotten up early this morning, pulled on the simplest costume she brought with her this trip, and they left the others sleeping in their room while they slipped downstairs.

"How'd you know?" she asked finally.

"You guys interact like people who have known each other a long time. Like you don't have to check where the other person is, you just know at all times." He sat back in his chair and crossed his legs. She thought the pose might be a tad defensive, like he didn't want to show his vulnerability.

"Yeah, that's the boyfriend," she confirmed. "Well, ex."

"It seems like he doesn't want to be your ex."

Melanie took another long drink of coffee. "I guess he's watched too many movies." With her. He'd watched those movies—where the man chases the girl to the airport or stages some kind of relationship intervention in the last few minutes that actually works—with her. This was her fault. Chris was trying to follow a script he apparently thought Melanie was crafting. Was she? She didn't know. When he walked into the hotel lobby last night—something happened to her insides, but it didn't seem like what she was *supposed* to feel.

She looked away from Matt so she could rein in the tears that wanted to erupt again. From one perspective, yes, it was sweet of Chris. But from the other—the reality—it was too late for a clearly reluctant grand gesture to save them from the consequences of the last year of their lives.

"In the movies, it would *definitely* work," Matt noted. He was right.

It was loud in the coffee shop. There were people in costume waiting in a ridiculously long line stretching back into the main hotel lobby. Most of them were looking at their phones, plastic swords or hammers or bows and arrows balanced carelessly on a shoulder or under an arm. She wondered how many of them were watching the video of Chris. It was at half a million views last time she checked.

"It's not going to work in real life," Melanie said, still watching the line.

"You don't sound very happy about that."

"No." Melanie couldn't look at him. She was terrified she was going to burst into tears. She wasn't sure if she was more upset that Chris did this or that it wouldn't—*couldn't*—work. "But it is what it is."

"Yeah. I get that." Matt sat forward and hunched over his coffee cup on the table. She knew, somehow, what he was about to say before he said it. "Look...I don't want to get in the way. You guys clearly have some stuff to figure out."

Melanie nodded. She was disappointed that he wasn't going to fight for her, but she didn't know what she really expected. Love triangles were the plot from yet another movie. They still barely knew each other. They'd kissed once.

Matt hadn't seen her when she had bacne or was burning something in the kitchen. He didn't know that she spent hours trying on her entire wardrobe every spring and creating a spreadsheet for her outfits. Chris knew all of those things about her and still cared about her. Enough to show up in Atlanta.

She couldn't quite name her emotions. She knew that what she'd been missing most in her relationship was feeling *wanted*. But Chris's one gesture—showing up here—didn't quite make up for how long she'd lacked that.

Still, it was too soon to go looking for that from someone else. Her favorite heroines would never. More importantly, that wasn't the kind of person *Melanie* wanted to be.

"Yeah," she told Matt. "We do. I'm sorry."

"Don't be sorry." He smiled, with only a tinge of regret. Then his smile widened a little. "We'll always have San Diego. And there will always be another convention."

She smiled and nodded. Thank goodness that was true, because this one was clearly a bust. She'd been really enjoying Dragon Con until last night.

She waited for Chris after Matt left, camping out at the little table despite her fellow geeks loitering around giving her seat envious glances.

He texted her several times from the line to get a badge to get into convention events. It took him 40 minutes. She saw him when he was talking to the security staff who checked him for sharp weapons.

His costume really was quite life-like. It was mostly true-black in color and the material of the cape was clearly high-quality. And it emphasized his height and size. Wearing it, he looked like he really could be a hero. Or a leading man.

It was easy to see a hero when you looked tall, handsome, athletic. *Are his shoulders actually a little bigger?* It was harder to remember reality. Chris had let her down repeatedly. She couldn't let go of that, even for one day, because she knew she'd wake up tomorrow disappointed. Again.

She hurried up to him because they were cutting it close to meet up with Emily. He saw her and strode toward her. His legs were so long that she misjudged where they'd meet and almost ran into him. She could smell his aftershave, even through the plastic outfit. Out of habit, she almost raised her chin to kiss him hello, but caught herself at the last minute.

Melanie had to pause and look out the glass front of the hotel for a moment to collect herself, shocked that she almost fell right back into thinking they were OK. Chris rocked forward on his heels slightly toward her, then caught himself as well, so at least she wasn't the only one.

"I like the outfit," he said, without really looking at it. Melanie could only think about how irritated she was that she was wearing one of her old costumes instead of something new, too unsettled this morning to focus on putting together a whole new look.

She was caught in between two realities, the one where she had a boyfriend who she kissed hello and who did favors for her friends and the one where she had an ex who was interfering in her plans. She hated that she had to find a way to mix and match parts of those realities in order to make this day work.

Plus, now she had to look around and see her friends hero-worship her ex-boyfriend and actively resist doing so herself.

It wasn't fair. And she blamed him.

Unknown number: (11:42 a.m.) Hi Chris, this is Alex from Fox 5. We'd love to talk to you about the Instagram video of you that's going viral. Would you give me a call back?

Unknown number: (11:55 a.m.) Hi Chris, this is Denise from WGCL. We think Atlanta viewers would love to hear a little more about your costume and heroic save yesterday. I'll call you again in an hour. Please let me know if you're interested!

CHRIS CONVINCED Melanie to meet him in the lobby after he waited in an insanely long line to get a ticket, then had to sort out the shuttle system in order to get from one hotel to another. She brought him a coffee and she was wearing her favorite outfit.

Melanie, obviously, looked hot in all her costumes but Chris was still trying really hard not to act like he was objectifying her. So he thanked her for the coffee and kept his eyes on her face.

He tried hard to not think about all the guys whose eyes were not staying on her face.

"I like the outfit," he offered, because he was trying to vocalize his thoughts more often, like his therapist suggested. "Didn't our two characters get together in the animated series?"

Melanie looked at him, half like she was surprised he knew that and half like he'd said the stupidest thing she'd heard all day.

"Emily's panel is in a couple hours but she really wants to do an Instagram Story with you before," she said, instead of responding. "Did you want to walk around first or should we go find her?"

Chris held out his hands, palms up. "I'm open to whatever. Lead the way."

Melanie nodded once and turned on her heel, expecting him to follow her.

Crowds of disorganized people made Chris claustrophobic. Even waiting in that long line for his badge was better than the chaos downstairs, as Melanie led him down an escalator to a huge ballroom filled with booths. There were thousands of people moving in all different directions, weaving between other people and in and out of aisles between poorly defined booths. He recognized a few costumes that were cool, outside of the obvious ones, including one woman who made him wonder how she rigged that demon baby to look like it was coming out of her vagina. Chris almost ran into someone while he was gawking.

But other people, mostly people not in costume, kept stopping him and Melanie, asking for a photo with or of the two of them together. The dudes kept asking the same dumb question and laughing at their own joke, too: "Where's the third hero?"

"He has a day job," he told one of them, which triggered good-natured laughter. Chris was putting a lot of work into having a good attitude about all this, since, after all, he flew to Atlanta to do exactly what he was doing.

But Melanie seemed to love the attention. She gave everyone a big, cheesy smile for their photos—fortunately, his caped character wasn't known for smiling, so Chris didn't have to—and did a three-quarter turn toward the cameras, one hand propped on her hip. Chris stood by her not knowing what to do with his hands.

"How do you do this all day?" he mumbled to her once they were free of the latest batch of admirers.

She shrugged, leading him through the maze. Chris was totally turned around and had no idea what direction they were going. "It's fun. And I take breaks, for panels and food and talking to friends."

It all seemed so superficial to Chris, but he knew better than to say anything like *that*.

They found Emily finally, standing in front of a booth somewhere in the back. She was wearing a costume but he had no idea who she was supposed to be. She was "thrilled" he was there, she said, as she introduced herself before Melanie had a chance. She came out from behind the table she was sitting at holding an enormous phone with a sparkly case.

"Omigod, you guys," she said, speaking to her screen. "Guess who's here. The hero who saved a child's *life* yesterday. You've seen the video, now meet the man behind the mask. Chris, what do you have to say for yourself?" She held the camera in front of both of them.

He waved shortly at the phone. "I don't know if I saved anybody's life. The car probably would have stopped before it hit him."

"*Probably!*" Emily shouted. "I don't think any mother would be happy with probably. You're so modest. Not very heroic of you, really."

"I'm not really very heroic," he responded.

"No? Then why are you wearing that costume?"

Chris grimaced. He glanced at Melanie, who was standing out of the way of Emily's shot and biting one of her cuticles. "To impress my girlfriend, I guess."

Emily laughed. Melanie looked up but at least she didn't look mad.

"What costume would you wear if you were choosing for yourself? What flavor of hero are *you*?" Emily asked.

Chris shrugged. "I've always thought the uniforms people wear to fit in—military, cops, firemen—were more interesting than the ones people wear to stand out."

Emily paused and looked at him, eyebrows raised. "Huh. Well there you have it, folks," she told her camera. "A very modest hero who looks up to real life heroes. So far this has been a very eventful weekend!"

She lowered her phone and turned to Chris. "Thank you so much for doing that!"

Not like he had a choice, but OK. "Sure," he said. "Any friend of Melanie's is a friend of mine."

Emily smiled, distracted by her phone. "Do you have an Instagram handle you want me to tag?"

"Um…" Chris shrugged, because he had one but he barely used it. He was more of a reddit person when it came to social media.

"I have it. I'll DM you," Melanie told Emily.

One of the other women behind the table in the booth, not wearing a costume, leaned over it and smiled at Chris. She was at the bar last night and he was struggling to remember her name. Hers was one of those smiles that women got when they were thinking about something else. "I'm surprised we haven't met before. You and Melanie have been dating a long time and she *loves* coming to conventions."

Melanie intervened, speaking over the other woman. "I guess we'll see you later at your panel, then!" she told Emily.

"Are you guys going to…hang out?" the other woman asked.

"I think Chris is a little overwhelmed by the convention so we're probably going back upstairs. Maybe we'll get lunch."

Chris was stoked to hear this plan because he *was* a little overwhelmed by the convention. It was also pretty great that Melanie noticed.

But, he realized, he was pulling her away from something that—like her overprotective friend said—she *loved*. He could feel the judgment of Melanie's friends without looking at them.

"You can stay if you want to," he told her. "Or, I mean, I can stay too. If you want to stay here."

She rolled her eyes. "You clearly hate it. Let's just go find some food. Now that you have your badge we can go in and out of the hotels more easily."

He followed her and started going over in his head the conversation he wanted to have.

~

From @emily_is_at_a_con:
Atlanta, Georgia
(video of Emily interviewing Chris)
The Costumed Hero aka @gamerchris_1989 speaks out after saving a child last night #DragonCon
Viewed by 1,001
Liked by @miz_anna_doll and 898 other people
@davenguyen1: That rescue video was sick
@ruthannleightman: I was there! It happened so fast, he literally scooped up that kid at the last second and acted so chill when the parents were freaking out. It was amazing
@kutabeary: He seems like an asshole
Reply from @dontcallmejolly to @kutabeary: He's being modest, why is that so bad?
Reply from @jezabellegreen to @emilyinarush @gamerchris_1989 you might consider that the interactions some of us have with those "real life heroes" aren't exactly heroic, more like horrific
Reply from @manlybubbles0190 to @jezabellegreen @emilyinarush @gamerchris_1989 You're not wrong. Still applaud the spirit of the comment
@aries_heart56: How did that kid even get into traffic? Where were the parents??
@mary_l589: Agree with @kutabeary
@mariewallaceauthor: Is he single?

@benedictfan398: this is cool - more interviews plz
@lau_spencer: I'd do him

THE PLACE in the hotel lobby that they went for lunch reminded Chris of his early dating days with Melanie, when she would say outlandish things about his beer—"it tastes like a brass doorknob!"—and share his fries and two hours would pass over a meal while they talked.

He couldn't remember the last time they went out like this together. But this was different from the early days in their relationship. Melanie even got her own fries. It was like a neon sign flashing: *She doesn't need anything from me anymore.*

She tucked a napkin into her boobs, which was disturbingly cute while also making him think of what it would be like if Melanie got grease on her cleavage and needed...help...cleaning it off again. He probably shouldn't stare. He yanked his eyes back up to her face before Melanie looked up again.

He didn't know how to launch this conversation, but he thought they'd been dancing around this stuff for too long already, so he went for it.

"So you know how you love Whiskey Brickle ice cream."

Melanie stared at him. It was weird having this conversation with her while in costume, and not only because it was uncomfortable sitting down in these pants. They were in a bizarre superhero movie where it was their relationship problems that were the supervillain.

He cleared his throat. "But you never tell me when you *want* Whiskey Brickle."

She was definitely glaring at him now. "I do so."

He suddenly remembered his therapist telling him not to over-generalize. "OK maybe not never. But a lot of the time."

"If I want ice cream, I tell you I want ice cream. I shouldn't have to remind you every time what my favorite ice cream is. I don't think, oh hey, I want ice cream but let's get the second-best kind. I'm not a *monster*." Melanie stabbed at her ketchup with a fry, clearly not hearing him.

"And I am? Is that what you're saying?" Chris could hear his voice raising and he knew they were getting off track.

"If the costume fits," Melanie mumbled, looking away and crossing her arms so her breasts bulged over them. It was super distracting.

Chris looked around to see how many other people were watching. All the dudes in this restaurant were pretending they weren't looking.

OK, focus, Chris. He takes a deep breath.

"All I'm trying to say is...I feel like we haven't been telling each other directly what we want for a long time and I think we should try that before you give up on us. Just...try."

She uncrossed and then recrossed her arms, looking anywhere but at him. Finally, she met his gaze. "I think it's too late."

Chris swallowed. His throat was dry, so he picked up his soda and drank it for a long time, trying to drown his panic.

"It's not too late," he said when he put his drink down. "We haven't tried everything. We haven't tried at all. That's all I'm asking. After nearly five years, don't you think it's worth trying?"

She shifted in her seat and dropped her arms. She wouldn't look at him. "Even if we try, there's no guarantee it's not too late."

Better. Not an outright no.

"I know," he said. "But I don't want to just...let go without something. Some effort. We used to work together."

She nodded, chewing her lip. "I know." She looked sad as she added, "I thought we were broken up."

This suit was making it hard to breathe, pressing on his chest everywhere the fake muscles didn't match up with his real ones.

Chris took another sip to loosen up his throat. "It's OK if you've...been with someone or moved on somehow. I understand. I mean..."

She shook her head. "That's not what I meant. We aren't together. We decided that already. So it's none of your business whether I've been with someone else."

He nodded because he had to. But he wondered if she would feel that way if the situation were reversed. *Wait.* He was doing the same thing he'd been doing that got them into this situation in the first place: Not saying what he thought. "Doesn't mean I like it," he said.

She stared at him for a long moment before she said, "I haven't slept with anyone."

His shoulders relaxed a little. He couldn't help it. He was glad.

"But I have been trying to move on," she continued in a rush, her voice defensive. "And I don't know if I can go back."

"We're not going back, though," Chris said hurriedly. This was something else he'd talked to his therapist about. "We're moving forward. To something new. Better."

She pressed her lips together, like she didn't believe him but didn't want to say so.

"What?" he demanded.

"I just don't see what's changed."

Chris sighed, because for a grand gesture that he thought would speak for itself, he was doing an awful lot of explaining. "Well I'm here, aren't I? I'm *trying*."

"But you hate it. How long is that going to last?"

Chris frowned. He didn't know the answer. He knew he couldn't stand wearing this hot, stiff costume much longer, that was for sure. It had seemed worth it to make Melanie happy...but she didn't even seem that happy now.

"I don't hate trying," he said carefully. "I do hate the costume and I hate that this whole thing is so commercialized."

She was looking at him closely but she didn't look mad. "OK," she said. "I get that."

"And I mean," Chris continued, knowing he should stop while he was ahead but still not doing it. "The way you do it is cool because you make your own but these people who spend thousands of dollars on their costumes?"

"Did you ever think maybe this is some people's sole self-care outlet and it's worth it for them?"

Chris sighed and tried to think about this. It still seemed unreasonable to him. Self-care shouldn't have to mean wasting a ton of money, right? But, OK, for him self-care meant getting off the couch and going outside once in awhile and he could see how that might give him a skewed perspective.

"Or," Melanie continued, sitting forward a little which told him this was important to her. "Some of these people wear these costumes multiple times a year. Think about that in comparison to, like, spending thousands on a wedding dress, that you only wear once."

Chris nodded. "Yeah. I guess you have a point."

"You guess?" she said sharply, doing the verbal equivalent of poking him to see if he'd fight. *Stay calm.*

"You do," he said firmly. "Have a point."

"But you still hate it."

"But I think I can find *something* about it to enjoy. I mean..." he paused, because his mind was blank. "I enjoy being with you," he said weakly.

She rolled her eyes. "Well you still have to go to Emily's panel. You promised."

"I wasn't going to bail," he protested, frustrated that she never thought the best of him anymore. He wasn't supposed to think in "nevers" but he couldn't help it.

"And I'll think about the rest," she said, chewing on her cuticle. He knew it was a habit she had when she felt overwhelmed, so he decided not to press. *Slow progress. Tiny steps forward.*

"OK," he said. "I'll take that."

~

Melanie to Costumes Are Squee! group chat: (1:34 p.m.) Can't believe my ex is here pretending to be something he's not

Roger: (1:36 p.m.) Hate to point this out, but none of us cosplayers are really here to be ourselves

Melanie: (1:37 p.m.) You know what I mean though.

Tim: (1:38 p.m.) Trust your gut

Anna: (1:39 p.m.) Maybe he's not pretending, he's playing? I'm a Pisces, it's all about play for me

Melanie: (1:42 p.m.) But playing at what?

Roger: (1:43 p.m.) Maybe he's just trying to figure that out, like all of us

Tim: (1:43 p.m.) I mean I just hope whatever he's playing at, it doesn't stay on this pro-cop propaganda track

Matt: (1:45 p.m.) Not defending the guy exactly but let's support Melanie here

Tim: (1:46 p.m.) Melanie hasn't made up her mind yet

Melanie: (1:47 p.m.) That's true

Melanie: (1:48 p.m.) Except I did break up with him

Roger: (1:49 p.m.) Over pro-cop propaganda?

Melanie: (1:49 p.m.) No! His dad's a cop, it's not like that

Tim: (1:50 p.m.) If I had a scar for every "it's not like that"…oh wait.

Anna: (1:51 p.m.) OK Melanie's not the bad guy here

Matt: (1:52 p.m.) Nobody's the "bad guy," take it down a notch guys

CHRIS CERTAINLY WASN'T GOING to make the long Uber trip back to his hotel located in the butt-crack of Atlanta, so he followed Melanie around for the rest of the day. They took a shuttle from the Atlanta Marriott Marquis to the Crowne Plaza Hotel to the W to some other hotel. He was thankful that they were almost constantly in air conditioning, because every time he stepped foot outside, the Atlanta heat seemed to melt the plastic in his costume.

He sat in the back and watched her speak with so much energy at Emily's panel. She was really excited about being there and teaching people how to make low-cost costumes. He was happy for her but in a distant way, like he was getting farther and farther away.

"I can be more myself when I'm dressed up as someone else," Melanie was saying. "Like the way some people feel more free to be distinctive when they're wearing a uniform."

His grand plan to show her he was a great boyfriend was not going so well. He knew so little about sewing and crafting and stuff like that, he couldn't even come up with a good question to get up and ask.

And then Emily called him out and invited him on stage. "One more thing, as a surprise for everyone. Our local convention hero is here, ladies and gentlemen. You know him from Instagram—the hero who saved the child!"

Reluctantly walking through what felt like gelatin to get on stage, he looked at Melanie, wishing for her to save him. Very superheroic.

"I was just in the right place at the right time," he mumbled.

Emily nudged the microphone toward him, as if everyone wanted to hear him stuttering. She raised her phone to record him again.

A hand raised in the crowd, from the second row on the end. It was a man with a boy who looked around 12 sitting beside him. He stood up and spoke loudly, without a microphone. "I was part of the emergency response yesterday. You might have been in the right place at the right time, but you still had to do the right thing."

Chris blinked, looking down into the crowd at the man, surprised by the support.

"He's right," Emily said into the microphone. "Could everyone hear that?" She waved at someone in a red volunteer shirt to pass the man a microphone, but they were all the way across the room.

"Come up here," Chris said into Emily's microphone, waving at the man. "You were there?" He had to keep waving for the man to approach, but he finally did. His kid trailed after him.

"I'm a first responder," the man replied. "EMT."

"Record *this*," Chris told Emily, and extended his hand to the man. "You're the real hero because you deliberately put yourself in places where people need help day after day."

"I, as a costumed hero, didn't do that," he told Emily's camera over his shoulder. Melanie had her phone out too. "Vigilantes only help when they feel like it."

He turned back to the front of the room and leaned into the microphone, hoping he was speaking into it the right way. "What is your name?" he asked the man.

"Derick Scott."

"Can you tell me a little more about what you did when you got on the scene yesterday?"

He did, and it was a little boring—no one was injured, so it was mostly paperwork—but Chris kept asking him questions and he could see from the expression on the face of Scott's son that it was having an impact. A superhero looked up to his dad; that meant something to him.

Finally this dumb costume was helping someone. He stood for *something*.

But he could tell the crowd, expecting a conversation about cosplay, was getting bored. He tried to wrap it up and tie it back to the theme Melanie was talking about. "And you wear a uniform to do your job. It's a little different from my outfit, but what about it do you think serves your work?"

Scott smiled, looking down at his kid, and leaned down to the microphone again. "People recognize what I do right away. My uniform is a symbol just like that costume is. In some ways, it hides my identity too, and puts the job first."

Chris shook hands with both Derick Scott and the younger Scott and turned away from the microphone, back to Emily. "Sorry I filibustered your panel."

"You were very entertaining," Emily said, lowering her phone. She went back to the front of the table and thanked everyone in the room for coming, ending the event.

Melanie stood up and walked toward him with a funny expression on her face. "You feeling OK?"

"I'm great, actually." He couldn't help the smile that bloomed across his face or the warmth in his chest. Was this what doing the right thing felt like? He needed water. His throat was dry from talking so much and so loudly for the rest of the room to hear.

She nodded, turning her phone over and over in her hands. "OK. OK. You just...kind of made a hero of that guy."

Chris wanted to ask if he'd messed up yet again, but decided to put it off, not wanting to ruin the moment. His costume *meant* something just now. It wasn't a dumb and useless gesture; it was a tool and he thought he'd used it well. His dad would be proud.

11

They flew home on the same day, but not the same flight. Chris thought it would be a little creepy if he hacked Melanie's email—even though he definitely could have—to get her flight information. And he thought there was a chance that, like last time, she wouldn't want him on her flight, even though this time they really were in Atlanta for the same purpose.

But they sat in the airport together waiting and watching each other's bags on bathroom breaks, which was nice and familiar from other trips they'd taken together at better times. Chris had more bags than normal, considering his costume needed its own. And it was *heavy*.

Less than an hour from Melanie's boarding time, Chris was in a cold sweat, trying to come up with a last-ditch way to salvage this trip. They were heading to the same destination, but he felt like once they got there, he'd be out of options for persuading her not to go through with this separation.

Oblivious to his freaking out, Melanie showed Chris her phone, holding it up so he could see the screen.

"Emily posted the video of you interviewing that paramedic. It's getting a ton of engagement and re-shares." Her voice was neutral, polite. Chris both hated that they had to stay impersonal in order to avoid fighting and appreciated that they were not currently fighting.

"Cool," he said, leaning in. He tried to keep a neutral distance between them. The costume did look neat on video if you didn't know how uncomfortable it was. "I guess she has the right audience for that. Because of the costume."

"It's actually a lot of people saying 'thank you for thanking a first responder' and that kind of thing."

"Really?" He took her phone and scrolled through the comments. There were a lot of them. "Do you think that's good?"

"Well, it seems like you struck a chord. I didn't really expect this," Melanie took her phone back, like she didn't really want him browsing it. Maybe all her text conversations were about him. "A lot of convention people are not super into authority figures, especially police. A lot of them have been hassled before, just for looking different or wearing costumes in the wrong place or whatever. And geeks tend to be pretty unconventional people."

"Except that they go to conventions, which you'd think would be pretty convention-al," he said, laughing at his own joke.

She shrugged. He couldn't tell if she didn't want to talk about this specifically or didn't want to engage with Chris generally.

"It's educational," Chris insisted, turning toward her in his uncomfortable seat. "Maybe this video shows some of the kids that go to comic con that they don't have to grow up to be a superhero to make a difference."

"I see your point," Melanie said, with a far-off look on her face, looking at the TVs above them showing flight times. He was not sure if he was allowed to ask her what she was thinking about.

Oh, what the hell.

"What are you thinking?" he asked.

She re-focused on him. "Oh, just...I don't know."

"No, what?" Chris leaned toward her, hopeful this could be a break-through.

"Well. That you should talk to some of my friends. You know, people who actually *like* cosplay. If you wanted to. Sort of balance this out." She gestured at the phone in his hands.

"You mean...because I have like a 'platform' now?" He made air quotes.

"Maybe. I mean, I don't know what it will look like. I know you admire your dad the cop and all, but if you really want to be educational, maybe you need to get some other perspectives." She shrugged and her shoulders drew together like she wanted to disappear. "I'm not saying you want a project. Just an idea."

And she got up to go to the bathroom.

It took Chris awhile—he didn't get it until he was halfway through his flight home, because he needed to be alone while he was thinking—but he realized Melanie's suggestion *could* be their breakthrough. It could be his path to understanding her, her friends, and why she loved cosplay.

And, he thought, by suggesting it, she also was telling him she *wanted* that.

Maybe he hadn't completely blown that grand gesture after all.

They rode home from the airport together in near silence. Chris was thinking hard about next steps and maybe Melanie was thinking about what happened next, too, because she stared out the window the whole way back.

Chris waited until they'd brought the luggage in before he told her, "I've been sleeping in our bed while you were gone. The couch got uncomfortable."

She glanced at him. "Hm," she said.

"It's just a little too short for me so my feet hang over the edge."

"Hm," she repeated, pouring herself a glass of water.

"I had this permanent twist in one ankle."

Finally, she turned to him. "We can share the bed tonight. But I'm not interested in anything more. I'm tired and feeling crampy."

He nodded. "Of course. Thank you."

She still looked at him like she didn't trust him. Maybe he

deserved that, but it was hard not to get angry in response. He took a few deep breaths in the bathroom and looked at himself in the mirror. He had this.

He thought about how he and Melanie were before all of this—they had amazing chemistry, they wanted a lot of the same things, and they had great sex—and he knew he had to convince her they were still on the same page.

Slow but steady. It was worth the trouble.

While he changed into clean boxer briefs in the bedroom, he thought he heard her crying in the bathroom and he worried about it. Did he make her cry? What had he done now?

He sat up in bed until she joined him, having stripped off her makeup so her skin looked uneven and rosy in patches. He could see that she was tired from the dark circles under her eyes and the way her shoulders slumped as she crawled into bed. He wanted to hold her.

He rolled toward her when she got into bed and turned her light off. She went rigid.

"What did I say?" she snapped.

"I just want you to know I'm here." He carefully put a hand on her arm and rubbed it.

She sighed and let him. He thought she closed her eyes but couldn't quite tell because of the dark. He kept gently rubbing her arm until it seemed like she'd relaxed again.

He thought about hearing her crying in the bathroom and how sometimes they could make up from fights with sex, the kind of sex where they re-established communication by trying new positions and laughing together.

He moved his hand down to her hip and she shot out of bed. "Seriously Chris?" she demanded. She grabbed her pillow and marched out of the bedroom without another word.

Chris laid in bed staring up at the ceiling for a long time, trying to decide if he should go out to the living room and—what? He got stuck every time trying to run through a conversation with Melanie in his head. She kept misunderstanding him and he thought it was because she was making an assumption about his intentions that he didn't know how to fix.

What he wanted to explain was that he didn't just love the dimple in her butt or the way she'd try any position in bed. He also loved that she broke up with him rather than accepting things as they were. Because she was being honest: they hadn't been *right* in awhile. And Chris had been ignoring the problem. He might have ignored it forever, unhappy but unable to confront what was wrong in himself and their relationship.

It wasn't that he was too lazy to find someone new. It wasn't that reaching this point in a relationship took a lot of work and he didn't want to do all that again. It was that he loved being at this point with Melanie. They were past the phase where they both pretended to be someone slightly better than themselves. Even now, when they weren't quite able to tolerate being in the same room with each other, he was still more comfortable with Melanie than he was with anyone else.

She slept on the couch and Chris kept waking up all night. He dreamed he was running through a maze of doors trying to find the right one and kept opening the wrong one by mistake, door after door after door.

~

Mom: (10:23 p.m.) Did you have a safe flight? Did you make up with Melanie? You lose your application + half your deposit if you cancel the lease on that apartment you know

Jenny: (11:02 p.m.) OK arranged to meet that guy and he bailed at the last minute AFTER I put on real clothes and makeup?!?! I'm deleting Hinge

Instagram @gamerchris_1989: 99+ notifications

DM from @gamerchris_1989 to @manlybubbles0190 @jezabelle-
green: Hi, I'm Melanie's bf/ex-bf. She pointed out your comments on
my video and I wondered if I could learn more
Reply from @manlybubbles0190: bf/ex-bf is the story of my life,
honey
Reply from @jezabellegreen: It'd be easier to talk in person. Coming
to the next con in NYC?
Reply from @gamerchris_1989: I'll be there

From @melly_89: I give up. I can't figure out how to make a realistic
leather uniform on a budget. Sorry #NYCC
From @mtinspace7: @melly_89 I feel ya, I've given up on mine too
From @miz_anna_doll: @melly_89 I think you should talk about this
on a panel. "Costume ideas that just don't work"
From @melly_89: @miz_anna_doll ask me again when I feel less
discouraged about it

Matt: (11:03 a.m.) How's everything at home?
Broken up with him (again?) yet? Asking for selfish
reasons, no pressure

Anna: (6:15 p.m.) Heyyyy haven't heard much from
you, everything going OK?

~

In: Drafts
From Greene, Melanie
To "Landlord Dan"

Subject: End of lease

Hi Dan, this is to give you 30 days notice we won't be renewing our lease at the end of November. Let us know what we need to do before move-out.

MELANIE HAD BEEN STARING at her drafted email for 15 minutes trying to figure out why she hadn't sent it yet. She didn't technically have to send it until the end of October, and she did tell Chris she would make the final decision at the end of convention season.

But considering they'd already broken up and were both looking for a new place—although, Chris said, apparently his new apartment fell through at the last minute—there was really no reason to wait. She needed to hit send and let the dominoes start falling.

Melanie was just having a hard time letting go.

It was inertia. Things had been easy enough at home and with Chris for the past few weeks since Atlanta. They hadn't had any huge blow-ups—at least since Chris started sleeping on the couch again—but that didn't mean they didn't still have all the same problems she confronted at the beginning of the summer.

Right?

Melanie re-saved the email draft without sending it and opened a new spreadsheet. She started one column for "Chris problems" and another column for "last time seen" and another for "how it makes me feel." Her complaints started with "tries to sleep with me" and ended with "makes me feel like he doesn't respect my wishes."

Melanie got a few rows filled in and then hesitated. Should she start a column for good things too? Like the fact that Chris was taking an interest in conventions now or actually taking out the trash?

Melanie sighed and Chris looked up from his computer, sitting on the couch across from her chair. She didn't look up to meet his gaze, because obviously she didn't want to talk about what she was working on. He looked back at his computer after a pause.

She typed a new sheet titled "good Chris things" and copied the last row she'd typed into it. Next to "tries to sleep with me," she wrote: "makes me feel wanted."

It was complicated. She didn't want to sleep with him, but she also did. She didn't want him to keep asking her for sex, but she wanted to know he wanted sex. It wasn't fair and it didn't make sense but that was how she felt.

Melanie closed the spreadsheet after that, because it was confusing her, and went back to the one where she tracked her costumes. She thought she was going to do another repeat costume in New York, because she'd tweaked her cape and makeup and it was much more realistic now.

Cosplay was so much simpler than her relationship.

CHRIS WASN'T good at planning. He could be an idea man or he could execute a plan someone else gave him. That was kind of his thing at work. Jenny literally called him The Executor. But connecting those two things, building a whole project from the ground up to completion? Never.

So he had no clue where to start and he did what he'd seen the people in UX at work do: Write down a lot of ideas in a messy storm of words. Except he decided to do it old school and got a whiteboard.

Melanie eyed the whiteboard in their living room with disdain the first time she saw it, coming home from work with the mail in one hand and her purse in the other.

"So you're...brainstorming," she said, like she was not quite sure the word applied.

He had written things like: Wear costume to fire stations? Hospitals? Parade?

"I'm *trying*," he reminded her.

"Don't do this for me. Do it if you want to but I'm not the one making you." She looked pretty serious when she said this.

He nodded. He got it—she thought if he only did it for her, he'd stop once he'd gotten her "back"—but of course she was part of why he was doing this. She was the inspiration. He did get excited when he thought about his project. He got excited because he *had* a project. It had been a while since he did something like this just because he wanted to and not for work. It'd been a while since he *wanted* to do a project outside of work. But would he do it without the motivation to please Melanie? Probably not. He still hated how it smelled inside that costume.

"I don't know what I'm doing though," he admitted. "I mean, I'm just trying to find my *thing* that's a piece of your world."

"There will be other people out there who are into what you're into, though," she said, and finally set her purse down, like she'd decided to stay. "That's how conventions started. Geeky people trying to find other geeky people. You don't have to force it."

"Am I geeky enough?"

She stared at him. "You're a gamer."

"Yeah but I don't play competitively or write reviews or sign up for all the indie bundles so I know the latest trends. That's why I thought, maybe..." He hand-waved at the whiteboard behind him. "If I just showed up in costume, I would fit in better. And people seemed to like the videos, so maybe more of them?"

She frowned. "You know I don't dress up in costume just to fit in, right?"

He hesitated. *"I never thought about it" seems like the wrong answer.*

"You really don't have to do this," she continued. "If you don't enjoy it, I don't want you to come to another con with me."

"No!" The last thing Chris wanted was to get shut out of Melanie's life again. But it was more than that. "It felt good. At that panel. It felt like I was making a difference, even just for one kid who looked up to me in that costume. I don't know what I'm doing yet, but I know there's something I can do that's good. Something I *want* to do, even if the costume was mostly for you in the first place."

Melanie's face softened, so his word-vomit must have made some kind of sense.

She was out late a lot over the next week and claimed to be at work. It was like a reversal of their usual schedules because Chris was now signing off at the end of his shift and refusing to check back in until the next morning.

But on weekends, instead of camping out in their room, Melanie started joining him in the living room to work on her computer or a costume. And then, slowly, as he spent time in the evenings tearing out his hair trying to figure out how to convince a local hospital he was a normal person who just wanted to dress in costume to delight the sick kids, she started sitting on the couch. And then she made him what she called a "content calendar" to better utilize Instagram for his project. It was a big step.

"Do I need more than one costume?" he asked her one night, thinking about how much he'd spent on one already.

She eyed him skeptically, clearly still not completely convinced he was into her hobby. "I wouldn't invest in another one until you're sure you like dressing up. Anyway, yours is a classic. He can become your signature look if you want."

"I'd rather be, like, a soldier of the Empire or something."

She almost dropped the button she was painting gold. "Seriously?"

Probably digging his own grave, he kept going. "They're the law enforcement officer of the galaxy."

"They work for the evil Empire."

"They're just trying to enforce the law as it exists. It's not their fault the policies are bad."

Melanie frowned. "You don't think they have some responsibility?"

He shrugged, uncertain whether this is one of those conversations where they were talking about more than what they were talking about out loud and he was accidentally taking a position he didn't mean. "Maybe there were some good things about the Empire, like some regulations that kept the water clean or space travel safe. It wasn't all evil."

"*Riiiight*," she said. But now she was smirking.

It was OK. They weren't fighting. He even thought he saw a slight smile on her face as she went back to her crafting.

He moved a Trello note into the "winning" column on his other whiteboard, the secret one he kept online called "Melanie ideas."

CHAPTER 12

New York City

It was not a love triangle if she'd broken up with one angle and stopped flirting with the other, right?

That was what Melanie kept telling herself as she sat between Matt and Chris at a panel for "Women in Refrigerators: Where Are We Now?"

The room, like most rooms in the convention center, was stuffy and lit by fluorescents. Melanie felt like hiding under the hood of her cape from the glare of the lights on the screen where they were showing clips of female trauma used as motivation for male protagonists.

It was an interesting presentation but she couldn't stop wondering what the men in the room—including the two sitting beside her—thought of it. Fortunately, one rather hairy man wearing a superheroine costume went up to the mic set up in a middle aisle and told the room exactly what he was thinking.

"Why do you think we don't see the reverse very often—a man killed to motivate a female lead—and would it be as offensive if we did?"

Melanie shifted in her seat, wanting to correct him. She leaned over to Chris. "It's an action movie trope," she said in an undertone.

Matt leaned over her, so that they were both whispering into Chris's space. "There just aren't as many action movies with leading women," he said, reiterating her point.

"Yeah, what about Angelina Jolie in *Salt* or Jodie Foster in *The Brave One*?" Chris said, keeping his voice low. "The male partners die in those and the women are out for revenge."

Matt and Melanie both looked at Chris, surprised he was on the same page as them.

"Good point," Matt said, quietly. He seemed surprised that Chris could keep up with their conversation, sparking a strange pride in Melanie's chest.

He leaned back into his own chair and Melanie could finally take a deep breath again without brushing up against him inappropriately. Then Chris leaned toward Matt. "Have you played *The Last of Us II*? Ellie's another good example."

Matt's eyes widened in excitement. "I just got it! You're right, that's a perfect one."

Chris had followed her around most of the day, pulling at the collar of his costume and blotting the part of his face that showed under the cowl. He seemed miserable, but he insisted he wanted to be here. He'd asked her to re-introduce him to Roger as well as Tim, who he'd only connected with on Instagram, so she'd texted them where they were.

"We must really like you to be here, Melanie," Tim said, settling heavily into the empty seat on Matt's other side. "I have nightmares about being fridged sometimes."

"I hope you don't think I would go on a murderous rampage to avenge you," Roger replied, sitting down beside Chris. Someone in the row in front of them turned around and hissed, "shhh!"

Roger made cat claws and hissed back at her. She turned back around to the stage.

"We heard you wanted some insight on the queer community," Tim said, leaning over Matt and Melanie to speak to Chris.

Chris opened his mouth, but before he said anything, Roger added, "Queer, here, meaning anyone who is not white, cishet normative and therefore does not meet the law enforcement definition of 'good citizen.'"

Chris closed his mouth again. "Ah," he said. Melanie waited to see how he responded. "Yes, I think I could use some insight into that."

Matt grinned, also leaning across Melanie. "Same."

Chris grinned back.

"This is my good deed for the day, but I'm not doing it for free," Tim continued. "Drinks on you at happy hour?" He challenged Chris with a bored face.

"Of course, happy to," said Chris. "You too," he added to Matt.

Matt reached across Melanie to bump fists with Chris.

On stage, the speaker was talking about the best examples of meta criticism for the fridging trope.

Melanie kept her eyes on the stage to deal with the discomfort of Chris and Matt carrying on a conversation across her body.

There should be a term for the men in your life liking each other more than they liked fighting over you. Bridging? She was the bridge for the friendly conversation her boyfriend—ex-boyfriend!—and her crush—ex-crush!—were having. Maybe they wouldn't be having it if she weren't here, but while they were, she felt completely irrelevant.

And she realized right that second that she didn't want to be irrelevant. She wanted attention and to be heard. But not by everyone, not by the public or this crowd; by a specific person.

Melanie sat back deeper under her cape, hiding the tingles she was having at her realization, and let the two men carry on having their conversation while she allowed her revelation to sink in.

~

Melanie's friends welcomed him into their circle like a clueless newb with money, which was totally fine. At least he was there at the bar with them, not watching it all on Instagram.

It'd been a long day. The Javits Center was massive and crammed with people who didn't move out of the way even when bumped into. All the cosplayers here, dressed as heroes who called New York City their hometown, seemed to have an *attitude*.

Anna had joined them, as well, and broke the ice by telling a story about the time she flirted with a voice actor who ultimately thought she was offering him work.

"I'm just bad at picking up men," she concluded.

"It's an art, it takes practice," Roger said.

"I wish it was possible to know what you needed to be good at ahead of when you needed to be good at it," Chris offered. He wasn't really talking about wooing, but he might as well have been.

"That's called avoiding vulnerability," Tim replied.

"It's the human condition," Roger added.

Chris grimaced and took a sip of his beer. It was not great. The only spot near the convention center that they could find with room for six was a pizza place with a small menu.

"Cut yourself some slack," Roger said, unexpectedly. "You're putting yourself out there. Those videos."

"Why would you make those, anyway?" Tim asked. Roger gave him a back-handed slap on the chest. "Ow. It's an honest question."

Chris took another drink of mostly tasteless beer. "I mean, someone put a camera in my face. And I just really believe there are real heroes out there," he said.

Roger and Tim both tilted their heads and said, "Aw."

He risked a look at Melanie. She was watching her friends' reactions, not him.

"Maybe you're just looking to the wrong people to be heroes," Tim said. "You know who needs a video made about them? The nonbinary person organizing inclusive bathrooms at the convention."

Chris nodded, because he had to acknowledge he hadn't even

noticed. "Another round on me?" he suggested, in lieu of apologizing for cishet men everywhere.

They took him up on it, which was enough for him, for now. He'd keep trying, and he'd get better.

He was crashing in Melanie's hotel room—which he'd thanked her for several times—and when they got back they were overly tired, hungry and bickering. Well, Melanie was bickering and Chris was "hmming" to keep the peace.

It was a small room with only one King size bed because everything else was booked. They hadn't done more than drop their luggage, get dressed and head to the convention when they got there that morning, so they hadn't talked about it. The sleeping arrangements. But Chris refused to do some kind of movie-guy thing like offering to sleep on the floor. Hotel floors were hard and inevitably nasty.

Melanie had been rubbing her eyes and her heavy mascara was flaking onto the white makeup around them. Her purple-grey lipstick was somehow still perfect, though, despite the long day.

She didn't bother to turn on a light when she walked in the door. She dropped her tote by the luggage stand and opened the window shades to the artificial light coming in off the street far below them. He dropped his cowl on the dresser. He couldn't wait to get out of this costume. He rubbed his face and his fingers came away covered in the black eye grease that he wore under his mask.

She put her hands on her hips and looked out the window at the New York skyline, continuing to make her point even though Chris had already agreed with her. "It's just kind of a privileged position to be pro-police."

"I get it and I am not disagreeing with you or Roger or Tim," Chris said, repeating himself. "I just don't think all police are bad. That's all I'm trying to say." His dad was retired now but Chris liked to think he'd been a good cop, not one of the bad ones.

"That's not all you're trying to say, though, is it," she said quietly, not turning around.

"Hmm?" Chris said again. He sat on the edge of the bed and started taking off his shoes.

"You're saying the heroes we love, that people like me dress up as, are stupid."

Chris sat back up, annoyed that she was putting words in his mouth. Again. "I am not saying anything's stupid!"

"You think real life is more important than imagination, than dreams and aspirations."

Chris glared at her back. This was so like Melanie, to assume the worst of him. "Stop putting words in my mouth."

"OK." She turned around, arms crossed. "So tell me what I'm not hearing right because that's what it sounds like."

Chris couldn't believe she was making him defend himself right now, at the end of a day when he'd done nothing but what she wanted. "Why are you trying to pick a fight with me?"

Melanie didn't change expression. "That's not an answer."

Chris sighed and pinched the bridge of his nose between two fingers. He was tired and he had to be careful not to overreact. "I don't know, OK, Melanie. I'm trying to figure out what I think. Is that so wrong to be an adult who doesn't always know his own mind?"

She jerked around and glared at him.

"If you don't know your own mind how the fuck can I believe you when you say you want to be with me?" she yelled at him, her whole body trembling. And then he got it.

"Oh," he said. He didn't realize that was what was really bothering her.

"'Oh,'" she mocked him. "You can't commit to anything! You don't know what you want! And here I've been just trailing along behind you for years..."

He jumped to his feet. "You have never just trailed along behind me." He got up close to her, but he didn't touch her. He'd thought she wanted to be touched before and that was a giant mess-up. But he couldn't let that kind of nonsense stand; if anybody was in the shadow in this relationship it was clearly *not* her. "You always know your own mind. Sometimes you just don't share it with me."

"And what about you?" she asked, a little more subdued. "What have you not been sharing all these years?"

It seemed like an honest question, not a poke at his defenses.

"That I'm...lost. Not always, but lately." He swallowed, looking down at her. This was much more vulnerable than those videos, and it was hard, but he'd wanted this conversation, so he pushed through. "That I'm not happy with what I'm doing and I don't know what would be better." Chris wasn't sure how to articulate the rest—the burn out, the therapist, the exhaustion that prevented him from doing anything about it and how now he was taking small steps he was still not entirely convinced would add up to big change. "But you're the only thing in my life that makes sense to me and is totally good in my life, Melly."

She paused, staring at his chest rather than meeting his eyes. But she was listening. That was something.

"Look...I take what you're saying seriously," he said, choosing his words slowly. "Just don't *yell* it at me. I'm trying to do something here that I think could be good. That could be *my* thing but that lets me hang out with you and your friends and be more present. And you criticizing me all the time—sorry, I shouldn't have said all the time, you've helped too—but you criticizing me makes me want to give up."

She flinched. Her eyes met his and in them he saw compassion. She uncrossed her arms and put her hands on his forearms. "I'm sorry, Chris. That's not what I meant to do. I guess I just...don't trust it. That this is something you really want to do and aren't doing just to be close to me."

Chris chose to ignore that, since it was obviously something he was doing to be close to Melanie. But not *just* for that. "You mean you don't trust *me*."

She hesitated and started to lower her hands. He grabbed them. "Just say it, Mel."

"No. I don't trust you." She wouldn't look at him as she said it.

And it wasn't that hearing her say this didn't affect Chris like a punch in the solar plexus, because it did. But he was also relieved to have it out in the open.

"That's something I'm trying to work on," he said. He looked down at her hands and rubbed his thumb over her knuckles. "But I need a little help figuring out what would earn your trust again."

She pulled her hands away from him, and he thought she was done. But then she put them on his face, on both sides of his jaw, and leaned into him so the clasp over her breasts dug into his chest.

"You can start by showing me you remember how to listen." She cut her eyes toward the bed. Chris could not have been more surprised if she'd told him she secretly hated cosplay.

"...In bed?" he blurted, like the old kids' game of adding "in bed" to Chinese food fortunes. He winced. It was the least sexy thing he could have done.

She laughed and dropped her arms. He could tell she was embarrassed by his less-than-amorous response and he wasn't going to let that last more than two seconds. He pulled her to him and kissed her. The texture of the makeup all over her face—and all over his—was kind of distracting, but he wasn't going to complain. He was finally kissing Melanie again and he'd missed this. It triggered a longing deep in his chest and the longer they kissed, the more the sensation built until he was about to explode with the need to get to more of her skin. He'd feared being too tired to want Melanie like this. But instead he was getting hungrier and hungrier for her.

"Can I start with your breasts?" he asked, whispering it into the skin around her ear.

She shivered. "I'd like that," she whispered back. He could feel her breath on the slightly sweat-damp hair around his temple. She shoved the detached purple cape back behind her shoulders so he could get at her top.

He fumbled with her costume a few moments before he gave up and let her shove down the top of her leotard. Melanie had great breasts. They were a little pointy and perfect in his hands. He palmed both of them.

He bowed his head and took one nipple in his mouth. He bit it lightly and she hissed. Then he licked and sucked it gently. He raised his head. "More?" he asked.

"Yes, please." She was watching his mouth on her boob. It was sexy.

He moved on to the other one. Melanie's sensitive breasts were like her game controller—if he got lost and forgot how to give her pleasure during sex, he could always come back to them and find his way again.

He ran the tips of his fingers down her side, over her hip, and along the line of the leotard over her sex.

"Can I take the rest of this off?" he asked after a few minutes, tugging at the leotard bunched around her belt.

"Only if you take off your pants."

He raised his eyebrows. "Just the pants?"

She smiled a little. "I might ask you to put the mask back on."

"Interesting." This was new. Melanie usually let him take the lead in bed. He liked her asking for what she wanted. He unbuckled her belt and let it drop on the floor, then unbuckled his own. "You are kinkier than I thought you were, Melanie."

She smiled wider, and he only then realized she'd been nervous to ask. "Glad I can still surprise you sometimes."

It took him too long to get his damn pants off, and it was a little silly just wearing the top half of his costume, but then he got the leotard off Melanie and she was standing there in her boots and purple cape. Like the Playboy version of a superhero.

"Who are you dressed as again?"

"She's a teenage superhero; best not to think about it too much right now."

"You don't look like any teenager. In a good way," he added quickly. He tossed her onto the bed so the cape spread out beneath her and he climbed on top. She gasped as they were suddenly in so much contact.

"Can I touch you here?" he asked quietly, his fingers sliding down her lower abdomen. She nodded, her head bobbing up and down repeatedly. He touched her between her legs and found she was already wet for him. Relief and arousal was a very weird mix. Melanie still wanted him.

She'd been letting her hair grow out down there, which he liked partly because it told him she hadn't been thinking about letting loose and having a lot of sex—not that he hadn't believed her when she said she hadn't been with anyone—and partly because it was new and different.

He slid farther down the bed, so that his feet were on the floor, and parted her folds with two fingers. She liked being held open like this when he rubbed her clit and anyway, this would keep the hair out of his mouth. "Tell me where," he said, and touched the tip of his tongue to her clit.

"Ohhh," she said. The muscles in her thighs seized up so hard she almost kicked him in the head. "Omigod. It's been too long."

"It really, really has," Chris agreed, before he put his lips back down where they were.

He made circles over her clit with his tongue and then started to move lower when Melanie grabbed his hair. "Be more consistent," she said. It sounded weird to him—what was this, a business meeting?—but he got that she meant "more" and he had told her he would listen. So he did. He kept drawing circles over her clit until his tongue felt like it was going to fall off but Melanie was moaning and thrashing around on the bed.

"Do you want to come like this?" he paused to ask. He pushed two fingers of his free hand inside her. She was so ready. His dick was so hard he kept brushing it against the bed for some relief, then remembering how gross hotel comforters were and trying not to. He would do whatever Melanie told him to do.

"Get inside me," she said, head thrown back, and he rushed to comply.

Wait. He hurriedly backed off her and off the bed.

"Where are you going?" she demanded, sitting halfway up.

He grabbed his cowl and pulled it back on. It was gross and sweaty in there, but he was going to make this good for her, damnit.

He turned back to her, looking through the narrow eye slits of the cowl. The whole room looked darker and she was all he could see. But Melanie was all he wanted to see. She stared at him, her pupils dark, and swallowed hard. "Um yeah," she said, and beckoned him back to her with one hand as the other went to her own nipple, squeezing it. She was incredibly hot like this, spread out with her boots braced on the bottom of the bed and pleasuring herself.

He stood over her, pulling her closer to the edge of the bed and nudging her legs even farther apart so he could stand between them. Then he leaned down and kissed her—turning his head far to the right so he could avoid hitting her in the forehead with his stiff plastic ears—and thrusting his tongue inside her mouth at the same time as his dick. He used one hand to brush her nipple with his fingers, gently tugging. She moaned.

"God you feel so good," he gasped, thrusting in and out. She was staring up at him, holding on with her hands on his shoulders where he couldn't really sense them through his suit. He was trying not to dig into her bare skin too hard with the plastic he was wearing, still standing so he could keep his upper half from bearing down on her with his full weight. Her pupils were so dark in her made-up face.

"I missed you," she blurted. "I missed us."

The words created a bubble of pleasure and he had to pause his motion for a moment so he didn't come too quickly.

"I missed us, too," he said, and reached down to touch her clit between them. She was so swollen, it wasn't going to take much.

"Shallow thrusts," she gasped, closing her eyes and sprawling back on the bed. She opened them again immediately, her gaze roaming his suit. He started rocking his hips more gently as he fingered her until she came, muscles clenching around him. He kept rolling her clit through it, and then let his rhythm pick back up again, thrusting inside her until he came too. Uncertain whether Melanie was still on birth control, he pulled out in time to make the kind of mess all over the bed he was afraid had happened many times on this same duvet.

They showered together, after. Chris, wiped out, leaned against the wall as Melanie helped clean off the black-grey makeup around his eyes.

"It's been a good day," he mumbled as they crawled into bed together and he wrapped his arms around her. They both slept hot; he'd have to let go at some point. But not yet.

"It has," she agreed, nuzzling into him.

And he slept the best he had in months.

CHAPTER 13

They were sharing a bed again. He remembered to take out the trash because he wrote himself a note and put it on his computer. He set a goal of making dinner together at least once a week and managed to stick with it. Melanie didn't give him that "what have you been doing all day?" look every time she got home from work. She even seemed happy. He hoped she wasn't hiding her unhappiness again.

He thought he would know if she were unhappy when he had her naked and upside-down in bed. It was the rest of the time when he was uncertain.

The week before they went to Baltimore, they ordered ramen and binge watched the TV show Melanie's planned costume was from.

"Will people even recognize her anymore?" he asked, mostly because he wanted to watch Melanie get excited about her costume plans.

"She is iconic." She sat forward on the couch and held up the DVD cover. "Plus the new spin-off just came out! People will get it."

He was watching her out of the corner of his eye. "The redhead is better."

Melanie huffed and he grinned.

"Clearly the superior choice if one was going to *date* one of them, I agree, but not for cosplay. I don't want to be covered in furs the whole time."

He laughed. "True. I wouldn't mind if one of your costumes was just you covered in furs for once, though." Then he winced internally because he didn't mean to say that.

"What?" Melanie looked at him closely, turning with one knee up on the couch. He wasn't sure if she was mad. "I thought you barely looked at my costumes."

Chris snorted. Like that would even be possible. "Why would you think that? I look at them as closely as every other guy at the conventions."

"What do you mean?"

"I mean...girl superhero costumes are all really sexy." That seemed safe to say. It was hard to argue with that.

Her eyes were on him, unblinking.

Chris squirmed, trying to dodge her gaze. "I mean I get a little jealous I guess, OK?"

"You do?" she said sharply, then pulled back a little, as if realizing she had raised her voice and didn't mean to. "I didn't know that."

"I mean I'm not telling you I don't want you to wear them. I wouldn't do that," he said in his own defense. He opened his mouth then closed it again because he'd probably done enough damage.

"What?" she said. He could tell they were both being careful with what they said because Melanie's voice kept swinging between sharp and even. What he didn't know was whether that care would make this a good and productive discussion or another way to not say things they needed to say.

"I just..." *would rather not everyone in the world got to appreciate your body*. But he only said, "You look really sexy in your outfits, is all."

"But you're the only one I go home with," she reminded him.

He smiled, because not so long ago he wasn't sure that was the case. It made him crazy to think of someone else touching Melanie. "True. I enjoy that too."

She didn't seem mad, but he wanted to make sure. "You're not mad?" he asked.

"No. I'm surprised. I thought you were immune to how I looked in my costumes."

Chris wasn't sure how to respond to this clearly ludicrous idea. When did he give Melanie the impression he didn't...how could she possibly...

"You said that before," he said. "What do you mean? Why do you think that?"

"Well you don't usually say or do anything to make me think you care. When I'm dressed up." She swallowed, looking away from him. *Oh.* She was upset about this. Of course, she would be; she was so proud of her costumes. She spent hours on them. Days. "It's like you don't even see it."

Chris wracked his brain to find how this misunderstanding started. "I guess I'm sort of avoiding saying anything because it's so obvious."

"My costumes are obvious?" Melanie frowned, looking up at him. This was going in the wrong direction.

"No, how good you look is obvious. To everyone."

She smiled a little at him. OK. He was glad they were talking about this and she wasn't getting mad. It seemed like the thing he did right was telling her he found her attractive. Could it possibly be that simple? Did Melanie need him to tell her more often that he found her gorgeous? It felt like he'd just solved a really hard game level with the simplest cheat code ever.

Then Melanie started picking at a thread on the couch. Uh oh.

"You're not, like, harboring some secret resentment of my cosplay are you?"

Chris blinked. This was not a question he could say "yes" to no matter what, but he paused to consider it fairly. He hated that Melanie's clothes gave other dudes certain ideas. He'd seen them size her up everywhere they went while she was in costume. But that wasn't her fault or even her problem. "Of course not. You love cosplay.

I like it because it makes you happy. I'm even starting to like it because it can represent something bigger than just wearing a costume."

She nodded, but he could tell she was still bothered. Old Chris would have brushed it aside and hoped the hard conversations went away. He reached over and paused the show that was still playing on their TV. "What?"

She kept picking at the fabric of the sofa. "I guess I just, suddenly, wondered...if you would still feel that way if we had kids."

Chris immediately wanted to rewind this scene and pause it rather than the TV show. They've never had this conversation before. They'd talked about kids briefly when they first started dating—"Do you want kids?" "I think so, maybe, someday, you?" "Same"—but that was it. It hadn't seemed relevant since then. Melanie cooed at babies, but otherwise he didn't think it was a conversation they would have for another few years. He figured that first they'd have to have the one about marriage.

Melanie rushed on: "Like...would you want me to stop spending money on conventions? Would you let our daughter dress up as whoever if she wanted to?"

"Um, OK, that's a lot of hypotheticals," he said, stalling for time. He found himself picking at threads on the couch like she was and intentionally stopped. Just because this conversation made him uncomfortable didn't mean they shouldn't have it. He didn't quite know why they were having it *now*. She'd surprised him. He needed a moment to focus on the fact that it was a *good* thing she was thinking about their future together.

But she frowned at him. She crossed her arms, which seemed like a bad sign. "Not really. Most little girls want to dress up at some point. Imagine what happens if their mom also dresses up in costume multiple times a year."

He pictured a mini-Melanie and mom-Melanie dressed up together. "That sounds pretty cute," he admitted. "But I guess I haven't thought about it before."

She nodded, and her arms loosened. "Yeah, I know we haven't really talked about it. I guess I was just thinking...if we're still going to do *this*..." she waved her hand around, encompassing their shared space and the two of them. "We should think about where it's going a little bit. What does the future hold beyond us, you know, staying together."

Chris nodded, slowly, because it was reasonable, but he didn't like being ambushed. It was like an alarm bell was clanging in his head and he wanted to make a run for the exit. He wanted to watch a movie in peace, that's all. He tried to breathe normally.

You don't want to lose this woman. Freaking grow up, man.

But he couldn't. He suspected she already knew what she wanted to hear, but she wouldn't tell him what it was and she wouldn't listen to what he thought. And he didn't know what it was he thought yet. Right now, what he thought and what she wanted seemed very far apart and the distance terrified him. They'd barely gotten back together.

He cleared his throat. He looked around the room, trying to ground himself. The living room was clean because he tidied up after work today before Melanie got home. He was taking the full two days off this weekend, so it made sense to create a clear break at the end of the work week. His therapist suggested that. She also suggested that Melanie wasn't the only one who needed to work on communicating needs.

"Can we talk about it more later?" he suggested. "I just haven't thought about it a lot. Yet."

Melanie nodded. She immediately backed off. "Of course."

Chris nodded too, and Melanie tucked her head into his shoulder and curled up by his side. They turned the show back on, but he felt like his brain was on pause now—frozen, uncertain, freaked out—the rest of the evening.

~

Mom: (4:13 p.m.) You look so cute in your hero outfit

Chris: (4:14 p.m.) It's called a costume, mom. And I'm not cute I'm badass

Mom: (4:15 p.m.) I don't use that word but you are that too, honey. But are you sure about the apartment? You know you're going to lose money on it

Chris: (4:16 p.m.) Yes. If I have to find something else, I will.

Jenny: (4:16 p.m.) If you get bored, I can definitely find you some work to do...jk jk but really if you want to work this weekend lmk

Chris: (4:16 p.m.) Jenny! Stop working!

Jenny: (4:16 p.m.) Have literally never heard you say that before (open mouth emoji)

Anna Marie Kendell (MSW, LCSW): Hi Chris, checking in on you since I haven't heard from you in awhile. How is your routine going? I'm here if you need any help.

MELANIE WAS RE-LOADING the dishwasher while listening to Emily's panel from Chicago's comic con on cosplay. It was nice that Chris did the dishes, even if he did them wrong. *Should I say something to him about the plastic lids needing to always go on the top rack?* Nah, she'd keep trying to catch them before the dishwasher was turned on.

The panel was talking about bodysuits and a woman suggested hairspray to prevent them riding up. Melanie wondered if she was the only person—well, only woman—who thought about ease of access when it came to her cosplay choices. She had picked her upcoming costumes for Baltimore based on her hopes for costume sex with Chris.

She wanted to ask him whether she could wear costumes at home, just for him, and if that would be as attractive to him as he said her costumes were when she wore them out to conventions. But it was embarrassing. What if he said their sex life was fine without them? Which it *was*. The sex had been good since they got back together. She didn't mean that they needed help, exactly.

But Melanie couldn't help wanting that high she got when she wore one of her outfits, after the whole process of planning, tweaking and putting it on. It wasn't that she felt like a different person so much as she felt like...art. She liked knowing she was designed to be enjoyed and the idea of designing something specifically for Chris to enjoy excited her.

But she couldn't figure out how to ask him. There were too many "what ifs." What if he wouldn't enjoy it at all? What if he thought it was weird that she would?

That morning, she got an S.O.S. from Anna telling her Roger and Tim definitely broke up—"or whatever they'd call it," she wrote—and couldn't be around each other at the next con.

"Completely rearranging sleeping quarters for Baltimore," she'd texted. "Are you and Chris definitely sleeping together now?"

That much Melanie was definite about, she texted back. She was sad about Roger and Tim, who had the kind of casually unconventional relationship Melanie admired. She wondered what had been their final straw. She wondered if they'd eventually get back together. She hoped they would by next convention season. She wanted her crowd of friends to get larger and more interconnected, not less. She even wanted Chris to be part of it.

Sometimes she worried that she and Chris were drawing out something that wasn't going anywhere anymore, just because they couldn't keep their hands off each other. She looked at signs—like

Chris not putting things back the right way in the fridge—and wondered which ones were important. *Does this tell me we're incompatible? Or is he just being a normal guy?*

She didn't trust herself to know, so she fell back on her spreadsheet. She probed Chris with hard questions sometimes, waiting for the answer that would prove her fears true. The pro/con lists were staying even so far. But eventually, something had to make up Melanie's mind.

From Chris on Slack:

(1:45 p.m.) Hi Nick and Jerry, I wanted to let you know I thought about the new position and I'm going to turn it down. I can send a formal email if that's best.

From Nick on Slack:

(1:50 p.m.) I'm sorry to hear that. And kind of surprised. You've really been on track to get this promotion. You sure you just don't need more time to think about it?

From Chris on Slack:

(1:55 p.m.) Thanks but no. Moving doesn't work for my life right now. And I am more interested in continuing to work on a project basis, which I can do better in my current role. I really appreciate the offer.

BALTIMORE

Chris had been to Baltimore Comic Con with Melanie before, so the train ride to the convention center and long lines to get in were all familiar at least. This convention center was practically in the middle of nowhere, in an industrial area. They took the MARC train to get there from downtown Baltimore.

He carried his cowl and gloves in his tote bag until they got inside because it was unseasonably warm out. Melanie posted a picture of him with the hashtag #climatechange.

They met up with Melanie's friends Laura and David in line. They'd been at brunch when Melanie and Chris got to the hotel.

Melanie had gotten a weird look on her face when she'd told him about sharing a room with them.

"What, you thought we were all going to squeeze into a King?" he joked when they dropped off their bags that morning and he saw Melanie's relieved face at the two queen-size beds.

"I just wasn't sure if their stuff would be all over the place," she said, and he assumed Laura or David or both of them must be messy. Melanie was an everything-in-its-place kind of woman.

Laura was dressed as an elf, sort of—she had the ears and a flowy gown but he wasn't sure that she actually looked like any specific character—and David as a tree. Everyone in line gave him a lot of space to avoid all the branches sticking out of his costume.

"I know it's not that sexy, but I like playing a character of few words," David joked as they all jostled to stay out of the way of his limbs. David seemed like a decent guy, and he had a girlfriend so Chris worried less than with Matt about the possibility he previously made a move on Melanie. He still hadn't worked up the nerve to ask her about Matt. Just because she hadn't slept with someone didn't mean they hadn't...done other stuff. But he figured it was better to make nice with the guy so he could guilt him out of ever trying to get with her again. At least he wouldn't be at this convention. Melanie's friends all in a group could be intense.

Once they were inside the convention center, Chris figured he and Melanie would go do their own thing, but Laura and David tagged along with them.

As usual, the convention center sprawled and was confusing to navigate. Chris reluctantly put the rest of his costume on. Laura put her hand on his forearm and murmured loudly enough for everyone to hear, "Don't you think you would be attracted to an elf, considering your outfit's cat ear fetish?"

Chris blinked at her in his peripheral vision, because the cowl made it hard to turn his head. "I've never thought of it that way," he said. He couldn't figure out if she was maybe a little socially awkward, like a lot of people he'd met at conventions, or if she was seriously coming onto him right in front of his girlfriend and her own boyfriend.

Melanie, clearly as uncomfortable as he was, laughed too loudly. She didn't say anything to Laura, though; she grabbed his hand and pulled him down the hall. The other two followed them.

They wandered through the booths on the convention floor, stopping to talk to Anna about her graphic novel about squirrels, which was the worst thing Chris had ever read but seemed to be selling well. People stopped them regularly to get pictures of one or all of them together. They attended a panel about mental health resources that Melanie picked from the packed convention schedule. They ate hot dogs and tried the convention beer—it was terrible, as most designated event beers were. The whole time, Laura and David stayed stuck to Chris and Melanie like vines.

Around 5, they were all exhausted and agreed to head out for happy hour and maybe an early dinner. Laura and David had pulled up reviews on a phone and were suggesting places as they walked toward the MARC station to head downtown. They passed a woman on a bench with her shoulders hunched, heaving into her hands. She was dressed like some cartoon character with a sailor-style outfit whose name Chris couldn't remember.

Melanie and Laura both winced and looked away. David didn't seem to notice. Chris paused a half-step. Was she sick? No, the woman wasn't throwing up but she was sobbing in the middle of a crowd. He glanced around to see if she was alone. He would really like to see someone nearby who could take care of her.

David paused a few steps ahead and looked back at them. Laura took her boyfriend's arm and pulled him to keep moving.

"Leave her alone," Melanie whispered, watching David and Laura get ahead of them. "I wouldn't want someone to point out I was crying in public."

Chris probably wouldn't, either, but he couldn't remember ever being that upset and alone in public, so it was hard to know for sure what he'd prefer to happen. "Shouldn't we see if she needs anything?"

Melanie ran one hand over her skin-tight costume. "I don't have any tissues, do you?"

Chris dropped his chin to look in her face and see if she was serious.

"How exactly are you going to help?" she hissed at him. Chris didn't know the answer. But he knew he couldn't keep walking on by.

Chris dropped Melanie's hand and walked over to the bench. "Hi, are you OK?"

The woman didn't look up and instead flapped a hand at him like she didn't want him to look at her.

Melanie had followed him. "Do you want to be left alone?" she asked. Chris was annoyed that she was trying to coach this woman into telling her what she wanted to hear when this was obviously a situation where everyone needed to slow down and let her say what she needed.

"I'm OK, I'm OK," the woman said, shoulders still hunched.

Chris looked around. People were side-eying them but going on about their business. David and Laura had stopped and were watching them.

He sat down on the bench, leaving plenty of space between them. His plastic suit squeaked a little as he did. "I don't think you're OK," he said quietly.

"No, don't worry." The woman started digging around in her tiny purse, catching snot in one hand. He really wished he kept tissues in his utility belt. "I'm OK."

"Are you with anyone? Can I call someone for you?"

She kept shaking her head, and finally found a tissue in her purse and held it to her face. One was not going to be enough.

Melanie was at his shoulder. She held her cell phone in front of his face and it took Chris several seconds to realize she wasn't trying to distract him, she was showing him the mental health resources from the panel earlier. There was a crisis booth at the convention run by a local organization.

Chris looked up at Melanie. She mimed making a phone call, raising her eyebrows, and he nodded, relieved she had a plan because he had no idea how to solve this problem. She stepped away with her phone.

"What's your name? How long have you been sitting out here?" Chris asked the woman.

She shook her head without raising it to look at him. "You don't have to sit here. I'm OK." She was trying to clean up her nose. If only this character carried around a mom purse instead of a tiny utility belt.

"Sorry I don't have any tissues. They don't go with the outfit," Chris said, trying to make her laugh. She waved him off again.

He hoped he wasn't making it worse. He only knew what helped him: Being asked if he was OK and forcing himself to talk about why he wasn't.

"It's OK," he said, and kept repeating OK like an idiot. "I know you're OK. But I'm going to sit here for a little while anyway, if that's OK with you."

She frowned and looked out over the empty space between the convention center and the train station, holding the tissue to her face. She didn't respond.

"What'd you say your name was?"

He waited.

"Elena."

"Are you having a bad day, Elena?" *Obvious understatement.* But asking questions seemed like the right thing to do and this was the only one he could think of.

She gave a small snort-laugh, which made him feel better. "I guess."

He was silent then because he wasn't sure what else to say. Eventually she added, in a low voice: "It's just... a lot."

"I get it," Chris said, also keeping his voice low. "Like when everything gets to be so hard that even the small things become overwhelming?"

She nodded, and he thought she might be breathing a little more evenly than she was earlier. So he kept talking, about having too little energy and how even getting upset was sort of a good sign compared to being too exhausted to react.

It took a long time for the mental health professionals to show up and Chris kept asking Elena questions for seemingly forever, hoping he didn't accidentally ask one that offended her. She got frustrated with him twice, acting like she was going to get up and leave. But then she didn't. She stayed there and he didn't ask her anything too hard, mostly because he wasn't equipped to handle hard answers.

"Hi there," said a woman wearing a red and yellow-striped scarf who eventually showed up holding a big tote bag. "Who's your friend?"

"This is Elena," he said.

"Hi Elena. I'm Kristen from a local behavioral health center. I'm at the con to make sure even geeks take care of their mental health. Is it OK if I sit down and talk with you for a little while? I promise I'm not going to make you do anything you don't want to do."

Chris stood and offered Kristen his seat. She waited for Elena to nod before she sat. "Thank you," she told him.

"Of course," he said, and nodded at them both before backing away, because he wasn't sure what else to do. He found Melanie standing with Laura and David far enough away to not eavesdrop and walked over to them.

"Thanks for waiting," he said. "And for calling them," he added to Melanie. "I didn't really know what to do."

Melanie smiled but he could tell she was thinking something else behind the expression. Her eyes were troubled. But he didn't want to ask her what was wrong in front of David and Laura.

"Should we go eat?" he said instead.

Laura stepped up to him and put her hand on his arm again. "That was so selfless to watch. I'm impressed."

"Me too. I just wear the hero outfits," David said. "And to be honest, I can't really sit in this thing so I was thinking more about that than helping out."

Laura laughed, but she was still eying Chris like he was a glazed donut. It was weird. His girlfriend was standing *right there* and Melanie was *her* friend.

"We don't need to make a big thing out of it," he said, taking a step forward to get out of the weird conversation and hoping everyone followed him. "I'm really hungry now."

"How unexpected of you," Laura said. She took David's hand and fell into step with him. Melanie said nothing, walking on his other side.

Chris pulled his gloves off and reached for her hand. She took it, but still didn't say anything. He could tell she was holding back and it gave him a pit in his stomach he didn't know what to do with. He didn't want to make her ditch her friends, but they clearly needed to talk.

Laura and David wanted to go to an English pub-style restaurant in Baltimore that was hosting a comic con special—two for one beers. They all sat in a booth in a dark corner and Laura and David retold the story of what just happened like it was a cinematic sequel they'd seen in a theater.

"First he saves children from reckless driving, then women from public meltdowns," Laura laughed, raising her beer stein.

"And all in costume," David added.

"Ready-made trending content."

"I didn't do it for Instagram," Chris said. He was hunched as far over his beer as possible, hoping no one else in the restaurant was eavesdropping. To make the whole situation worse, Melanie was being oddly quiet.

"It doesn't hurt, though. Instagram loves you." Laura pulled out her phone. "I've never had this many likes. Ever."

Chris grabbed for her waving hand. "You posted that on Instagram?"

"Just a picture of you on the bench. Don't worry, you look great." She let one finger drift down Chris's and he yanked his hand away, letting go of her phone.

"I didn't..." Chris swallowed and heaved a deep breath. He wanted to say he didn't give her permission but didn't want to sound like a girl who had to approve her image any time her friends posted it online. He cast his eyes at Melanie to see if she found this inappropriate. "What about her privacy?"

"If she wanted privacy, she shouldn't have been sobbing on a public bench," Laura shrugged, head down and scrolling through images on her phone.

Chris's shoulder muscles locked up. It was such a cavalier response, as if showing emotion meant someone giving up their right to consideration. He didn't want to be here anymore. He didn't like these people.

"In fairness, it was a public place," Melanie said quietly. "But also, people who are going through a hard time deserve compassion. And space to recover."

He couldn't believe how neutral she was being, like she refused to take a side even though one was obviously right. This wasn't the goddamn United Nations. He wanted to get up and walk out of this restaurant. He didn't think he'd ever been this disgusted by someone else's behavior before.

David put his arm around Laura's shoulders. He was eying Chris like he knew what he was thinking. Good. "That's a good way to put it, Melanie. Compassion like Chris showed. Don't you think so, Laura?"

Laura raised her head from her phone. She looked from David to Chris and nodded slowly, like it was dawning on her that she was being a bitch. "Of course. But sharing mental health struggles on social media is normalizing. It helps people understand everyone goes through shit."

She put her phone face-down on the table and re-crossed her legs under the table, kicking his ankle lightly in the process. "You're so passionate, Chris. It's sexy."

Chris lowered his chin at her. Melanie sighed. David and Laura exchanged a look. Chris glanced at Melanie but she still refused to meet his eyes.

"It must be such a turn-on when he gets worked up like this, Melanie," Laura said.

"Don't you think, Melanie?" David asked.

Everyone looked at Melanie. Melanie had her chin propped over one elbow on the table. She picked up a French fry on her plate and swirled it in the ketchup, moving it around and around in a circle without picking it up and eating it.

"Sometimes," she said finally.

Laura smiled. Her foot kept knocking Chris's under the table. He didn't think it was by accident anymore.

Chris kept his eyes on Melanie. She still wouldn't look at him. What was happening here? He wanted to grab Melanie's hand and take her somewhere they could talk away from her friends.

"I think I'm going to head out," he said. He reached for his wallet and hoped he had cash. Waiting for their server to run a credit card was going to make this so awkward.

"Oh come on, don't overreact," Laura said.

"Chris, calm down," David said at the same time.

He was too angry to respond. He didn't like being told what to do.

He stood up and threw down some cash—thank God for Melanie constantly telling him he needed cash to travel—and looked at her to see if she had anything to say. She finally lifted her head and gazed back at him mutely.

Was this who she was now? Silent for fear of controversy? Maybe she'd been right all along. Maybe they were too different.

He was afraid to ask her to get up and leave with him. So he didn't. He walked out, climbing the stairs back up to street-level and standing on the dark street unsure what to do next. He needed to get away from the situation.

He started walking.

He walked until he found an empty bench under a light and sat down and pulled up Instagram on his phone. Laura had tagged him in her post. The woman on the bench with him probably wasn't identifiable because her head was down. That was something at least.

He realized at that moment that he left his cowl in its tote bag with Melanie at the restaurant, so he was sitting there in the dark in just part of a rubber costume.

He felt—and this was becoming familiar—like an idiot. But he was also mad. Furious, even. He couldn't believe he'd been following Melanie around like a lovesick puppy only to end up like this: Melanie off with her posse of idiots and him sitting alone with no comfortable clothes.

He wanted to make Melanie happy by taking care of her. But was it so wrong that he'd expected to be taken care of in return?

He flipped his phone camera toward his face and started recording.

～

From @lauraloowho:
Baltimore Convention Center
(picture of Chris sitting on a bench next to a woman)

This hero doesn't just save kids at #DragonCon he also gives #mentalhealthadvice at #baltimorecomiccon @gamerchris_1989
Liked by @miz_anna_doll and 2015 others
@aries_heart56: I think these were BOTH a set-up. Who does this guy work for?
@benedictfan398: is he going to be speaking on a panel?
@manlybubbles0190: Now THIS I can get behind @gamerchris_1989 @melly_89
@lau_spencer: I'd do him

MELANIE COULDN'T STOP WATCHING the front door of the hotel, waiting for Chris to come back. When they got back from the restaurant, Laura bodily turned her into the hotel bar. Laura kept ordering more drinks and making Melanie taste them all, even though Melanie had barely finished her wine. David went up to the room when they got back and texted Laura that Chris wasn't up there.

Was it possible Chris got an early flight and flew home? Would he do that?

Laura, still holding her phone after reading David's text from their room, turned it to Melanie.

David: (9:18 p.m.) Tell Melanie she might want to check Instagram

Melanie sighed. "I think I'm going to need more wine first."

Laura pushed something blue in a daiquiri glass toward her and raised one finger for the bartender.

"Melanie, if he makes you so unhappy..." she began.

Melanie held up her hand and shook her head. "We both know you were making him uncomfortable."

"And you think it was..." Laura paused. Melanie raised her eyebrows. "For good reason? As in, he was right to be uncomfortable just because we might make sexual choices he doesn't agree with?"

Melanie rolled her eyes. "Don't do that. This isn't some issue of biphobia."

Laura dabbed up a few drops of moisture on the bar with a drink napkin. "Are you sure?"

"I'm sure," Melanie snapped. Chris might not always get everything right, but his heart was in the right place. It was about consent for him, not acceptance. She took another gulp of her new glass of wine.

"OK, OK." Laura smiled easily, like they were just making small talk and she wasn't trying to make Melanie break up with her boyfriend. She took another sip of a drink, the peppermint one. "But you know...just saying he's not interested is a lot more mature than walking out."

"I don't think it was that. It was...me." Melanie rested her elbow on the bar and put her forehead in her palm, rubbing at her temples. "He wanted me to...he needed me to speak up. Defend him."

"He can't defend himself?" Laura sounded skeptical. Melanie raised her head.

"He doesn't know you. You're *my* friends."

"But we don't have to be *just* your friends. That was the whole point."

Laura raised her eyebrows at Melanie. Melanie hated the way she acted like her argument was impossible to refute and Melanie needed to be guided to a conclusion she'd already reached. Right now, Melanie didn't like Laura very much.

"It's not all black and white, Laura. So you and David don't get along with Chris. Or he doesn't get along with you, whichever," she hurried to add, when Laura opened her mouth to argue. "That doesn't make any of you the bad guy. And just because I get along with you and he doesn't, that doesn't mean Chris and I aren't compatible." Melanie wasn't entirely sure she *did* get along with Laura and David, anyway. She'd rather be talking to anyone else about this.

Laura shrugged and uncrossed and re-crossed her legs, adjusting on the backless bar stool. "So you're definitely back together, then?"

Melanie took the glass out of Laura's hand and drank the rest of whatever it was. She'd been mixing her liquors, trying to squash her emotions, but now she was queasy. "I don't know anymore," she said, thinking about how she didn't even know where her boyfriend was right now. She worried he was going to do something macho like sleep on a park bench or at the airport.

After another half a drink, Melanie left Laura at the bar to go to the bathroom. She locked the door of the single stall behind her and pulled out her phone. She opened Instagram and saw that Chris had posted a video.

In it, he was outside and looked like he was standing under a streetlamp. She didn't recognize the street or buildings behind him.

He was agitated, talking about how he saw a woman who was upset at the convention earlier. "You may have seen it on Instagram, without my permission," he said. "If she saw it, I want her to know I'm sorry. I recognize that in cities, we live our emotions in public places. But at a convention, we're supposed to be in a community. Someone told me that's the point of a comic con—to gather around like-minded interests. I wear a costume. So do a lot of people who go to these things. It's funny how these cons have normalized wearing a costume to the point where the possibility we're all hiding behind them isn't even discussed."

The video wasn't well produced. Chris's face went in and out of the camera view, and the lighting got worse and better as he walked and talked, clearly gesturing as he did so with his phone hand.

Melanie closed Instagram after watching it for another minute, not liking the whisper in her head that said: *You are small and unimportant to him.* Why did Chris turn to Instagram to vent his feelings, rather than talking to her?

What if, without intending it, she'd been expecting Chris to be who *she* told him to be and not himself. He was being himself in the video in a completely new way and it was uncomfortable because he was speaking his mind on subjects she'd talked about a lot without asking his opinion.

How could she be with him when she wasn't certain she knew who exactly he was?

Melanie walked back out to the bar and glanced at the front door of the hotel one more time. "Let's go upstairs," she told Laura, picking up her coat.

Laura was holding her phone and Melanie suspected she'd been watching the video on Instagram.

"I don't want to talk about it," Melanie said, preemptively. She obviously should have just *told* Laura and David that she and Chris weren't interested in sleeping with them—but at the time she'd been afraid of hurting *their* feelings. *Stupid.* She should have thought about *Chris's* feelings instead. And her own. A foursome was not her thing and it should have been OK to say that. She kept trying to please other people and she didn't know why.

"OK," Laura said, putting her phone away. Judging her, or maybe Melanie was projecting. Maybe Laura didn't think she was weak for not announcing her boyfriend's actions were unacceptable and she was leaving him. But Laura stayed silent as she unfolded from the bar stool and followed Melanie to the elevators.

Melanie regretted this whole shared room situation as she waited for Laura and David to get ready for bed in the one bathroom. She eventually washed her face and changed into pajamas, keeping her phone on the sink where she could see it the whole time. Chris never responded to her text asking where he was.

Stupid to text him at all, like giving up the high ground. Or maybe she gave that up back when she let him walk out of the restaurant by himself. She wasn't sure anymore.

She crawled into bed and turned out the bedside light to prevent Laura and David from starting any conversations. But then Melanie laid there for what must have been hours, staring at the wall on her side of the room.

She didn't know what she'd do if he didn't come back to the hotel room at all. Was that the end? Were they really over now, for good?

She tried to figure out what she wanted or needed to say to Chris when she saw him again. But she couldn't seem to map out a conversation in her head. The truth was, she didn't know what he was thinking. She wasn't sure when she stopped having a clue what was going on in his head.

Anna: (7:15 a.m.) WTH happened last night? It looked like it went DOWN on Instagram

Matt: (7:34 a.m.) Are you guys OK? Whatever happened, I bet it was Laura and David's fault

Anna: (7:44 a.m.) Just chatted with Matt. Don't listen to him! We were all having a great summer until Chris inserted himself (no pun intended)

Matt: (7:50 a.m.) Don't listen to Anna. Just talk to Chris and ignore all of us

WHEN CHRIS WOKE up the next morning, he felt stiff all over from trying not to touch Melanie all night. Everyone was in bed when he got back to the room, sleeping or pretending to, and he laid there rigid and hating the world for hours. He thought Melanie was awake too, but neither of them crossed the gap between them, either not wanting to wake Laura and David up or afraid to have the conversation they needed to.

The room was deathly quiet as the others started getting up, using the bathroom and getting dressed. Chris could hear brief murmurs between the three of them as he laid in bed using his phone to look at changing his flight home.

And then, unexpectedly, David and Laura left and he and Melanie were alone in the room.

"Are you going to get up? We're going to get breakfast," Melanie announced, standing at the bottom of their bed. "I at least need coffee before we talk about this."

Chris heaved his legs over the side of the bed and stared at the carpet for a few long seconds before he got up. Coffee did sound like a good idea, even if he didn't really want to have a fight in public.

And they were definitely going to have a fight.

CHAPTER 14

Chris was a McGriddle kind of guy when it came to McDonald's breakfast. Melanie liked Egg White McMuffins, when they were available, which they weren't always—something Mel ranted about surprisingly often.

He knew these details because he and Melanie had been dating for years. But history didn't always add up to much. Chris was beginning to realize that, despite his paralyzing fear of change and his fear that there was only one woman in the world he wanted to spend the rest of his life with.

He wished they had a car to sit in; instead, they ended up half-hovering over a yellow-painted concrete parking stop in the lot out front of the restaurant, knees nearly up to their chins and coffees sitting on the asphalt at their feet.

"I saw your Instagram rant," she began, looking down at her sandwich as she unwrapped the paper.

He nodded. He wasn't sure he'd call it a rant, but didn't have a better word for it, so he said nothing. He picked at the cheese that was sticking out of one side of his sandwich.

"I agree with you that there needs to be more mental health

accessibility at conventions. But the rest of it seemed kind of pointed."

"It was, I guess," he acknowledged. He took a bite because he knew from experience that if he waited too long, the sandwich became nearly inedible.

She didn't even take her sandwich all the way out of the wrapper. "At me?"

Chris kept chewing, even though his stomach was already protesting this small bite. He'd swallowed too much tension already. So he opened his mouth and let some of it out: "At your friends who thought it was just a photo op."

"They didn't think that. Just because somebody puts something on Instagram doesn't mean it meant less to them than someone who didn't."

Chris sighed. He wished that, for once, Melanie could cut him some slack and maybe try to understand where he was coming from, instead of constantly pushing back on him. "I guess that's technically true," he said. He wrapped the sandwich back up.

"I don't like your friends," he said finally. "Some of them, at least."

"Yeah, I'm getting that."

"All they seem to care about is what they can get out of any situation."

She said nothing, so he kept talking.

"And I guess I'm wondering if that's what you're like, too."

"Oh, thank you very much, Chris," she snapped, her voice raising. She looked up from her sandwich, which she still hadn't eaten. "You've known me how long? You've lived with me how long now? And now that you've discovered altruism for the very first time you suddenly think you're an expert?"

Their discussion already seemed so pointless. His concerns were valid, weren't they? Yes, maybe they were sort of new—at least talking about them was—but that didn't make them any less important. And Melanie obviously wasn't going to take any responsibility for the situation, even though she was the one that led him into a difficult situation and abandoned him there.

"That's not fair," he said. He didn't bother to put any heat into his denial; what did it matter?

"Isn't it?" Melanie's voice wasn't as apathetic as his. "That's kind of our thing, after all. You start something for good reasons and then I have to make the logistics work."

He was surprised by the bitterness in her voice. Instead of getting defensive, like he wanted to, he tried to think back to an example of what she was talking about. She did step in to call someone to help with that woman yesterday. And there was the time—still a fond memory—when she brought him something to drink while he talked to the police in Atlanta. Although both of those situations were the product of circumstances and not entirely his fault.

"Thank you for helping me yesterday," he said.

She frowned, like he'd caught her off guard. Then she nodded. "That wasn't quite what I meant, but OK."

Exactly. "I'm not sure what you mean most of the time, Melanie, that's kind of the problem."

Melanie flinched and looked away. Chris's nose suddenly itched and he rubbed at it. He felt terrible that they were doing this in a McDonald's parking lot, with the smell of hot asphalt to accompany their grievances.

"Maybe we should save this conversation until we're home," he suggested.

"You don't get to decide what we're going to do all the time," she snapped. She put her sandwich down on the ground and brushed off her knees. "I'm sick of this. I'm sick of having to change what I want to do because of you. This was supposed to be my summer, my convention season."

"Like I haven't changed anything for you?" he demanded, thinking of the past weeks of wearing that stupid costume and traveling more often than he preferred.

"Don't act like you're some kind of martyr for wearing a costume." Her arms were crossed again, which meant this wasn't going to be a conversation. Melanie wanted a fight.

He scowled, because the suit had started to smell like sweaty plastic inside and he did hate it. "It's never enough for you."

"Don't say *never*," she snapped, looking at him like she never wanted to see him again. "Like you know what I'm going to do or say every time. Like you know what I feel before I do."

"I don't know what you feel because you don't tell me!" Chris said. He knew his voice was getting louder, but he didn't stop because he didn't want to. Clearly all that therapy stuff wasn't working. Hadn't he been trying? Hadn't he done his best to guess what Melanie wanted and do it? "Then you drag me to these stupid conventions and make me hang out with your stupid friends and alls you want to do is buy more and more crap to hang on our walls or refrigerator and, apparently, do weird sex shit and ignore people who are sobbing on public benches!"

"Weird sex shit?" she repeated, her voice reaching a screeching level, and Chris took a step back mentally, because he did just say that didn't he. He wasn't being very articulate about how much he'd hated David and Laura treating him like a toy.

His self-doubt evaporated in a poof of anger. "I don't like being manipulated into stuff I'm not into! So sue me!"

She glared at him. "I never asked you to do anything you didn't want to do. That was all *your* decision. I can't help that you're a robot who doesn't enjoy anything! And just because I don't want to interfere in a private moment doesn't make me a bad person!"

"Yeah, just like dressing like supervillains doesn't mean anything to you," Chris mumbled. He picked up his coffee and took a loud, slurpy sip, trying to drown out his own pettiness. He couldn't seem to stop talking. At least they were arguing here, in the open air, in his own clothes, not in a stale warehouse wearing plastic. For months, he'd been focused on winning her back, afraid to say anything she might not like, but no longer. He was unleashed.

She straightened. "*Excuse* me?"

"It's like you never think about what anything means. Like, oh, this costume is cute and shows my butt, I'll wear it," he said, hating himself and feeling relieved to let it out at the same time. "Well guess what, Melanie, I wouldn't want our daughter to dress up like you do because all those costumes are sexist and too revealing and I don't want our daughter to buy into the machine!"

"Are you kidding me?" Melanie jumped to her feet. "This is what you really think?"

Chris stood too, holding his coffee. He scratched his forehead with a free finger. He believed what he'd said, at least mostly, but he hated how he was saying it. His voice had gone all mean without intention, mocking her and mocking himself for being with her. That wasn't what he'd meant to express at all. He'd gone back to the hotel last night and started this day determined to tell Melanie that while he didn't always agree with her, there was more to their relationship than having the same point of view all the time. We need our own room, he'd planned to say. We need to check in with each other more.

"Well I enjoy my costumes and I get to choose what I want them to say, not you," she said, and started picking up her food from the ground. She stomped over and dumped it all into a trash can. She walked back and looked him in the face and Chris felt a sense of dread wash over him. "And you don't have to ever look at it or listen to me again because we're done, Chris. It's over."

Then she walked away and Chris stood there holding his cold coffee and unable to take it all back.

~

From @manlybubbles0190:
Baltimore, Maryland
(photo of Roger looking directly into the camera)
Comic cons need more #mentalhealthawareness HT @gamer-chris_1989

From @jezabellegreen:
Baltimore, Maryland
(photo of Tim looking directly into the camera)
Cosplay doesn't always equal OK. Comic cons need more #mental-healthawareness HT @gamerchris_1989

MELANIE HAD HEARD of writer's block, and she supposed that applied to any kind of creativity, but this level of mentally constipation was new. She couldn't even focus on her costumes.

Instead, she worked on her spreadsheets. She updated the one she kept for her cosplay. It included each character and the different parts of each costume—the pieces that crossed over into multiple costumes or could be reused that way, as well as the pieces she was still missing or wanted to replace, like bullet bracelets or white boots.

Reluctantly, she also tallied up the cost of each costume, which had grown larger for every costume she'd put together this summer.

Perhaps, she thought, Chris was right to criticize her. She *was* materialist. She should have been saving for her moving costs. Or she should have only spent on costumes and not on all the merchandise that was sitting in her closet.

But, she reminded herself, these cons were her vacation for the year. And it was *her* money, not his.

She wasn't even sure the overindulgence was what he was criticizing, but that was the seed that was planted from his fury. He seemed so disgusted with her choices and habits and it fanned the flame of Melanie's own insecurities about investing in her hobbies.

And about enjoying the *weird sex shit* that some of her costumes represented.

That was exactly why she hadn't brought up her cosplay fantasies. And why she was going to split up with him at the beginning of the summer. He didn't enjoy the same things she did.

I shouldn't be with someone who makes me feel guilty for being who I am.

She had doubts about that summary of why their relationship failed. Something about it didn't fit quite right. But it was easier now to tie things up in a tidy bow and put "the end" on it.

To cement it and make her resolution more real, she started telling people they were over.

"I broke up with my boyfriend," she told Max at her office, when they were talking about why she couldn't work that weekend.

"Do you still live with him?" she asked, dumping cream in her coffee, stirring, then dumping more. "That happened to me once. I couldn't afford to pay double rent so I ended up living with him for months. Very millennial of us."

Melanie nodded. "The lease is almost up. Just another month to go now."

She'd sent the email to their landlord that morning. He'd responded "sorry to hear that" and sent a few times he could come look at the place to size up how long the turn-around would take.

At home, she and Chris were separating. His clothes were packed, although he seemed to be in a constant state of repacking as he pulled things out to wear and then wash and then repeat the cycle. He was putting his games and records into boxes. She went through the boxes after him to make sure he didn't pack anything that belonged to her. Yesterday, she found a box of porn and felt good for the rest of the evening about dumping him.

But this morning, she had doubts again. He had tried, hadn't he? And sometimes, when she was thinking about other things, she wondered: *Did she?* Before she announced her plans for the summer to Chris, she'd barely brought up the problems they were having. She'd expected him to know she wasn't happy. And then when he showed up in Atlanta, she'd let him keep trying to figure it out alone.

But the things he'd said to her in anger—things he'd clearly been thinking before, not only in the heat of the moment—those seemed irreconcilable to Melanie. Impossible to overcome.

She went home that night and the apartment somehow smelled both sweaty and greasy from the pizza he probably ate for breakfast, lunch and dinner. She looked at him, hunched over his computer monitors, and imagined coming home to an empty apartment. It would be as clean as she left it in the morning. She would light a candle and make dinner and listen to nothing, if she wanted to, unlike Chris who constantly had music or games or TV playing.

She remembered, nearly five years ago when she was single, wishing for a partner to help her put together furniture and bring the groceries in. But at least when she was single, she didn't expect any help. If she didn't go to the grocery store, she didn't expect to have any food in the house. If she didn't wipe up the sink before she left for work, she had to deal with it when she got back. But no one else made the mess and then left it for her.

Then she walked into the kitchen and saw that Chris had taken out the trash. And there was a serving of leftover pizza covered in plastic on a plate in the fridge. All the pepperoni had been picked off it. She hated pepperoni and Chris knew that.

Melanie leaned her forehead against the cool refrigerator door and tried to hold both of these scenarios in her head and tally up the pros and cons to see how it calculated, but it was difficult because she'd lived with Chris so long and she wasn't sure she even knew how to live by herself anymore. She didn't remember what it was like to come home to an empty apartment and no pizza. She wasn't sure she really wanted that.

Melanie ate a piece of pizza cold and took a glass of wine to the bedroom. She texted Matt. Turning to him as an emotional crutch was wrong, but not as wrong as not telling Chris "thank you" for the pizza.

She and Chris had barely spoken since Baltimore. "Thank you" would feel like a concession, like reopening a door she closed a thousand miles away.

She'd been drinking wine in the evenings and texting Matt ever since they got back, because she couldn't seem to focus on anything else. The atmosphere in the apartment was tense, even though Chris was clearly trying not to get in her way. It felt as though they were both moving around in their own personal bubbles, afraid to bump up against each other's space.

She told herself that as much as she regretted that things were ending this way, the thing needed to end. Sometimes the only thing to do when you were in pain was keep pushing through it. Stay the course.

> Melanie: (7:39 p.m.) So Laura and David propositioned me in Seattle

> Matt: (7:40 p.m.) !!

> Matt: (7:41 pm.) Did it work?

"How cute are you, but no," she typed, then erased it. Too flirty.

> Melanie: (7:42 p.m.) What do you think?

> Matt: (7:43 p.m.) Probably not, but only because I don't think you'd kiss and tell

She paused and took a couple sips of wine slowly. She didn't have anyone else to confide in who understood the cons, how people started to act like their costumes and reality got looser late at night.

> Melanie: (7:45 p.m.) But then they sort of came on to me and Chris in Baltimore

> Matt: (7:45 p.m.) Yikes! Guessing I don't have to ask if that went anywhere.

> Melanie: (7:46 p.m.) Why?

> Matt: (7:46 p.m.) Because Chris.

She studied his response, letting it settle in. But Melanie had known Chris for years and she didn't know how he would respond to

Laura and David's advances. It should have been a joke to him. He should have brushed them off, holding Melanie's hand, and ordered another beer. Maybe, if he hadn't been so unhappy to even be there at all, it would have been.

> Melanie: (7:50 p.m.) He hates the cons

She waited for several minutes, until her phone's screen went dark and she set it down. Her sister would say it was silly to break up with someone over a hobby. They didn't have to enjoy the same things. It wasn't the key issue to a relationship. Probably.

Her phone lit up again.

> Matt: (6:52 p.m.) It's more than that, though, isn't it?

Melanie nodded, alone in her bedroom. It was more than that. It was fundamental. It wasn't the cons, it was how and why and how often and what she did there. It was the fact that she wanted costumes and geeky references and friends who thought those things mattered to stay in her life.

Melanie put her phone down and slid out of bed. She opened the closet door. It was far emptier inside than it used to be, without Chris's clothes. She took another sip of her wine and put the glass down on the dresser before she pulled her plastic costume bins out from under the bed. She started taking her costumes out, one by one, and hanging them up where she could see them.

Letting her hobby take up space.

~

From @melly_89: Taking a break from social media for awhile, friends!

~

CHRIS SAVED his expensive costume from the trash collection at the last minute. He woke up that morning in a panic and ran out to the curb to pull it out of the trash can before the truck came by, even though the night before he'd thrown it away in a rage and even gone so far as to take the trash out to the alley to make sure it was actually gone for good.

But in the light of day, the costume inspired rare sentimentality.

He spent a lot of time and put a lot of effort into that costume.

Maybe he wasn't quite done with it yet. He could always throw it away later.

He smuggled it back inside the apartment while Melanie was still asleep and put it in one of his boxes, then took the box out to the trunk of his car. He knew she was going through everything he packed. For some reason, he didn't want Melanie to know he was keeping it.

She might think he was doing it for her. And he wasn't.

Since he was up, Chris made coffee and threw together his favorite breakfast casserole with eggs and bacon and hash browns. He sat down at his computer with his mug while breakfast was cooking and checked his email.

He had the reply he'd been waiting for:

"Dear Chris, we would love to see what you can do for us. Are you open to discussing becoming our brand ambassador? Let's get together and come up with a trial period that works on both sides. We won't be able to pay you anything right away but I'm hoping this can benefit all of us and we might be able to revisit payment in the future."

Chris leaned back in his leather chair and swung it back and forth a few times, grinning.

This was why he saved the costume. But this time, he'd make sure he got to decide when he had to wear it.

He heard the rustling of bedclothes in the bedroom but didn't call out to Melanie because he knew she hated being talked to in the mornings.

He went into the kitchen and stirred the casserole, then put it back in the oven.

Chris: (8:14 a.m.) I'm in. They're interested.

He didn't expect a response right away, but he'd forgotten Matt was an early riser. "Of course they are!" he responded. "Did you tell Mel?"

Chris: (8:20 a.m.) No. I don't want her to know about it.

Matt had sent him a DM on Instagram after Baltimore, telling Chris he had struggled with panic attacks at cons before and wished organizers gave more thought to mental health services.

"Have you ever felt so claustrophobic in your costume you wanted to peel it off right in the middle of a crowd?" he'd asked. "Because I have. I felt like a crazy person."

"You're not crazy," Chris had replied. "I feel that way at every con."

Most of the time, Matt didn't ask about Melanie. They talked about games—they both agreed *Final Fantasy 6* was the best game of all time—and Chris's plans to move out and Matt's second attempt to take the GRE and how much he hated studying for it. They didn't talk that often, until lately when it had become every day. Chris was excited about his new project and the silence in his own apartment had become oppressive. Melanie seemed to fill every bit of space he'd freed up packing his things almost immediately, rearranging as though he had never been there.

Melanie came out of the bathroom. "There's coffee made and breakfast in the oven if you want some," he called to her without turning around.

She made a grunting sound, but he didn't take it personally. Melanie was not a morning person.

He heard her pouring coffee in the kitchen, and that was enough acknowledgment. Then the oven timer went off and he could hear her turn it off and take the dish out. She took her mug and plate back to her room in silence.

Chris was going to miss this: The simple tasks of maneuvering around another person when you knew their routine. It was a silly thing to feel nostalgic about; he'd get used to a new routine. He'd have to.

But he didn't want to. He knew all the noises coming from the bedroom that corresponded to Melanie's habits: The way she put a paper towel down on the dresser before she set her hot dishes there; how she bent over and brushed her hair upside down; the flip of the light switch in the bathroom as she reached for the headband to pull back her bangs while she washed her face.

These everyday, shared tasks made him happy. When they argued, weren't they just disagreeing on their ideas about ideology—how they thought things should be done rather than how they actually did them in reality? It seemed so foolish to create a rift based solely on ideas.

He supposed his opinion didn't matter. The decision was made; they were going to part. He gave it his best shot at convincing Melanie their relationship was worth fighting for. If they couldn't agree on that fundamental fact, they couldn't agree on anything important.

Anyway, Chris had his project. It was enough to distract him from the bleakness of moving out and starting over on a very large part of his life. That, at least, was something he could pour effort into.

He opened the spreadsheet Melanie made him for content planning a month ago and started making revisions.

〜

Max: (3:20 p.m.) If you need to get out of your apartment, I have an extra bedroom you can have until you can sign a new lease

> Matt: (4:15 p.m.) Hey, I'm going to be driving through Denver this week. Want to meet for drinks or coffee?

> Anna: (4:55 p.m.) FaceTime soon? I miss you and gotta fill you in on all the social media gossip you're missing.

> Anna: (4:58 p.m.) Seriously, Roger and Tim are both promoting this mental health for geeks thing but still barely speaking to each other

> Mom: (5:15 p.m.) Are you sure you and Chris are over? Your pictures have been so cute on Facebook

MELANIE'S E-FILING SYSTEM, which she would have sworn was already tidy, had never been as organized as it was now. She went through her email folders and cloud drive in between tasks at work, when ordinarily she might have been looking at an online craft store.

At home, she went through her closet. She had so many outfits that screamed "fitting in" to her. They weren't her style at all. She used to think she didn't really have a personal style, but once they were hanging side-by-side with her flashy costumes, she realized that the cardigans and A-line skirts definitely were not her.

Her group chat wanted to know what she planned to wear for Halloween. It was usually the last chance she had every year to wear a costume. But she had no plans to dress up this year. At work, people often dressed up for the day, but most of her costumes were too sexy to be work appropriate.

Sexist and revealing, she heard Chris's voice saying in her head.

Melanie held up the leather catsuit, the sequined booty shorts, the purple cape and leotard. She had the parts she needed to whip up a brand new costume, by repurposing the pleather catsuit and adding some accessories. But that didn't seem work-appropriate, either. She could create something new if she hurried—she could gender-bend a male costume, perhaps. But doing so would be a concession, like saying that only a male hero's costume was modest and appropriate to wear at her desk.

Melanie flicked through the cosplay gallery on her phone and found an unused picture from New York. She posted it on Instagram with the hashtag #tbt and a long caption: "Thinking about work-appropriate Halloween attire today and realized most of my costumes reveal more female parts than many offices would accept. Do men have this problem? Female parts should not = inappropriate."

She posted it and immediately wondered if Chris would see it and what he'd think.

Melanie: (6:15 p.m.) Oops, social media cheat day.

Anna: (6:17 p.m.) Love it and you're so right!!

Anna liked her post. Melanie looked at it, remembering the way she and Chris connected over sex while she was wearing the purple-caped outfit. She didn't understand how that kind of intimacy one minute could deteriorate into talking past each other the next.

Melanie sighed. She could borrow Chris's hero suit for Halloween. That'd be modest. But, of course, she didn't want to ask him for it. She hadn't seen it since Baltimore. Had he thrown it away?

She hated that he was suddenly taking out the trash and cooking food for both of them. Why did he have to make her life easier just when he was about to exit it?

Melanie sat on the end of her bed, picking at the fraying hem of the pajama shorts she was wearing. Chris seemed happier now, like it wasn't an effort for him to do those things.

Did she do that by breaking up with him? Was he happier and more like his old self because he was almost rid of her?

She didn't want to think about it. Melanie got up and went to the bathroom. Chris was still sitting at his computer in the living room, with only the desk light on. She'd warned him it was bad for his eyes and would usually go out and turn on another lamp for him, but not this time. Not anymore. She closed the bedroom door and slid into bed, but she couldn't concentrate on her book so she opened her computer and started going through her shared cloud files. There must be some redundant files in here she could clear out. She was on a roll.

The first file she saw was the spreadsheet she made Chris when he was trying to learn how to schedule content on Instagram. She assumed she could delete it now; his project was done, judging by the fact he hadn't posted to Instagram since Baltimore. But she could see that he'd accessed it recently.

Melanie's mouse hovered over the file for nearly a minute before she double clicked it.

When the spreadsheet opened, she realized he'd been working on it a lot. He'd changed it entirely. It was now a schedule for posting content to the Instagram account of the nonprofit behind their local comic convention. The nonprofit also ran a literacy program. Chris had dozens of ideas for content to promote it online.

The list began:

Signed donated graphic novels
New website
Halloween costume event

Melanie closed the spreadsheet, suddenly paranoid Chris would know she opened it. It was a violation of his privacy to know he was working on a new, con-related idea without her. She closed the computer and set it aside.

So he hadn't completely thrown out everything having to do with superheroes or conventions just because of their break up. Did that mean he actually enjoyed the hobby without her?

Melanie picked up her phone and looked at her Instagram likes from the last post she did. Chris was not among them.

She wished she knew what was going on in his head. Suddenly, his silence over the past few days seemed less angry, like she'd thought it was, and more thoughtful.

Perhaps Chris had changed. But did it happen before or after their argument? Did she miss the signs while she was busy with costumes and cons and finding herself?

~

Matt: (7:45 p.m.) Do you want me to come?

I_T WAS_ a generous offer from Matt, texted on Saturday with Halloween on Monday.

Chris knew what he should do: He should ask Melanie to help. But he couldn't. It was almost a physical disability. He could *not* ask Melanie for help. At this point, their relationship was not fully dissolved—they were still living together—and he wouldn't be the one to try to weave a few threads back into a relationship, even one that was superficially amiable. He tried. He failed. He gave up.

But he really did need help. He put out the call on the organization's Instagram: "Costumed heroes needed on Halloween." But without free booze—which they weren't licensed for—or a cool venue—a church basement probably didn't count—he didn't have a lot of hope people would show up.

He probably oversold his influence with the costumed "community" to the nonprofit, but he really wanted to help a good cause. His ideas were good, he was certain, but his execution had to work too.

"No, dude," he finally typed back, even though he did want Matt's help. "But if you know anyone closer who would be willing to show up…"

"I know someone in the next room," Matt replied.

Chris sighed and rolled his eyes.

Chris: (7:50 p.m.) Stop playing matchmaker, it looks terrible on you

Matt: (7:51 p.m.) You're stereotyping, asshole. Just because I'm not female or gay...

Chris rested the phone on his chest as he stared at the ceiling above the couch. Surely there were enough people out there looking to help a good cause these days to round up a few in two days. No, not "people." Geeks.

He sat up and jotted the phrase down as it came to him: Geeks for a cause.

His phone vibrated.

Matt: (7:52 p.m.) Try reddit? Twitter? And don't forget you have some reach on your own Instagram. I'll reshare anything you post.

Chris would try reddit, but he was avoiding his own Instagram because of Melanie. She basically won Instagram in their divorce. That platform was hers now.

"Thanks," he typed back. Matt seemed like a cool guy, but Chris was still not completely convinced he didn't want to sleep with Melanie, so he wasn't sure he wanted to be indebted to him. That would really suck for him if the two of them ended up hooking up after Chris was officially out of the picture.

Chris put his head in his hands. He kind of missed the days of numbness. Now he had to manage excitement about ideas and disappointment when they ended up being out of reach. Now there was regret for messing up, because he'd tried. Now he beat himself up for every idiotic thing he'd said to Melanie, like bringing up hypothetical children and acting like he knew any better than she did how they'd raise them. Now he wanted to make things happen and got stymied when he didn't know how.

But no. He had a mission; he didn't need a girlfriend. He needed to work harder and stop being scared of looking like an idiot.

❧

Anna: (9:43 a.m.) Are you going to sleep with Matt???

Melanie: (9:44 a.m.) At a coffee shop??

Anna: (9:45 a.m.) Omg you know what I mean

Melanie: (9:46 a.m.) I'm still living with Chris

Anna: (9:46 a.m.) AND you still love him

Melanie: (9:47 a.m.) I thought you wanted me and Matt to get together!

Anna: (9:48 a.m.) I want you to be happy

Anna: (9:51 a.m.) (gif of a squirrel hopping on another squirrel's head before running away) Just remember you can't hump and run Matt!

MELANIE MET Matt in a coffee shop where they didn't put flavors on the menu because the coffee should "stand by itself." Melanie didn't realize this when she picked it. She picked because they had gourmet donuts and local art on the walls and there were leather benches behind tall bookshelves in the back. She got there early and claimed one of those booths as well as a couple donuts.

Matt kissed her cheek when he sat down and thanked her for getting him coffee. "Sorry I was late."

She waved him off. "When did you get in?"

"At like 1 am. I left after work and drove straight through. I have meetings today at noon." Matt guzzled the black coffee, and she could see why.

"Well it's nice to see you. We missed you at Baltimore."

"I heard it was quite eventful." Matt raised his eyebrows, popping a piece of donut in his mouth.

Melanie crumbled a bit of her cake donut between two fingers.

She wanted to know what the grapevine was saying, but she was also afraid to hear. "What exactly did you hear?"

He smiled. "Well, I follow your ex on Instagram, so...I heard a lot." He eyed Melanie over the rim of his mug. "Ex? Boyfriend?"

"Hard to keep up, I know," she said. She was excited to see Matt again but sitting down with him out of the context of conventions and costumes lacked context. She barely knew him as a normal person. She didn't feel comfortable pouring her heart out to him.

"Nah, I didn't mean it like that. Just wondering how things stand." He ate another piece of donut. Melanie's wasn't tasting very good on her unsettled stomach, so she pushed the napkin toward him.

"Ex," she finally said, giving them a label. He nodded. And then he licked the icing off his fingers and put an arm out, like he was inviting her in for a hug.

Melanie hesitated.

"Come on, you look like you need one." He waggled his fingers at her.

"Is it that obvious?" she ducked her head and leaned into Matt's side so he didn't see her eyes filled with tears. She'd lost her boyfriend, all her friends were so far away and she didn't have anyone to talk to, much less lean on. Her own mother had been trying to convince her she didn't want to break up with Chris. Her sister, who never approved of anyone, thought she was an idiot for leaving him.

"No one's perfect, but doesn't he show up for you most of the time?" Lynn had asked. Since Melanie told her the news, she'd sent a series of "what about that time..." texts reminding Melanie of the good episodes in her relationship. Like Chris wasn't always on his best behavior in front of Melanie's family.

"Your father and I always enjoyed very different activities," her mom had said. "But what made it last was we trusted our differences made us stronger and didn't let them pull us apart."

Melanie bet Chris's divorced and overprotective mother-of-the-year, Maggie, wasn't giving *him* such a hard time about moving on. She was probably helping him find a new apartment.

Matt rested his chin on the top of Melanie's head.

Matt smelled like sugar and oranges; Chris smelled like Cheetos and Dr. Pepper. But that was the smell she missed, for some reason. Her senses were attuned to Chris and anything different was wrong. She pulled away. Matt let her go but his forehead said he was puzzled.

"I'm sorry," Melanie blurted. "It just doesn't feel right. I'm sorry."

She put some distance between them. She could tell from the heat of her skin that her cheeks were flushed. She blamed Anna for putting ideas in her head before she arrived. Of course she wasn't going to sleep with Matt. Even if he wanted to, which he probably didn't. She wasn't even close to over Chris. He was like a magnet she was still attached to, and until she could walk away without that pull he exerted on her, she couldn't possibly try to pair off with someone else. It wouldn't be fair to any of them.

She and Matt both peeked down at their mugs of coffee for a long moment. It was agony trying to figure out what to say next.

"No, this is on me," Matt said finally. His voice was wry. "I may not be technically breaking the bro code, since I knew you first, but I'm definitely not being a good friend. To either of you."

Unaware Matt and Chris were *friends*, Melanie frowned. "Either of us?"

Matt pulled his phone out of his jeans pocket. "I think you should see this."

ARMED WITH A LOT of advice from Matt, a new fire extinguisher and the flour he found in the very last cupboard he searched in the kitchen, Chris felt like a newly minted superhero. Just call him The Planner and Executor. He'd workshop the name once he successfully implemented his plan.

He had everything he needed. He just had to do it now. He

bounced around a little on bare feet in the empty kitchen before he picked up his phone and went for it.

From @gamerchris_1989:
Denver, Colorado
(photo of Chris)
"It's what I do that defines me." Join me IN COSTUME for a special event on Halloween serving meals to the needy. Link in bio
Liked by @mtinspace7 and 21 others

MELANIE WAS PRETENDING to listen to her coworker Susan, who was talking about brewing her own kombucha.

"I can't get it as fizzy as I want it," she was saying. "I've tried everything. Ginger, narrow bottles—you know those ones I mean? They have a special name."

Penny's boyfriend, Dan, was nodding over and over, as though he was really engaged in this monologue about Susan's experiments with carbonation. But he was also about four beers in and Melanie wasn't sure he was focusing on anything at all, really.

The bar had its garage doors up, even though it was a little chilly for it in late October. It was attached to a bakery and featured beer and pastry pairings. Everyone was eating carbs so they could drink longer. Melanie and her coworkers had arrived right after work and been there long enough for it to get dark out.

Melanie only went out with these people because she didn't want to look pathetic by staying home alone on a Friday night in front of Chris. She didn't know if he was home alone, currently. She made a point of not texting him to let him know what she was doing. Because she didn't owe him anything anymore.

Penny had left for the bathroom at least half an hour ago. Melanie smiled and gestured that direction as she stood up, taking her purse with her.

Everyone else standing in line for the single stall down a narrow hallway had their phone out, faces lit up by their screens. She was supposed to be taking a break from social media, but that kind of resolve could never withstand a line for the bathroom. Melanie pulled out her phone.

She looked at Facebook, browsing the other events currently happening that looked more fun than her night. She looked at TikTok, but it was too noisy for public viewing. She looked at Twitter, where she replied to a few people about the latest gossip from the set of the movie version of her favorite show and replied "Squee!" to Anna's tweet announcing a sequel to her squirrel book, this time remaking a Native American tale.

She opened Instagram and got a notification that Chris was live. She clicked on it before she could think about whether she wanted to see it and there he was, in their apartment kitchen, baking cookies and talking to the camera.

Melanie's perspective shrank to just the phone in front of her face, oblivious to anything else going on around her. She held the phone closer, trying to hear it. Was she drunk? She had to think carefully about how to move her feet before she could step forward to stay in the slow-moving line.

She hadn't seen him all day and it was like he'd transformed into a gorgeous stranger overnight. Chris was using captions. Since when did he know how to use captions on Instagram? The captions read: "I thought I better put my money where my mouth is and do something geeky for a cause so here I am attempting to make cookies, which I've never done before, for the party we're throwing on Monday. My ex would be shocked but I just tasted the batter and it's pretty good. Now I'll attempt to use these geeky cookie cutters—also borrowed from my ex—and see what happens."

His ex was shocked indeed.

He was wearing her favorite shirt of his, the clingy black one, her superhero apron and...boxers? He was wearing black boxers. He looked hot. He looked like a sexy male centerfold from a magazine called Hot Dudes Baking. He was getting a ton of heart eye emojis on the livestream.

Melanie suddenly realized he could see that she was watching and exited the stream. He'd posted again on Instagram within the last hour. It was a picture of him wearing that outfit, holding a cookie cutter and a pint of beer with a quizzical look on his face. The caption read: "Calling all #geekforacause. I'm trying something new by baking tonight (!) - why not join me for the results on Halloween? Throwing a party in Denver. Costumed heroes wanted. Link in bio."

She went to the link. It wasn't a party so much as a gathering at a church providing free dinner to the needy on Monday night. The convention nonprofit was funding the meal. Chris wanted costumed heroes to serve the food.

The line shifted again and Melanie slid forward, one shoulder still leaning against the wall as she read from her phone.

"Are you OK?" Penny was in front of her, looking at Melanie with something near concern on her young face. Melanie realized she'd slumped against the wall, all her focus on Chris's feed, and straightened up.

"Yes," she said, and cleared her throat. "Sorry. Yes. I'm fine."

"We're going to go. Do you want to share our Uber?"

Melanie smiled. "I'm fine. Thank you though. I'll probably leave after I use the restroom."

Penny tilted her head, looking skeptical. "We should do this again sometime?" her voice went up at the end, like it was a question.

"Sure," Melanie said. "That'd be fun."

She didn't know what she was talking about; all night she'd struggled to find anything in common with her coworkers. But Penny seemed like she could be cool, under different circumstances. And Melanie wanted more friends who were local. She should *try*. "Actually," she added, channeling her inner brave Amazonian princess. "No, let's try something different next time."

Penny smiled a little, not enough to actually raise her lips but enough that Melanie could tell she liked that answer. "Something less basic?"

Melanie used her butt to push herself away from the wall and straightened her spine. Hero pose. "I spend most of my free time dressing up in costume and going to conventions. Anything but *basic*."

Penny scanned Melanie up and down, like she was evaluating her street clothes for their costume quality. "Really."

"Really," Melanie said. "It's a lot of fun. You should try it."

Penny put one hand on her hip. For a moment, Melanie thought she was going to scoff. Then she said, "I wouldn't know where to start."

Melanie smiled. "I can help with that."

Penny pursed her lips. "Now that'd be fun," she said. "Text me." She smiled a little and gave Melanie a waggle of her fingers before she walked away.

Melanie went back to Instagram. Matt had reposted Chris's post. So had Laura and David, who shared an account.

"If you're in Denver, wear a costume for a good cause!" read Laura's post.

Melanie texted Matt: "Wtf is going on with Chris and Instagram."

> Matt: (8:49 p.m.) (laughing crying emoji) Told you. Isn't it great? It's like expecting to see a car crash and ending up watching a Fast and Furious movie

> Matt: (8:49 pm.) You're going right?

Matt told her Chris was planning an event. He hadn't given her the flour-coated details. She typed: "He didn't ask me." Then she erased it because that implied she wanted to be asked. It wasn't even fair; she hadn't spoken to Chris since Matt told her what he was up to. She hadn't confronted him. And it wasn't her business what Chris did. Besides, she didn't care. It wasn't her job to support his projects anymore.

> Matt: (8:52 p.m.) It looks really cool

He wasn't wrong. And who helped Chris figure out how to livestream on Instagram anyway? And how did he find the flour? He was a good cook, but he'd never baked anything in the entire time she'd known him.

It was like the man she'd lived with for the past two years was suddenly a completely different person. He'd...grown? He'd educated himself without her help.

She looked at the photo post again, the one of him wearing boxers, an apron, and a clingy t-shirt. She felt something. It wasn't lust. Well, not just lust. It was also jealousy. Because she suspected she wasn't the only one looking at this picture and lusting over her boyfriend. Ex-boyfriend.

> Melanie to Costumes Are Squee! group chat: (9:01 p.m.) Wtf is going on? I am so confused. Are you guys seeing this

> Anna: (9:04 p.m.) O.M.G.

> Anna: (9:05 p.m.) We're talking about Chris on Insta right

> Roger: (9:05 p.m.) I'm welling up. Look at him go

> Tim: (9:06 p.m.) You know I hate to agree but I agree. Talk about being vulnerable

> Roger: (9:07 p.m.) It's like he actually heard us

She was the next person in line for the bathroom. She locked the door behind her and leaned against it. She opened the livestream again. Something was clearly burning in the kitchen behind Chris while he waved a towel frantically in the air, his butt toward the camera, which she could tell was propped up on their counter. As she was watching, the phone slid down off whatever it was propped on until it was tilted up at the ceiling. Disaster. His viewers started disappearing. She closed out of the stream quickly, hoping their apartment hadn't burned down by the time she got home.

Should she go home immediately? Should she help?

It wasn't her job to help Chris anymore.

But she wanted it to be. She *wanted* it to be her job to help Chris. She wanted to be behind the phone filming him right now, handing him the vanilla and pointing at the timer he forgot to start.

When they first met, Chris's ideas pinged off the walls like an arcade game every time they talked. He never followed through on any of them, and that became Melanie's contribution to their relationship. She sifted through Chris's ideas, picked the ones she liked, and made them happen. Chris never once asked, "why this idea and not another?" He acted thrilled every time she plucked an idea out of the ether and turned it into reality. His ideas had stopped springing in clusters out of his head over the past year or so, but it seemed like they were back. *He* was back.

Was it possible it wasn't their relationship that had stalled but them as individuals? That Melanie needed to take a hard look at herself and Chris, too, needed to find himself again?

Melanie bit her lip, looking at herself in the grey-tinged mirror over the bathroom sink. She was aware there were people waiting for her outside the door, but in her mind that problem was far away.

He'd hurt her. But he'd also pulled himself out of a dark hole and shown up to support her in a hobby he didn't particularly like. When was the last time she did something like that for him?

From Greene, Melanie
To: <all-office>
Subject: Halloween costume event

On October 30, 4:56 p.m.
Thanks for agreeing to help out tomorrow night! It's going to be a
great event for a great cause. Please send me:
Your clothing size (top and bottom)
Your preference ranked 1-3 on costume you'd like to wear
Time when you can pick it up from the office
Attached please find a spreadsheet of your costume options,
including photos of me wearing every outfit.

CHAPTER 15

Chris's limited ability to turn his head in the cowl was hampering his ability to take a full victory lap. He could barely believe what little he could see. It was *working*.

The church basement was filled with costumed heroes. It was an old, Catholic church with a grey stone exterior and a surprisingly bland basement that looked like any other below-ground event space. There were folding tables set up in rows surrounded by metal chairs and another row of tables filled with food at the front of the room by the doors. The costumed helpers were lined up behind the tables, serving food to a line of people coming in from outside.

Jenny was there, dressed as Bill Nye—a true superhero, she insisted—volunteering to run refills back and forth between the kitchen and the tables of food.

But there were also a dozen other people he didn't know. As they came in, dressed as blockbuster movie leads as well as a couple characters he didn't recognize, he asked if they'd heard about the event on social media.

"I think so?" one 20-something woman said, vaguely. He supposed social media was like that—people were so immersed in it that it could be hard to trace information back.

"Thanks for coming. I like your costume," he told another woman dressed in a purple wig and cape. He remembered that one because Melanie wore it in New York.

"Thanks, it's borrowed," she replied, taking the gloves and hairnet he handed her.

He was filling tiny paper cups with powdered tea or lemonade or water at a table positioned in an "L" shape with the food table. From there, he could see—and take pictures for Instagram on his phone— a masked girl and a white plastic soldier and a be-leathered devil all serving lasagna and green beans and rolls. Next to him, a random fairy was pouring hot chocolate.

This was amazing. And the photos were terrific.

The people with plates looked amused. "You've sure got a pretty smile," one of them told the masked girl.

"Is that your girlfriend?" another asked Chris, referring to the only other person wearing bat ears in the room.

"My ward," he replied seriously. He didn't think that was quite the right backstory, but he didn't care. He couldn't stop grinning. He couldn't believe he pulled this off. Deena, the volunteer coordinator, was thrilled. She promised him complete access to the nonprofit's social media channels after this, and they'd already set up an appointment to talk about his other ideas. Like building them a badly-needed new website. But he'd ease into informing them theirs sucked. *Finally, a project that meant something.*

"That wasn't exactly canon, that ward comment," the character who was *totally* his character's ward said, wandering over to him after the line began to clear.

Chris shrugged, although his suit barely moved as he did. "I know, but it's hard to keep them all straight. Multiple wards, and then some other random relationships. These people don't have all day for the break-down." He smiled at her. "Thanks a lot for coming."

"Of course," she replied, and he suddenly realized the lower half of her face was familiar. "We might not always get along, but we didn't want to be the reason you and Melanie broke up."

Chris blinked. He'd stepped into a parallel universe. "Laura?"

She spread her cape and did a tiny curtsey.

"You saw my Instagram post? Or Matt's?" Chris looked over at the the red devil, suddenly realizing who he was. Matt gave him a two-fingered salute from one leather gloved-hand then went back to scooping beans and providing rolls in Laura's absence.

The suit was suddenly even warmer than usual. Chris was so shocked he kind of wanted to sit down for a minute. People he knew actually showed up for his crazy idea. People who didn't even *like* him.

"That was really, really generous of you, Laura."

Laura smiled, a slow curve of her red lips. "Don't get all sappy on me. I know you don't like me. But that's OK. I did it for Melanie. And because I get wanting to be with someone you don't always like all the time."

"Uh," Chris put his hand to his head to push back his hair, a nervous habit that didn't work in this costume. He ended up just fondling his plastic ears. "You know Melanie and I broke up."

Laura didn't change expression. "Did you?" Her red lips curved as she shrugged. Then she sashayed away, back to the food table.

He stood there numb, unable to process suddenly having all these things in his life—friends? Hobbies outside of work? How did this happen? He'd never thought all those baby steps could add up to getting almost everything he wanted. But it was bittersweet because he couldn't share it with the woman who prompted him to take action in the first place.

Chris followed Jenny into the kitchen as she went to tell someone they needed more coffee. It was chilly outside tonight and he wanted everyone to leave with a warm beverage. He pulled out his phone once he got behind the wall and texted Melanie.

Chris: (5:33 p.m.) Thank you for your help on the event. I can't believe Laura and Matt came all this way.

Melanie didn't respond immediately. He waited a minute, then put his phone back in his utility belt.

"Don't touch anything," Jenny was telling another woman who was dressed as a warrior princess. "We're just supposed to transport and serve, we're not allowed to have anything to do with food prep."

"Thanks, Jenny," Chris said, appreciating that she even applied her take-no-prisoners attitude to volunteering. "Thanks, uh, ma'am."

The other woman was yanking at the top of her outfit. "Sorry," she said, both hands grasping the fabric above her breasts. "No one tells you this is wildly uncomfortable. It feels like it could fall down at any moment." She added in an undertone to Jenny, "Wrong kind of free service if you know what I mean."

"Maybe if you loosened the belt it wouldn't pull on the top so much," Jenny offered with oblivious practicality. Even Chris knew not to comment on how a woman's clothes fit. "Is it not your size?"

The woman glanced at Jenny irritably. "I borrowed it from Melanie. Oh." She looked at Chris sharply.

"That's Melanie's? My Melanie? I mean-my ex?" Chris looked at the costume more closely. He should have known. The details were clearly hand-made. He'd definitely seen that belt buckle before.

"Yeah," the woman said. She shrugged and continued, like she accepted that the secret was already out. "I work with her. Several of us do."

"And she asked you to come? That's so nice of her," Jenny said. She turned to Chris with narrowed eyes, like he'd been keeping this from her. "I thought you really broke up this time."

"We did," Chris said. He didn't quite know how to react. Grateful and slightly relieved? He was so afraid of Melanie finding out about his project—his tentative steps toward building something of his own —and judging his motives. He thought she'd only look at his actions through a filter of anger.

Jenny raised her eyebrows. "Wow, after my break-up, I was doing more digital stalking and spreading rumors about STIs than favors.

You guys are so mature. Maybe this is why I'm still single," she added to the other woman in an undertone.

The woman laughed but she was still fidgeting with her top and glancing at the door like she was anxious for an exit from the conversation. Jenny came on a little strong sometimes.

The full scope of what she was saying slowly washed over Chris.

"Melanie loaned everyone here costumes?" he asked, suddenly realizing how many of the costumes out front looked familiar.

"Not everyone but, yeah, a few of us." She smiled slightly. "I couldn't believe it, to be honest. I didn't know Melanie was into cosplay."

Jenny laughed. "SO into cosplay. Like, spends all her time and extra money on it."

"Can you tell Deena we need more coffee?" Chris interrupted, directing the question to the stranger. Jenny knew about Melanie from what he'd told her but he wasn't sure how much Melanie wanted her coworkers to know about her hobby, especially second-hand. She didn't reveal the full extent of her hobby to him until they'd slept together more than once. He was shocked that she would tell anyone at work about it at all. "The one in the checked apron. Thanks."

She nodded and moved away from them, past the steel shelving where there was another plate of warmed rolls waiting to be taken into the other room. Chris went to pick them up, not wanting to fail on the project when it was going so well.

"Did you ask Melanie to help?" Jenny asked, following him.

"No." Chris paused. "I can't believe I thought I got all these people here by myself. There's no way this would have been such a success without her."

"Hey! I'm here because of you," Jenny countered him, putting her hands on her hips. "Stop beating up my friend Chris."

"Right and I appreciate it but..." He shook his head. "I mean, this was so last minute. I just..."

He paused and thought about what Melanie said during their

fight: *That's kind of our thing. You start something for good reasons and then I have to make the logistics work.*

He groaned. He'd done it again.

"What?" Jenny demanded, looking around as if a phantom villain had punched him in the stomach.

"I jumped into something and she had to make it happen. Again. No wonder we keep fighting, Jenny. This is always our dynamic: I come up with an idea and she makes it happen."

"Maybe she likes making it happen." Jenny shrugged, like he was overreacting.

"She wants to be my girlfriend, not my...*helper*."

"Are you crazy?" Jenny punched him in the arm. "That's what a partnership is."

"OK fine," Chris batted her fist away. "Then it should go both ways. When do I ever help Melanie?"

Jenny frowned at him. "Dude, that is a question to ask yourself. I have literally never been to your apartment. I don't know your life." She wrinkled up her forehead. "Are you actually a sucky boyfriend and I don't know it? Do you leave dishes in the sink and forget her birthday?"

"I've never done that! The birthday thing," Chris added. "The dishes yes. I also...criticized her costumes and told her I didn't want to raise a daughter who wore..." He trailed off, watching Jenny's face fall like he was becoming increasingly difficult to defend. "Never mind."

She was shaking her head at him. "This is disappointing. Even the good ones are kind of terrible. I'm going to remember this lesson next time I make a pro/con list. The cons are always going to be longer. I guess you just gotta decide how much shit you'll accept in a relationship."

"Gee, thanks," Chris snapped. "You're making me feel great about this."

"Well, but you have a lot of pros, Chris. You try hard. You make her feel wanted—right? You do that?"

"I think so?"

"Well, most girls just want to feel wanted." Jenny went to punch him again and he ducked away. She hit too hard. "You might want to think about that next time you're criticizing her outfit."

"Yeah well you should put 'enjoys punching people' on your next Tinder profile." Chris waved her away and stepped over to the rolls that were starting to cool. "I have to work! Go do something!"

"Maybe I will!" Jenny stuck her tongue out at him and stomped away.

But Chris couldn't stop thinking about what she'd said. On work projects, Jenny could look over what he turned in and predict the one issue that was going to bother the client, and maybe she'd zeroed in on the problem between him and his girlfriend. Melanie had told him she thought he didn't find her sexy in her costumes. But was it possible it went deeper than him not saying "you're beautiful"? Was it possible that every time he forgot to take out the trash, he was saying "I forgot about you" to Melanie?

He took the rolls out to the front room and replaced the empty aluminum tray on the table.

"Better keep an eye on this soldier, might be up to no good!" called out a man who hadn't taken his backpack off. He was wearing two coats and holding a tray filled with the last of the rolls on the table. He used his fingers to point from his eyes to the person in the white full-body plastic costume, cackling. "Look out, Batman!"

The soldier put hands on hips. "Well the Empire's soldiers were just law and order for the galaxy. It's not their fault the laws were unjust."

Chris blinked. He looked at the costumed character who had Melanie's voice and his own words.

He clomped over to the food table in his noisy plastic boot covers. He stared into the shiny visor of her helmet. "Melanie?"

The silent helmet stared back for long enough that he became uncertain. Surely Melanie would never cosplay in something that didn't even have a wig and left her completely dressed.

Then she reached up and pulled off her helmet, and Melanie's sweaty hair fell around her face. She smiled at him. "These aren't the droids you're looking for."

He had never seen anything this sexy. For at least half a minute, Chris couldn't speak. He couldn't believe Melanie showed up for him. In this costume.

Chris swallowed and took a deep breath. "Why did you come?"

Melanie flinched, which was not the reaction he meant to get.

"I thought it was a good cause," she said. "I thought it might be nice to wear a costume for a cause for once."

He grinned involuntarily and turned his whole upper body so he could take in the room again, proud of this moment. There was a small woman right behind him, staring at him and waiting for him to move so she could get some lasagna. Chris took her plate and held it out for Melanie to put a serving on it. Then he handed it back.

"But why in that costume?" Chris asked, turning back to Melanie.

He could tell from the way her neck moved that she shrugged, even though her costume didn't move. The plastic must be as stiff as his. "I thought it was the opposite of sexist and revealing and you'd like it."

Chris grimaced. That was sharp.

"You look just like the real crusader when you do that," Laura said, leaning into their conversation to make a face at Chris, then drawing back to her serving station next to Melanie's. He hated that they had no privacy, but not enough to stop their conversation. He needed to know why Melanie was here and what it meant. He had to unwind the knot in his stomach that kept asking: *Can I be happy now?*

Melanie smiled. "She's right, you do. I like it," she added, and bit her lower lip for a second. Chris nearly lost his train of thought entirely, watching her lips.

"Is this...a grand gesture?" he asked.

Melanie snorted. "It's just a *nice* gesture. I didn't do it to be romantic. I truly wanted to help." She paused. "Well, maybe this costume was a little bit 'grand.'" She made finger quotes around the word.

He cleared his throat. "I'm sorry about what I said," he said in a low voice.

Melanie opened her mouth.

"What was that?" Laura leaned over again, cupping a hand to her ear. Matt, on her other side, reached over and pulled her away by the shoulder. "Sorry, sorry," Laura said, clearly not sorry at all, as she straightened back up at her position at the tables.

Melanie met Chris's eyes again. "You had a point," she said. "But I think my reasons for dressing up are valid, too."

Chris nodded. "I know they are."

Melanie opened her arms to encompass the room. "But this is amazing. Your vision for how much more cosplay can be is...really cool, Chris."

"I never would have thought of it without you," he replied.

Melanie smiled, but it was a small one. She looked down at her hands and fiddled with the spoon in the lasagna tin. "But cosplay just to *play* is also really cool, Chris."

"I know." Chris spoke quickly. She nodded, and then waited. He struggled to find his tongue again. They both had to be real with each other. "It's just not *my* thing."

She nodded again, eyes still on her latex gloved hands on the table.

"I'm sorry I wasn't supportive."

"You *were*," she said. "You just hated it."

"No, I..." Chris swallowed. He looked at Melanie in all that white plastic. It was probably at least as uncomfortable as what he was wearing. She did that for *him*. "I've really been struggling for the last year, Melanie. But trying to make everything easier on me wasn't fair to you."

"Easier," she repeated. She frowned, and he couldn't blame her for being puzzled. It sounded stupid in retrospect to say, *My lifeforce was draining out of me and I was so wrung out I didn't even know how to fight back.*

"Yeah," he sighed. "For once, I had a problem you couldn't help me with. But I'm getting help now. I'm *trying* again."

She nodded slowly. "I'm trying, too, Chris."

"What are you trying at?" he asked, surprised. "You're...Melanie, you've always been exactly who I want."

She smiled a little, and he thought it must have been the right thing to say. Laura leaned over again and said, "Awww."

"I've been hiding, though," Melanie said, ignoring Laura. "Not speaking up, not telling you what I want. Not telling anyone what I love. I depended on you to see who I really was and when it felt like you stopped doing that...I wasn't sure who I was anymore, I guess."

Chris held onto the edge of the table, rocked by how badly he had let her down. A skinny man next to him cleared his throat loudly. Chris automatically took his plate and Melanie put a scoop of lasagna on it.

"I'm sorry," Chris said to Melanie after handing the plate back.

"You should be!" the man said, before he walked away grumbling to himself.

Melanie smiled at Chris. "No, you don't have to be sorry for not reading my mind. I am working on letting more people see who I am, because that's a big burden to put on you."

"Well I think *trying* is all we need, really. That and the fact that I love you." Chris kept swallowing, because his throat was dry or because this costume was swelling around his neck.

"I love you, too," Melanie said. She came around the table and reached for his shoulders. They clunked chests hard.

Chris laughed. Out of the corner of his eye, he saw Laura was pulling her phone out, probably to take their picture and post it without asking again. But right now, he didn't care. He leaned down and Melanie put one hand around the back of his cowl and tilted her head far to the left so she could get in under the nose of it.

Kissing Melanie when he thought he might never kiss her again felt exactly like one of those kisses that resolved a romcom movie, or like seeing Obi-Wan again as a spirit in *The Empire Strikes Back*. Like everything was going to wind up OK.

Chris only let go when he couldn't hold his breath anymore. His nose was covered in rubber that didn't breathe at all.

Melanie stepped back and gestured down at her outfit. "I hope you like my unsexy outfit. I know it's not running through the airport or saving a child from danger, but...it was really expensive to rent this costume at the last minute. And it's super uncomfortable."

Chris almost said, "tell me about it," before he stopped and eyed the boxy white plastic. He wanted to tell her how she made him feel, showing up like that. She was right that it wasn't the *most* sexy outfit she'd ever worn. But for a few seconds, he let his dick think about what parts of that costume come off and whether he could put Melanie across this table and...

Nope, getting an erection in this costume was not pleasant, as it turned out.

"You know what?" he said. "Let's go get you out of it."

Melanie looked at him, startled. "But your event..."

Chris looked at Laura. "You'll stay and help clean up, right?"

Laura sighed dramatically. "I guess I can manage that. By the way, we're crashing at your place."

"In that case," Chris said, and walked around the table to take Melanie's hand. "We definitely need to go right now. Because I cannot *wait* to get you out of that." He picked her up by the waist and hoisted her over his shoulder. Plastic met plastic with a creaking sound and an "oof!" from Melanie.

Chris managed to carry her out of the church basement into the hallway before he had to put her down or drop her on the stairs.

"It's still a grand gesture, right?" he asked, as Melanie clutched her stomach. He pulled his cowl off and sweat started dripping down his face. They were a mess. But they were a mess *together*.

"Oh yeah," she said. She leaned up to kiss him. She put her hands in his sweaty hair and bit his lower lip. Ow, this costume was so tight around his groin right now.

"Melanie," he whispered, leaning into her so she stumbled back against the wall. "I want you." He'd say it over and over if she needed him to.

She moaned under her breath. Her hand was on his hip but he couldn't feel it there. "We're in a church," she whispered.

"It's not being a church just now," he said, blowing the words into her ear so she shivered. "It's an event center."

He opened the door behind her. It was a windowless storage room.

Melanie's eyes opened wide at him. But then a sly smile crossed her face. She was right there with him. She slid across the wall and backed into the room, her eyes a dare.

Chris grinned and followed her, already unbuckling his utility belt. He slammed the door behind him, hoping it didn't lock automatically. He backed Melanie up against the metal shelves lining one wall. "Hold on," he said. She reached above her head and he started pulling at her hard clothes.

It turned out the pants did come off her costume and Chris's costume provided some helpful support when he was on his knees. But when she returned hers, she would have a hard time explaining the scratches all over the white plastic.

From @lauraloowho:
Denver, Colorado
(photo of Chris and Melanie, in costume, kissing)
My kind of crossover #HEA #geeksforacause
Liked by @miz_anna_doll and 2670 others

From @mtinspace7:
Denver, Colorado
(photo of Matt and Jenny)

Science > vigilantism (she made me say that)
Liked by @miz_anna_doll and 36 others

EPILOGUE

Denver – next summer

Melanie was still standing under the big blue bear statue that peered into the glass-fronted Denver Convention Center when she got her first picture request.

"Your costume is amazing!" the mom said, holding hands with a little girl dressed as an ice princess. Melanie complimented the little girl's outfit in return. "And is that your real hair? Because it's really good."

"It is." Melanie smiled. She missed wearing a wig, but her hair was already short enough that this year, she went for it and got it cut and dyed for real. It took her a whole year, a lot of patience and a lot of asking for help to get this costume right. Melanie planned on wearing it to every con she went to this year.

She made it to the convention floor five photo ops later and headed for the education area, a roped off pen in the middle where people mostly dumped their kids while they stood nearby and ate or took a breath or both.

This year, it was even more crowded than usual. There was a faux light saber fight taking place on stage with Roger narrating the plot using a microphone off-stage.

Chris stepped on stage in his new costume, which suited him much better than the last one. He grabbed one of the fighters by the scruff of her neck. "You belong in jail!" he yelled, dramatically.

"And so he took the Rebel off to jail. But in jail, do you know what happened?" Roger continued, with dramatic flair.

"No," all the children chorused.

"The Rebel learned to read!"

Melanie watched some of the parents smile at each other from the sidelines.

"The Rebel read comic books and graphic novels and anything she could get her hands on. And by learning to read, she learned all about Good Guys and Bad Guys. And learned she did the wrong thing when she stole from the Good Guys. You know what else?"

"What?" said a little girl.

"The Rebel learned that she was a Bad Guy."

On stage, the robed Rebel put both hands to her face like she was crying at the revelation. Several children "ohhh"ed.

"But it's OK!" Roger continued. "Because she also learned she doesn't have to stay that way. And that's when our hero came back!"

Chris reappeared from behind a cardboard planet and waved cheerfully. He was so much more comfortable playing a superhero than an antihero. And he still looked hot in his red underwear on the outside of his tights. No need for the children—or their parents—to know how they'd used that costume in the privacy of their bedroom last night.

"And he helped the Rebel get out of jail, once she'd served her sentence, and become a Hero like him."

Chris and the Rebel held up their linked hands and bowed.

The crowd of children clapped. Chris walked up to the microphone and said into it, "While our little skit might be simplistic and aimed at the kids, we are raising funds today for a great cause: prison literacy. Every product on display on the front table was donated and proceeds go to this cause, so to the parents here—and whoever else enjoys watching grown adults lightsaber fight, no judgment—please check them out. And we'll have another skit in a few minutes. Here's some music for now."

Chris hopped down off the stage, red cape billowing behind him, and waved at Melanie as an ad started playing on the screen behind him.

She stepped over the cardboard fence roping off the area and gave him a quick kiss, half on the jaw to keep it family friendly. "That was great."

"We're getting better," Chris agreed. His cape caught on the back of one boot and Melanie flicked it so the fabric fell correctly down his back. "Thanks mostly to hiring an improv person to be my narrator."

"One of your better ideas," she commented. He smiled and waved at a kid wearing a *Where's Waldo?* shirt who was staring unabashedly at them. Melanie waved too.

"You are blowing that kid's mind right now."

Melanie turned. Matt was standing on the other side of the cardboard barrier with Jenny. They were dressed as the doctor and a blue British police box.

"Don't even say it," Jenny said, holding up her tweed-covered arms. She tugged on the sides of her bow tie with a flourish. "I know we're ridiculously cute."

"You are," Melanie and Chris said at the same time.

"That giant box looks really hot, though," Chris said to Matt, whose could only be seen as eyes inside the blue box. "Is it as bad as this outfit?"

"Well, I'm not wearing anything under this, so I actually stay pretty cool."

Jenny smacked him where his stomach would be under the costume. "There are children here!"

"I'm kidding! I'm wearing underwear."

Melanie laughed, but Chris seemed distracted, keeping track of the person operating the video and microphone. He was becoming quite the manager.

"Hey guys!" Anna bounced up, wearing all red. "I just took a picture with the best cosplayer. I mean, his muscles were smaller than mine but his fake claws were amazing."

She held out her phone to Melanie. "I've got to remember to send this to Tim. He's so pissed Roger got this con in the break-up." In the same breath, she asked Chris, "How's sales?"

"Your stuff is almost sold out. Thanks again for donating."

"The franchise stuff or the squirrel stuff?"

"Both!"

"Really?" Anna rubbed her hands together like a supervillain. "Are you selling mostly to grown men with fades?"

Chris grinned. On the screen behind him, a clip of an upside-down kiss started playing. It cut to a montage of other superheroes and their inspiring girlfriends.

"Uh oh, sorry, kids!" said Roger into the microphone. "This segment's for your parents. These scenes come *after* the fighting, if you know what I mean."

"Just a second," Chris said, and hurried toward the stage.

Melanie raised her eyebrows and handed Anna's phone back to her. "Always chaos around here."

Chris hopped up on stage and took the microphone in both hands. He turned around and said into it, "Melanie."

Melanie's eyebrows shot up. Behind her, she heard Matt, Jenny and Anna rustle and someone giggled. And she *knew*. She knew what this was and she knew the reason why he was doing it this way—in public, despite her fear of being in the spotlight!—was his promise that their relationship would always be open to trying something new.

They'd had the conversation around Christmas—"do you want to get married eventually?" "yeah, eventually" "do you feel like we're getting close?" "yes, but I'm not in any hurry because we have a really good thing already"—so maybe she should have expected this. But she hadn't.

"Melanie, I'd like to say you're the MJ to my Peter, the Peggy to my Steve, the Catwoman to my Batman, the Lois to my Superman. But that's not quite accurate to who we are. You and I don't always tell the same stories, or read the same books, and sometimes we even struggle to get on the same page. But I love your stories. And I love that you always listen to mine. I think you and I make a pretty good crossover pairing." Chris paused and wiped one of his hands on his leg. "And yes I had to get help for some of those references because I am not the super-nerd in this relationship."

"Not *that* kind of super-nerd maybe!" Matt called out from behind Melanie. She threw an appreciative smile over her shoulder at him, clearly at least one source of super-pairing answers for Chris. He was also on their group chat, now, so it could have been all of them.

Anna was holding her phone up, hopefully getting every word because Laura and David would murder her for letting them miss this if she didn't share it later on Instagram.

Chris nodded. "OK, OK. Yes, I'm also kind of a nerd." He cleared his throat. "Anyway, Melanie, I hope you keep crossing the page to appear in my story and letting me do the same for yours. Because I think together, we are writing a pretty great book."

Melanie put a hand to her face to hide her giant smile.

Chris waited to make sure Melanie was looking at him and popped open a pouch on his yellow belt. He pulled out what she assumed was a ring. "Will you marry me?"

Melanie nodded, holding both hands to her face now.

"You have to come up here," Chris said.

Melanie grimaced. She wiped at her eyes and glanced around the crowd, which had swelled with people drawn in by the public proposal. It felt like the entire convention center was watching them and it made her nervous. But Chris was standing there, inviting her out on a limb, knowing what it took to keep the adventure alive in their relationship. She wondered what her character would do. She laughed to herself, because for once she would rather do what Melanie wanted and go jump into the arms of her new fiancé. She walked toward him, picking her way carefully to avoid stepping on any children's limbs.

"You're going to marry *him*?" one little girl said. Her face telegraphed that she wasn't sure that was legal.

"I sure am!" Melanie told her. She finally made it to the stage and held out her hand to Chris. He put the ring on her finger but she forgot to look at it. She was too distracted gazing back at Chris, finding his familiar eyes under that temporarily dyed black hair. They were shining, and not just from the glare of the lights in the convention center.

The crowd started clapping for them.

"I love you," she said, quietly enough that it was just for them.

He squeezed her hand. "I love you too."

Then he threaded his fingers through her spiky hair, cape flapping around both of them, and tilted her head so he could move in for the epic kiss.

The End

FREE NOVELLA!

Want to read Jenny and Matt's story? You can find "Level Up: A Gamer Romance" online or through my newsletter at aliciawilder.com/newsletter

My mailing list offers tidbits about being an indie author, comic con events, book recommendations, and news about my upcoming releases. I only send emails when I have news or freebies.

Otherwise, the best place to find me is Instagram. Come say hi: https://www.instagram.com/aliciabwilder/

Thank you for reading! Please consider leaving a review if you liked "Cosplay Cupid."

For Erik, who not only believed I could publish but poured hours into making it happen.

Thanks to the writers, therapists and (ugh) bad exes who inspired me to write love stories in order to reclaim the joy of romance despite trauma.

Also to my early readers: Regina Black, Hannah Olsen and Jessica Calla. To my current writing group, Valerie Pepper (who helped me through some last-minute revisions—not all heroes wear cosplay), Kat Webb and Ivy Fairbanks. And to these and many others who have supported my writing and publishing journey: Sarah T. Dubb, Jessica Miller, Kharma Kelley, Brooke Seipel, Emily Whitten, Chelsea Harlan, Jonathan Easley, Vanessa King, paparouna, Josh Barber, Kate Tracy and Emilie McConnell. I have also attended panels and conferences and participated in writing communities that helped me in large and small ways.

To Rhianna Bowyer, who taught me so much about design.

This is also dedicated to my mom—who is never allowed to read the sex scenes—for always supporting my dreams.

ABOUT THE AUTHOR

Alicia Wilder is a journalist and a cosplayer IRL. She loves moderating author panels at comic cons while dressed as Wonder Woman. She lives in Colorado, has a cat, and believes happily ever afters are for everyone.

For updates, visit: aliciawilder.com

instagram.com/aliciabwilder

tiktok.com/@aliciabwilder

goodreads.com/aliciawilder

ALSO BY ALICIA WILDER

Telluride Temptations

The Hookup Holiday: A Christmas novella

High On Love: A 4/20 novella

Aim For Love: A small town adventure romance

Leave No Trace: An enemies-to-lovers romance

Colorado Geek Series

Cosplay Cupid: A second chance, geek romance

Level Up: A gamer novella

Mountains & Monuments Series

Photograph Me: A forced proximity novella

Breadcrumbs: A fake dating novella

My Secret Vice: An escapist political romance